HOMECOMING

BY

GILLIAN OGILVIE

Published by Anvil Authors UK
LA14 3AT

Copyright © 2014 Gillian Ogilvie

The right of Gillian Ogilvie to be identified as the author of this work is asserted in accordance with Sections 77 and 78 of the Copyright Design and Patents Act 1988

This book is copyright. All rights reserved. Reproduction by any means is forbidden without express permission.

This book is a work of fiction. Except where actual places, events and characters are being described for the storyline of this novel, all persons, places and situations in this publication are fictitious and any resemblance to living persons is purely coincidental.

ISBN 978-1-291-82548-0

Also by Gillian Ogilvie

Lost in France
Broken Wings
Living without Lucy
Dragonfly Crossroads,

Murders like Buses
Murders like Pyramids

Non-fiction
Shared Thoughts on Random Themes

Artwork by Gillian Ogilvie
Graphics by Graham Troth

This book is dedicated to all those coming home

And to my good friends Wilma and Lachlan Ross without whose wonderful hospitality this book would never have been written

The Strath, Sutherland 1570

Morag Murray's heart was filled with rebellion and worry. She straightened up from her toil to ease her aching back and shoulders, shielded her eyes with her hand and gazed down the strath towards the town of Dornoch. Where were they? It was four days since a neighbour had ridden up to the farm on his sweating garron to tell her father the news. It had sent all the menfolk off roaring 'death to the enemy'. Which enemy it was Morag wasn't told. Her father had bidden her stay and tend the place until his return. No use asking Ruairidh Murray what the fuss was all about. Any questioning of his orders or doings was likely to earn her a skelp round the head – if she didn't move fast enough. Women had no place in a man's world other than to feed him and breed his bairns, tend to his wants and obey his orders.

These were uneasy times. All her life there had been trouble between the Murrays and the Earl of Caithness who was a cruel tyrant. She knew all suffered under his rule over the whole of this great area. He had the power of life, death and banishment and used it widely for his own ends. No doubt this was the latest skirmish in the struggle against his unfair dealings. So they had gone - her father, her two older brothers, Hendrie and Kenneth, and their neighbour, Andrew Mhor. Gone off, in haste and excitement, leaving her to cope alone.

In haste and joy, thought Morag as she turned back to her work. Not for them the drudgery of everyday toil to keep body and soul together. Like bairns they had always to be seeking some new distraction. Father had rustled cattle when young and even Hendrie had felt it necessary to prove his manhood by taking a couple of steers from a neighbouring clan. Why he wanted to bring trouble so close to their door was beyond Morag's understanding. But that was men. No thought for stability and safety, always fight and argue and let the hot blood flow.

As she bent to spread the shining seaweed over the lazy-bed that would grow food for them the following Spring, Morag's angry thoughts revolved again in helpless chafing against her fate. Her mother, Mairead, had died when Morag was twelve years old. Since then she had kept the house and done all the women's work. She had seen to the cattle and the fowls, spun the precious thin wool of the small sheep she tethered close to the steading, and grown and gathered food to feed her father and her three brothers. When Hendrie and Kenneth married it was true she had help, and enjoyed the female company and a brighter future. But when the bairns arrived Father helped the boys build homes of their own at a distance. He made it clear Morag would remain at the farm to look after him all her days. Duty he called it. But she was no better than a bondservant.

She dashed the back of her hand across her eyes and fought back the tears. She would not weep - even though last week she had heard of the betrothal of her best friend from childhood. At fifteen Ephie was two years younger than Morag. Ephie's father was a simple cottar holding his small croft from Morag's father. Morag was by far the prettier of the two girls, yet it was Ephie who would become a bride at Samhain. Morag would dwindle into an old maid tending her irascible father, unloved and with no bairns at her knee.

All the while she worked and seethed with discontent, a nagging worry lurked at the back of Morag's mind. Where were her brothers and her father? Why had he sent no word? There was no-one she could discuss this problem with. Her sisters-in-law and her youngest brother, Rabbie, were all up at the shieling, so the cattle could benefit from the summer pastures on higher ground. With the other women and children, they encouraged the beasts to eat all the sweet hill grass to be found, and made cheese and butter to store against the winter. Only Morag had been left behind.

'Ho! Morag!'

She raised her head at the call. Alarm raced through her nerves. In these uncertain times it was foolish to drop one's guard, even so close to home. But, when she saw who greeted her, Morag smiled. It was Willie 'Bairn' - a young loon who wouldn't hurt a fly. He wandered the smokes taking food and shelter where it was offered and was never turned away. His brain might be weak but his back was strong and he had an affinity for beasts that made others marvel. Often she had watched him coax a 'cross-lain' calf from a nervous first-time mother cow. His small yet strong hands and gentle voice soothed the terrified beast and eased the calf into the world.

'Hello, Willie,' she called and spread the last heap of seaweed at the corner of the lazy-bed. There it would rot down nicely in the sun and rain until it provided much needed goodness in the soil for next year's planting. Perhaps if she were less successful with her crops her father would not hold her so tightly at his side?

She wiped her hands on the hem of her skirt and stepped across the ridges of the infields to where the young man stood smiling at her.

'Come away in,' she invited. 'I've a pot of nettle soup ready for a hungry loon.' She laughed as she watched his face light up and led the way indoors. It took a moment for her eyes to adjust to the gloom of the house. Although the shutters were fastened back from the windows, the stone walls were thick and the window apertures small. She threw a handful of ground bere into the soup to thicken it and make a more substantial meal, then stirred the peats and swung the cauldron across to have the benefit of their heat. 'Have you news from Dornoch?' she asked the boy and was disturbed to see him shrink into himself as he sat on the stool near the fire.

'Bad mens,' he said. 'Bad mens.'

'What do you mean, Willie?' she asked quietly. 'Come now,' she coaxed. 'There's no-one here to hurt you. What bad men? Did you see them?' The boy nodded. 'Where?' demanded Morag, her voice sharpening in spite of herself.

Willie shook his head. 'Bad mens,' he muttered again. 'Bad mens by Hamish's beasts.'

This made some kind of sense to Morag. When the weather was warm, Willie preferred to sleep in the fields with the beasts. But Hamish's croftland was only the other side of the small smoke at Evelick - too close for comfort.

'What were they doing, Willie? Where did they go?'

'Killed Hamish's coos. Went to the big toon.'

Morag frowned. Perhaps her father hadn't been so foolish after all. The cows would normally come down from the shieling for Samhain, but this year, the weather had been wet and warm. Lowland grass had grown lush, so Hamish had brought his cattle down early and urged Father to do the same. But Father would take no heed. His kine stayed at the shieling. Only now were they getting ready to return; cattle, women, children and cailleachs - the old women who carried the history and wisdom of the clans in their memories. Poor Hamish had already recovered his beasts from the hill and now, it seemed, had lost them. But at Evelick? So close. What were raiders doing there? And who were they?

Surely not wild youngsters out to prove themselves? They would have driven the cattle off, not killed them.

'Why kill them?' she murmured to herself.

But Willie had sharp ears. 'They eats them,' he assured her.

'Of course,' she said. If indeed a large force was attacking Dornoch they would have come from far and would need to be fed. But what were they doing this side of the town? They could only have come from the North, so why stray as far as Evelick, well to the West? Morag chafed at her inability to leave the farm. If she went to find out what was happening there'd be no-one to watch over the remaining beasts. The sheep would soon need milking and someone must tend the fire if she was to be away any length of time. Then she smiled. Willie. Of course. He could stay. As long as he didn't feel too afraid he would stay and guard the hearth.

A short while later Morag strode down the strath towards Evelick. She would avoid any contact with the people there for they were known to owe allegiance to Caithness's allies, but in that area she would find paths often trodden between the strath and Dornoch so the going would be easier. The hot sun was at her back and brought out the smells of whin and heather. Her skirts brushed the wild garlic that grew in profusion along the way and all around her the late summer colours glowed. Had she not been so worried Morag would have revelled in an hour of freedom to wander along and collect Nature's fruits and herbs to augment the food she could produce.

If she crossed the River Evelick by the stepping stones close to home and left Skibo on her right she could reach the beach and follow it into town. Walking there would be easier than pushing through the rough undergrowth here. But Willie had said the 'bad men' had gone, and by way of Evelick was the most direct route to Dornoch. There she hoped to find her father or at least news of what was happening. As she hurried along she drew her plaid around her shoulders and frowned. The day had been hot and bright, but ahead was a louring sky. Perhaps its sullen mien lent force to the feeling of foreboding that nagged at her mind? September just past, and the days should still be long enough, but to the east the sky was growing darker by the minute.

She kept well clear of the bounds of Hamish's land and saw no-one. Then on she went following the shorter grasses along the raised beach using bushes and small clumps of wind-pruned trees for cover. Her bare feet gave her a sure grip on the sandy soil. Soon a breeze blew into her face. Morag stopped and sniffed. She frowned. A fire? But there were no smokes in this area. Hamish's was the last habitation of any size this side of Dornoch. A couple of cottar's had their huts down near the water where they supplemented the harvest of their miserable soil by netting fish but with the wind in this direction there was no way she could smell their fires. And this wasn't peat smoke, so sweet and comforting. This air had an acrid smell and a taste that made her want to clean out her mouth. Morag's heart beat faster as she hurried, now careless of concealment. What did this mean? She stopped and strained her ears sure she had heard someone call. Were Father and the brothers on their way back? Had they seen her and called a greeting? But no. There was nothing, only the wind gaining strength and now the glow of the setting sun reflected on the low clouds. Morag stopped - eyes staring. The sun set in the west and she was facing east - east towards the town of Dornoch. The clouds were flame lit. Dornoch was burning.

With a sob in her throat Morag pulled her plaid closer round her body and hurried on. Head low against the wind she stumbled along the barely visible track. As she drew closer she heard shouts, screams, and could make out voices cursing. She hid in the undergrowth as a group of men ran across her path. Their voices were strange to her ear, not local men. Gathering her courage, she crept forward. The thudding of her heart beat against her bodice. Here was the edge of the township. Everywhere there were houses aflame. As the wind whipped the smoky clouds back and forth she saw the top of the cathedral tower outlined against the livid sky behind it. The sight of its solid strength gave her the courage to creep from one shadow to another seeking her family. She choked back a cry of horror as she almost fell across the body of a man lying dead by the wall of a smouldering hut. She bit her lip and moved on. But as she penetrated farther into the town there were more and more signs of defeat. The bodies she saw were nearly all Murrays, men and a few women who had had no time to flee or been too old to run. And the noise ahead was increasing in volume. By the sound of it someone had found the ale-house and plundered the contents.

Morag hesitated then reluctantly drew back. With cautious steps she retreated to the edge of the town then with one more backward glance fled towards the strath and the comparative safety of her home.

When she could bear the stitch in her side no longer Morag dropped to her knees her chest heaving. What should she do? It was hopeless to try and find her kin in the holocaust of fire and smoke Dornoch had become. What if they were all dead? She shook her head. That she couldn't and wouldn't believe. Her father was too canny to get trapped in a burning town. To her knowledge he had taken part in several skirmishes, always knowing when the race was lost and withdrawing in time to fight another day. Strategy he called it. She had heard him teaching her brothers. 'It is worth losing a battle to win a war.' They would return – all three of them. She knew it.

As her breath steadied Morag felt her heart race but not with fear. This must be what it felt like to be a man. To be seized by a kind of madness that put aside all thought of personal safety in order to achieve a goal. On the heels of that feeling of freedom and power came the knowledge she could never enjoy that kind of life. She was always aware of consequences and besides she was a female, a chattel at her father's bidding. The bitter truth rose like bile in her throat. She hawked and spat it aside, scrambled to her feet and made her careful way around Hamish Beag's land.

Thirst took her to the river where she had so often paddled seeking the fresh-water mussels to rob them of their harvest of small pearls. Her dowry she had called them. Morag's lips tightened at the thought. If her father had his way she would have no need of dowry. She sighed and reached forward to scoop the sweet water into her mouth then she plunged her hot face beneath the cool surface. If only her problems could be washed away as easily as the sweat and soot on her skin life would be wonderful. Gasping she lifted her head and smiled at her thoughts. How simple that would be. But life was not like that.

As she dried her face on her plaid she froze at a sound nearby. A human sound. She was not alone. There it was again. A groan of agony. Fearfully Morag glanced around. She could see nothing. She had left the murk of the burning town behind her and now the shortening day was almost gone. Shadows in the gloaming could hide any number of desperate men. She held her breath and waited. The groan came again. Friend or foe? She could not tell.

'Water! For the love of God. Water!'

The voice was strange to her ears. A man she was pretty sure but not one of her kind. She turned her head to peer into the darkness of the riverbank. There! A flash of paler light. Skin perhaps? Tense, she looked around again. Was this a trap? But who would want to trap her? No stranger would know the river bank was here. The sides were steep and topped by a grove of trees. At sound of that heart-rending plea again Morag cupped her hands together and tried to lift as much water as possible between them. Then she made her careful way towards the noise.

It was a boy. Or at least a young man. No great warrior he, but someone nearer herself in age who turned agonised fearful eyes towards her as she knelt where he lay. She tipped as much of the water as she could into his open mouth but it was clumsy work and most of it splashed onto his face. 'Wait,' she said, then smiled at her words. This fellow was going nowhere. She hurried back to the water's edge and dipped the end of her plaid into the water until it was sodden and dripping then retraced her steps. 'Open your mouth,' she commanded and as he obeyed she squeezed as much water from the material as she could. He swallowed with difficulty but managed to croak his thanks.

She repeated her ministering three times then used the damp plaid to wipe his bruised and bloody face. By now she could scarcely see him but her gentle exploring fingers found a gash on his head. 'Can you get up?' she asked. 'I can help you to the water's edge. Then you can drink your fill.'

'I can't,' he replied. 'I am wounded in the leg.'

'Wounded?' Once more she was alarmed. Her breath caught in her throat. 'Are there more of you here?'

He managed to laugh. 'No mistress, only me. You need have no fear. As usual I have fulfilled my father's high opinion of me and made a noble mess of everything.'

Morag's heart warmed with fellow feeling. 'How have you done this? He surely cannot blame you for being wounded. How many of the enemy were there?' For a moment she forgot that it was he who was the enemy to her kin.

The young man laughed again. 'My father was wrong. He said I would never draw blood in battle. This raid was my chance he said, to prove him wrong – and I did. Unfortunately the only blood I drew was mine own.' By the light of the rising moon, now peeping through the branches above them he saw the puzzlement on her face. 'I was hurrying after my brothers, last as usual because I was adjusting the set of my dirk. I tripped on my plaid then on a tree root, lost my footing and fell down this bank. I felt the blade of my claymore slice into my leg then my head met stone and I knew nothing more.'

Morag could see just how it had happened. Above their heads the bank had eroded until its rim ran close to the roots of the trees. Any stranger seeking cover to advance would be unable to tell how near he was to the edge. She pressed her lips tightly together trying to quell the rising bubble of mirth but in vain. Her giggle was echoed by the stranger's shout of laughter abruptly cut off by a gasp of pain. 'What is it?' said Morag.

'It hurts when I laugh,' he replied, 'and when I breathe and when I move and when I try to do anything.'

'I understand,' she smiled. 'I'm sorry I laughed but the picture you showed me was so funny. Let me see your wound,' she went on as she started to run her hands over his legs starting from the ankle. 'What's your name?'

'Dougal. Dougal Mackay.'

Morag stiffened. The Mackays were no friends to the Murrays. But their lands lay far away to the north and east. She'd heard them spoken of with admiration as brave fighters. But what were they doing here?

'I've no more idea than you,' Dougal said in reply to her question. 'Apparently it's politics. The great ones say fight and we answer - who? We're Mackays of Strathnaver and why we should be here is a mystery to me. No doubt some feud or slight will be at the back of it. There were Sinclairs with us and some said Sutherland of Duffus was in it too. I neither know nor care. I can't see why we had to come so far and in company with them but John, Maister of Caithness, called and I suppose we must have owed some debt of honour. My father bade us come and here we are.'

'Honour!' Morag was scathing. 'You call it honourable to set fire to homes and murder women in their beds?'

The hapless Dougal then blundered. 'Women don't understand war. It's not like that at all.'

Morag sat back on her heels fisted her hands on her hips and glared at him. 'And you my great warrior, how many battles have you fought? Have you even seen a town that has been sacked by an invader?'

'No, but . . .'

'Well I have. These are my people.' She described the pitiful sights she had seen in Dornoch that day. As she did so the reality and enormity of what had befallen her kinsmen hit home. She bent her head and wept. Some of those dead would surely be known to her.

Unable to move from where he lay Dougal reached for her hand to comfort her. 'I'm sorry. I'm a fool speaking so glibly of things I know nothing of. I copy my brothers and I ought to know better. They boast and lie about the stupidest things. They must surely be ignorant of the pain they inflict.' He fell silent waiting for her tears to cease. 'I'm glad I was such a poor warrior on my first foray. I'm glad I fell and injured myself. I would not want to harm your kin.'

His words reminded Morag he was wounded. She resumed her gentle exploration. His stifled groan told her when she was getting close to the spot. Even without it she would have known. The flesh of his thigh was swollen and hot to the touch a sure sign of putrefaction. She frowned. 'How long have you lain here?'

'I don't really know. I told you I hit my head and swooned. How long I was out of my senses I know not. It had been dusk when we approached this spot. We were to come to this side of the town and spring a surprise while the main body attacked from north and east. For hours we had lain above watching the lie of the land and biding our time. When I came to my senses it was daylight but of the next day or another I don't know. I had a raging thirst that has consumed me for the last two or three days – I think.'

'You think?'

'Time seemed to play tricks. The sun was never in the right place when I opened my eyes. Maybe I have lain for four nights maybe five?'

'No wonder your wound has gone bad. It needs immediate treatment.'

Dougal grimaced. 'The treatment I would get from any of your kin would be immediate enough. A dirk across my throat or a claymore through my heart.'

'But you have done nothing wrong.'

'Neither side would agree with that. Your kin would rightly say I had no business here and mine would demand why I hadn't killed the enemy?'

Morag thought for a while. There must be something she could do for this likeable young man who seemed to suffer from a father's ire as she did. Of course, being a male, he had no idea of real suffering at the hands of his sire. She would wager he had plenty of freedom. Perhaps he was his mother's favourite as this was his first outing in anger? Had a doting mother interceded for him to remain with her until now?

'What are you thinking?'

'I shall tend your wound. You are safe enough here if you keep quiet. Few come this way. But you will have to trust me. I cannot return before mid morning tomorrow. I know it is long but I have duties to perform and . . .' from hoping her father and brothers would hurry back she now wished their return would be delayed. 'I may not be able to get away when I wish.'

'Of course not. Where is your man? What is he thinking of to let you wander alone in these troubled times?'

Morag hesitated. If she confessed her unmarried state she was leaving herself vulnerable. But honesty had been between her and Dougal from the beginning. She compromised. 'I am not wed but keep house for my father and three brothers.' There. She had told the truth but also explained she was not without kin who would avenge her should any man harm her.

Dougal smiled. 'I don't believe it. Have the men in these parts no eyes in their heads. Your mirror must tell you what a bonny lass you are. May I know your name?'

'Morag. Morag Murray.'

Dougal's eyes widened. 'And you give me succour, Morag Murray?'

'We are not unfeeling monsters. But now I must go. I have been too long already. I won't drag you nearer the water. You are better concealed where you lie but drink once more from my hands and I will leave you my plaid to keep you warm. You'll stay dry. There'll be no rain this night.'

Dougal smiled up at her. 'How do you know?'

She shook her head in pity. 'I'm a country woman. We know these things from our cradles. Rest now. I will return.'

Back at the farm Morag found Willie curled sleeping by the hearth. He had milked the sheep and covered the pail. He stirred and smiled at her. She thanked him for his work and offered him more broth to eat while she cooked the rabbit she had taken from the snare at the edge of the pastureland. This was one rabbit that should not eat Murray crops.

While her hands went automatically through the motions of gutting, skinning and jointing the rabbit for the pot Morag's thoughts were confused and contradictory. What was she thinking of, aiding an enemy? If ever her kin found out she would be - at the least - beaten senseless - at worst - cast out forever from the lands of her clan. Yet could she leave him to die? Die he would if that badness in his leg was not excised. It would gradually creep through his body poisoning every part. And such a handsome body too. Morag smiled as she remembered the feel of Dougal's strong muscled leg when she searched for his wound. He had a bonny face and the smile of a mischievous angel. For a while in his company she felt she had a friend. She had relaxed in the time they had spent together. And tomorrow she would see him again. But what if he were discovered before then? He would be killed or captured. And what of her plaid dyed and woven by her hands? Someone might recognise it. She wore it each day. Would Dougal cover up for her? Say he found it or stole it perhaps? If he were ever given the chance to talk before they slit his throat.

That night sleep was a long time coming to Morag and fantastical dreams interrupted her rest. She flew through the air yet how she did not know. Below on one side there were great forests strung through with a necklace of lochs leading to rocky outcrops and then a shining sea. On the other, most of the trees had disappeared. Fields took their place and the smokes that marked dwellings were crowded with more people than Morag had ever seen in one place. These smokes were joined by wide hard paths where people and wagons passed each other always hurrying. Where were they going? And always ahead of her was Dougal his white teeth flashing in his sunburnt face. He held out his hand to her but she was afraid to take hold of it. Something held her back. Morag woke in a foul mood next morning.

She cut Willie a chunk of porridge from the drawer and gave him some of the sheep's milk to break his fast and to act as a bribe to remain at the farm. He helped her rush through her chores and promised to milk the sheep again that evening. Morag sent him on an errand to check the traps around the farm and keep his eyes open for any hens laying away from the house. It was too late in the year to let them get broody. While Willie was gone Morag gathered together what she would need and tied it into a bundle she could carry easily. The sweet-natured loon made no comment when she told him she would be away on an errand for some time but he promised to remain until her return at least.

With care Morag approached the spot where she had left Dougal. Her heart pounded. It would not do to be seen here. She was no longer her mother's darling daughter allowed to roam with her friends and paddle in the Evelick river seeking pearls. Questions would be raised if she were seen away from the farm through the day in these dangerous times.

She crept below the shelter of the overhanging trees and saw the strain on Dougal's face. He had raised his head as he watched to see whose arrival the rustlings heralded. He closed his eyes in relief as he recognised Morag. His whole body relaxed and his grateful smile was reward enough for her unquiet night. She spread out her bundle beside him and busied herself making a small fire.

'Is that a good idea?' he queried. 'We don't want to give away our position.'

'It is necessary and I have very dry kindling here that will not smoke but burn with a strong heat. Any stray wisp of smoke will disperse through the undergrowth and tree branches above us.' She placed a small pannikin of water on the glowing wood which was bone dry and burned fiercely. It came from her precious store gathered along the beach and kept under cover indoors. Next she pushed up the plaid covering Dougal's thigh. He winced at her touch gentle though it was. From knee to just below his groin the whole was swollen, the stretched skin glistened red. A livid patch of ugly yellow spread from the centre of the wound where the skin had closed over it. Morag dipped the corner of her plaid into the river and cleaned the place. 'I need heat to clean your wound.'

Dougal grimaced and spoke through gritted teeth. 'That doesn't sound too comfortable.'

She regarded him seriously. 'It won't be. But the only other choice is death. If the wound is too bad it may be I should take your leg but I have not the skill or strength to do that...'

'I thank God for it,' Dougal exclaimed with a grin.

'... and you I think would not survive in your present weak state.'

The young man's face whitened. His eyes grew round with horror. 'I hoped you were jesting, yet know you do not. I had rather die than be a one-legged cripple.' The words burst from him at the thought.

Having got him into a suitably serious frame of mind Morag patted his shoulder. 'Pray it will not come to that. I think the fire is hot enough now. How sharp is your dirk?'

Dougal looked alarmed. 'Why? I thought we were safe enough here.'

'It's not for fighting but healing – I hope.' Morag took the dirk from its scabbard on the ground by his hand. He had been ready to defend himself if discovered. How long she wondered had he lain through the night straining eyes and ears for warning of approaching danger? She thrust the tip of the blade into the heart of the fire then knelt and blew into the embers. The heat reddened her cheeks. Her eyes watered and she closed them tight but did not give up on her task.

At last she was satisfied. From the items in her bundle she took a piece of thick leather bent over along its length and bound with twine to form a hard rod. 'Bite on that,' she commanded. With wary eyes Dougal clamped the leather in his strong white teeth and watched as she withdrew the dirk from the fire. 'Perhaps you should look away,' Morag suggested, but his gaze was fixed on the glowing tip of the blade. Morag sent up a prayer for help to her mother, a noted healer in her day. If only Morag could remember just how Mairead had healed her family's wounds. With all her courage she drew in a deep breath pursed her lips and drew the sharpened blade firmly through the hideous mass on Dougal's thigh. With a groan of agony he closed his eyes. She exhaled on a sigh spared him a glance and saw the sweat start out on his brow. Then she bit her lip and continued her work.

Having reopened the wound she next used a piece of fine lawn taken from her mother's wooden kist, wet it in the simmering water of the panninkin, and by dint of swabbing and squeezing she encouraged the stinking pus to leave the infected thigh. As she worked her way deeper into the hole his claymore had torn open Dougal groaned again and fell into a swoon. One worried glance Morag spared him then worked faster taking less care now not to hurt him but using to the full the advantage of his unfeeling state. She dropped into the pannikin her mother's proudest possession a fine metal needle together with the piece of twine attached and once she was satisfied the wound was clean she poured the remainder of the hot water into it patted it dry and began to sew the edges of the wound together. She pressed lavender flowers against the join and bound up the whole. Then she poured broth from her flask into the pannikin and waited anxiously.

'Holy Mother of God,' groaned Dougal. 'Have I died yet?'

Morag smiled. 'So you're back with us are you?'

'Yes and would rather not be,' said her ungrateful patient.

'I think you'll live. Here take some broth.' She supported him against her shoulder and held a bowl to his lips. He drank carefully at first and then more greedily. She spooned into his mouth the pieces of rabbit she had thrown into the cauldron. He chewed with relish.

'I have died and gone to heaven,' he declared. 'Is there more?'

She fed him another bowlful anxious to give him as much nourishment as possible. He would need all his strength to recover from what she had done to him. 'That's enough for now. I have black pudding for you here. It's meal I've ground myself and the blood from our cows is full of goodness. It will soon have you well again. Take half now and save the rest for this evening. Here is water in the flask and a piece of porridge for tomorrow until I come again.'

'Don't go,' he begged. 'Stay awhile with me.'

'Not today. You have need of rest. Now you have eaten I hope you will sleep. That is the best healer I know. Tomorrow I shall try and stay with you a while. Sleep now,' she smiled. Already his eyes were heavy. The good broth and food would work their magic and give him much-needed strength. The sooner he could walk, the safer they both would be. She must get him to leave as soon as possible but she wanted to give him the best chance she could. Why save his life only to see him cut down?

The following few days were the happiest Morag could remember since her mother died. Dougal rapidly gained strength and appetite. Eagerly he devoured the food she brought him. Once his needs were met natural curiosity emerged. He would know more of his rescuer.

'You say you are not married but how can that be? Even if the menfolk around here were blind or you so hideous you could sour the milk, from what you say your father has a fine farm so you cannot be dowerless. And I know you are a grand cook and healer. What more can a man ask in a wife?'

His artless question opened the floodgates of Morag's unhappiness. Into his sympathetic ear she poured her woes. 'I know my own worth,' she exclaimed bitterly, 'none better and I would make any man a good wife . . . if I was let. But my father sees me only as an unpaid servant and intends me to stay by him and tend to his house all his life. By the time he dies I shall be truly an old woman to be pitied, with neither chick nor child, for the farm will go to my youngest brother.'

'But your father must value you highly,' suggested Dougal in a vain attempt to cheer her.

'Och, aye! As highly as a fleet garron or a heavy cow that will bring him coin at the cattle fair at Muir of Ord. He doesn't see me as a person with hopes and dreams but just one more of his possessions to make him either richer or more comfortable.'

'Would your brothers not speak for you?'

'Not they! He made them in his mould. Only Rabbie is my friend and that because I raised him. My mother died in childbirth when I was twelve years old. Suddenly I had a home and child to look after. The wet nurse took the baby for six months. I thought my father couldn't bear to see the wean that had robbed him of his wife but one day he brought home this bundle and laid it in my lap as I sat by the hearth. It was Rabbie and father bade me tend him.'

'Was that so very bad? I should like to have a younger brother. I am the youngest and the butt of all my brothers' jokes. I know my mother favours me and perhaps they are a bit jealous. They are rough but not really unkind.'

'My older brothers are married and live apart from us. My father keeps his own counsel. Ours is a silent house except when he is out. Then Rabbie will sing and play the fool for me.' She smiled. 'When the men are ploughing it is Rabbie who goes backwards in front of the horse-gang to encourage the beasts to pull. His capers even make my father smile – sometimes – but you have to judge his mood. When we were all small he sub-let some land but the smokes are higher up the strath. I rarely see the folks who bide there. And he made sure the boys live at a distance. He cannot be doing with noisy bairns around his hearth. I am as isolated by that as by my position.'

'I don't understand. What position?'

'My father is the richest farmer this side of Dornoch. As the mistress of his house people respect me yet in their eyes I see pity. They know my situation.' She turned towards Dougal. 'When we harvest the first sheaf of corn cut is called The Maiden.' He nodded. The same custom pertained where he lived. 'It is a privilege to be given this sheaf. The lucky girl will usually be wed within a twelvemonth. But in the strath the sheaf is always given to me.' She lowered her head so Dougal would not see the tears that threatened to fall. 'I hate it. I hate it,' she muttered so low he had to lean nearer to hear her words. 'It is a constant underlining of my unmarried state. And each year it will be the same. My father insists on the sheaf being awarded to me. As his daughter it is my right – but only until I wed.' She raised her head. Angry eyes glared into Dougal's face. 'He mocks me,' she cried. 'And at the end of harvest when everyone is working faster to get their allotted amount done he will take me from the field on some errand and put any female on whom his wrath has fallen to take my place and be the shamed cutter of the last sheaf, the Cailleach - to be avoided at all costs. It is said to bring ill omen or disgrace. And it is me they blame for it. I hate him. I hate him.' Her voice rose. She fisted her hands at her breast. 'But what can I do? I'm just a woman. I know he has turned away three good men who wanted me and I would have accepted at least two out of them. They were not uncomely and good strong workers. These days I'd take Willie Bairn himself if only I could get away.'

Dougal frowned. 'Who's Willie Bairn?'

Then Morag had to explain who Willie was and this reminded her it was past time she got back to the farm.

The day following her ministration Dougal's leg had been cooler, but still stiff and sore. Morag was relieved to see the swelling appeared to have gone down considerably. On each visit she cleaned her handiwork and rebound the leg, fed the ravenous Dougal and then settled down for an enjoyable spell of stolen idleness.

'You haven't lost your appetite then,' she remarked.

He grinned and answered her with his mouth full. 'Don't you worry about my appetite. My mother says she'd rather keep me for a se'ennight than a month. Now you've sorted my leg I'll do fine. Another day or two and I'll be ready to go.'

Morag felt a pang of envy as she heard his words. What joy to be free to come and go as one pleased.

'Your food is wonderful,' continued Dougal. 'I feel stronger with every mouthful.' He chewed on the last of the latest rabbit Morag had saved for him. Willie had found yet another in the snares and it now lay stewing in the pot at the farm. Good broth from the stewing water would help to build up the invalid.

Morag smiled at her thoughts. Anyone behaving less like an invalid than Dougal would be hard to find. Already he was talking about walking on the morrow.

'Don't overdo it and burst my stitching,' she warned. 'Are you very close to your mother?' she added wistfully.

Dougal's face softened. 'I am her ewe lamb,' he acknowledged. 'Poor woman, she tried to keep me a child as long as she could. But I was raring to go off with my brothers all the time. Consequently, between her chiding me and them not wanting a tagger-on, I learned to make myself invisible at an early age. Too invisible sometimes,' he added with a shout of laughter. On being asked to explain he told her how he had fallen while spying on his brothers' games. No-one had known of his presence and so he had lain for hours with a twisted foot until his mother organised a search party to find him. 'Poor woman,' he said again. 'So many alarms I gave her.' His expression grew serious. 'I wonder if my father and brothers have returned to her with news of my death?'

'All the more joy for her when you arrive safe and well,' Morag hastened to say. 'How old are you, Dougal?'

He smiled. 'You think me younger than my age perhaps because I tell you the foolish things I did in my youth. But I have twenty summers at my back and I have seen wonderful things.'

'How is that?'

'My mother sent me to my kinsman Mackay at St Andrews to be educated. I spent some time at the university there and went with him to court while he was trying to reclaim title to Strathnaver from the devious Gordons.' Dougal spat upon the ground in his disdain for that hated clan. 'When I was sixteen I was at court with my cousin when the Queen gave birth to her son. What feasting there was - what rejoicing. But I was glad to leave. I am an honest man with a simple mind. Court intrigue was not to my liking no matter how exhilarating others might find it. You Murrays enraged Caithness when you helped young Earl Aexander escape to join his uncle Huntly. He vowed revenge. No doubt that's why we are here.' He smiled at Morag. 'You Murrays! Poking your noses in where they're not wanted.'

'Young Alexander wanted us well enough,' she retorted. 'I hear on all sides the cruelty of Caithness. Too many young men have died suddenly at his castle of Dunrobin.'

Dougal sobered. 'You are well-informed, Morag.'

'When you have no voice it is well to keep your ears open. That way you learn how, when the loyalties of great men change, trouble can come to disturb your own hearth.'

'That is true. It is a wise man who keeps a quiet tongue and an open mind.'

Morag nodded then shivered as a chill breeze sneaked through the shelter of the trees. She looked up at the sky then jumped to her feet. 'Heavens! The time has gone by so fast. Poor Willie, I have left him too long. I hope he has milked the sheep.' She smoored the fire and gathered together the pots and flasks she had brought to sustain Dougal. 'I will come again tomorrow. Rest easily and you will heal more quickly.'

But on the following day she brought disturbing news.

'What is wrong?' cried Dougal as he saw Morag's worried expression.

'Bad news,' she answered dropping to her knees and undoing her customary bundle. 'There'll be no fire the day. Your people have won,' she said bitterly. 'Butchers! The townsfolk are dead or fled and your kind lay siege to Dornoch Cathedral.'

Dougal's eyes opened wide. 'How can this be? Why a siege? If Caithness has won the day why does he not loot the place and withdraw? Why stay?'

'There are defenders barricaded into the cathedral tower it seems, defiant to the rule of Caithness and determined to stay put until reinforcements arrive. Perhaps they think Huntly will come to their rescue?' she added hopefully.

Dougal shook his head. 'I doubt it. He has bigger fish to fry and higher matters on which to bend his mind. A few townsfolk will not engage his head or heart to come to their aid.' He thought for a moment. 'But he will be glad of it!' he cried. 'While Caithness is engaged in this affair Huntly has one less worry at his back. He will not want any siege to be quickly lifted. But what has that to do with us?'

'They are my people who are dead and gone,' Morag cried.

Dougal reached out and gripped her hand. 'I know. I am sorry for it and I would wish it were otherwise but you are agitated for something closer to your own hearth.'

Morag let her hand lie a moment in his then withdrew it and began to get food for him out of her bundle. 'I got word of these doings from a neighbour passing our farm last night on his way back up the strath. He had lain in hiding for two days fearing for his life before he dared to sneak back home.'

'And is there any news of your kin?'

'Aye,' she nodded. 'It seems they have suffered lightly - gashes and bruising. Perhaps one has a broken arm. Andrew wasn't sure. But the worry is they are on their way home.' She looked with anguished eyes at the man lying helpless on the ground before her. 'Once they return there is no way I can get succour to you. If I left the farm they would follow and find you – and kill you without a second thought. If I leave you now there is no way you can regain your strength enough to escape from here. You don't know the land. Not everyone is fled, only the townsfolk and those nearest the smoke. You'll be seen and caught. And all my fine handiwork gone for nothing,' she ended on a sob of laughter.

'Where are your kin now?'

'Andrew Mhor thought they had gone to the shieling to protect our women and cattle and bring them home when it was safe. They should be there by now or at latest tomorrow. A day of rest and maybe a bit longer for wounds to heal - then two maybe three days to get back to the farm with all the bairns, wagons of cheeses and chattels. It will take some time. But they were due to return next week so already those at the shieling will have started preparations.' She wrung her hands desperately trying to judge just how long it would be before her father's return.

'Then you think we have three days clear before they come back?'

'Yes. No. I don't know. Father may send one of my brothers on ahead to guard the farm - although we should be far enough out of the way to escape any Dornoch raider's attentions. Two days, perhaps. We have two certain days.'

'Then in two days I shall leave.'

'Lucky you,' she cried unable to bite back her envy of his freedom.

Dougal looked at her. 'Come with me,' he urged. 'Strathnaver is a good land with rich farming and rivers full of fish.' He saw the doubt in her eyes and hurried on. 'Come as my friend and companion. You have all the skills of a woman grown. If you wish to marry there will be plenty of offers. You can take your pick,' he smiled.

She shook her head. 'You're havering, man. I am a Murray. You think your kin will welcome me with open arms?' she laughed scornfully.

'My mother would,' he answered quietly. 'You saved my life. But for what purpose if I cannot get back to my own place? I am being honest, Morag. I need you. I need you to flee from this place. But I am offering you a chance of freedom from the old life you say you hate so much. Or was that just wild talk?' he concluded.

She shook her head. 'No. It was the truth. But you don't know what you ask. You would have me leave my comfortable home and those I do hold dear, the bairns, and our people who come to me for help and advice. Who will intercede for them with my father?'

'It will not be your problem. They'll find another way.'

'And how would we manage?'

Wisely Dougal held his tongue.

'You say your mother would welcome me?'

'Aye. Indeed she would. Like the daughter she never had.'

'But - what of your other kin?'

He laughed. 'I am vain enough to believe my father and brothers have a fondness for me. They would thank you and they value bravery highly. They would not make light of what you have risked for me.'

'Where do you stay?'

'To the south of ruined Borve Castle. My mother was dowered with a fine farm from her grandfather. Added to the holdings of my father's family we have quite a settlement with my brothers and their families close by. Feast days are full of laughter and no-one goes hungry from a Mackay's door. Believe me, Morag, there will be room in plenty for you in my father's house. A woman who knows how to cook and tend the land and beasts must always be welcome, but I doubt you will remain long with us. I have lusty cousins who are looking for wives even now.'

'And they would wed with a Murray?'

'Why not? Fresh blood is good for breeding. Every farmer knows that.'

Morag laughed, then sobered quickly as more problems crowded into her mind. 'But you? Will you be strong enough to travel in two days? You must!'

'Bring me a stout stick cut with a fork at the top, long enough to go beneath my shoulder and I shall whittle myself a good crutch. Do you know the land beyond Dornoch?'

'I am sure I can take us as far as Littleferry but beyond that I don't know. Do you know the way home?'

'No.' He laughed as he saw her face. 'But it will be easy enough. I know we must strike North. Once past the head of Loch Fleet we are nearly in Mackay country. Far enough in that direction, and then we trek eastwards until we reach somewhere I recognise. Don't fret. We'll get there right enough.'

'And you say you have twenty summers? You talk like a bairn.'

'How so? Are my directions not correct?'

She pondered a moment. Truly she had heard Strathnaver covered most of the land to the north of Dornoch, and Strathnaver was Mackay country. It seemed too easy to just head north and then east and hope to find Dougal's home, but was it? Somewhere along the way there must be some of his kin. They would give them food and shelter and guide them on their journey. If she had the courage she could travel to this new land of which he spoke with such glowing eyes. She looked across to where he watched her. 'I'll think about it,' she promised. 'In the mean time you must start to use your leg – but gently. Try and bend and lift it before you put any weight on it at all. Tomorrow I shall help you to try and stand. Only then will we have any idea if your plan is possible.'

As she hurried back to the farm, fed Willie, completed her chores and settled the beasts for the night, Morag's thoughts sloshed round in her head like buttermilk in the churn. Should she go? Should she stay? Could she go? What would happen to her father and the farm if she left? That was the easiest question to answer. If he chose to re-marry he wouldn't be short of willing partners. Or perhaps he would simply load Morag's chores onto the shoulders of her sisters-in-law? Or in a very few years Father could encourage Rabbie to marry and bring a new woman into the farm to answer to his beck and call. At least Rabbie would stick up for his wife and not let their father bully her.

But that wasn't the root of Morag's problem. Did she *want* to go? It would mean leaving behind all she knew for a strange country maybe with different customs certainly with a difference in language although Dougal was easy enough to understand. Perhaps that was because he was educated? All this talk of University and the Queen's Court. Morag had her letters learned at her mother's knee but that was all, beyond the wisdom of nature. What would these folk of his be like who had such grand kin? Would she get the welcome he believed to be her due? Or would they scorn an uneducated country girl? Would any man be willing to marry a dowerless Murray? At this she lifted her head proudly. Dowerless she may be but as good in her own place as any fine lady. Then Morag's busy hands stilled. She smiled. She was not dowerless. She had her pearls. The linen bag in which she kept them at the bottom of her wooden kist was heavy with the harvest of her childhood. Over the years she had added to them on the odd occasion she could steal an hour to herself to paddle in the Evelix and remember happier times when her mother was alive.

But the questions remained. Did she want to go and was such a journey feasible with a man she scarcely knew and who was sorely wounded? Strangely it was not her ignorance of Dougal before these days that bothered her but more the actual doing of the deed. Instinctively she knew she could trust the young Mackay. If only he would heal rapidly in the next two days she would be quite content in his company.

Next day Morag found Dougal standing to greet her beneath the trees. He hung on firmly to a branch above his head. She noticed he let little weight press on his wounded leg but it was a great improvement to lying on the turf.

Having succeeded in impressing her he was quite willing to lower himself to the ground again and attacked her offering of food with relish. 'I swear it is your good victuals that make me strong,' he declared. 'Did you get the wood?'

Morag showed him the pieces she had managed to chop, nearly breaking the simple axe.

'It would have been better to get pieces less green,' Dougal observed. 'They would bend less and be easier to whittle.'

Hands on hips Morag stood, mouth open ready to blast him for his churlish lack of appreciation, then shook her head. He had no idea. No idea how hard it was for her to get to the river to tend and feed him without being seen and rousing comment. No idea how difficult it was not to let slip a wrong word to sweet Willie Bairn who, simple though he may be, was beginning to wonder where Morag went each day. To add the hard toil of chopping a specific shape of stout branch well away from the house and steading had been wearisome physically and a strain on her nerves. Any moment she expected to be discovered. 'You'll have to make do,' was all she said. 'I brought you a bundle of rags to pad the end of your fine crutch.' She held out the cloths and was rewarded by his flashing smile. She wondered how often it had got him out of trouble. 'I can't stay today. I have too much work to do. Here is your food and I have brought you a flask of milk. There's goodness in it,' she added as she saw his lip curl in distaste. 'Be grateful.'

Again that smile. 'I am Morag. I am. So much you cannot guess. Have you . . .?' He broke off his question as she stiffened her back and pursed her lips. 'I'll not moither you,' he promised. 'I'll look for you the morn's morn.'

When Morag returned to the farm she was dismayed to find Willie Bairn nowhere to be seen. Ah, well! The loon had stayed longer than he usually did unless there was lambing or farrowing to help with. He loved to help bring new lives into the world. In some ways it was as well he was not here. She could make her preparations in peace.

First she put a great quantity of oatmeal in the cauldron to cook over the fire. She intended to empty the drawer for their journey so must replace the porridge taken with fresh for the family. Tomorrow if there was a rabbit in the snare she would cook it to take with them. If not - she looked up into the rafters where the sleepy hens roosted – did she dare take one of them? Why not, she asked herself? Had she not raised them? But to kill a beast while there was still feeding from the land was a heresy. Winter was the time of slaughter when precious feed both for man and beast had to be eked out until the grass grew again. Sometimes the Spring was late and cold. Then the cattle preserved grew so weak over the hard winter months it took three men to carry them out of the byre to the welcome warmth of the early Summer sun. But this year the harvest had been good. There were bere and hay in plenty and father would buy more oats with the coin he would get from the cattle he did sell at the mart. Yes, there was enough to make sure the two-legged and four-legged inhabitants of the farm had full bellies through the harsh dark days of the winter to come. Morag shuddered at the thought she might be lost in the Northlands with Dougal Mackay when winter came, then thrust aside such cowardly feelings.

Mentally she made an inventory of what she would like to take with her in her flight. Then with a sigh she became more practical. Only what she could carry and perhaps a small lighter bundle for Dougal would be possible so she must choose wisely.

Her grandfather's old sporran she could belt around her waist and fill with porridge. That would keep them going for a day or two until they were far enough away to light a fire in safety and cook whatever they could catch. The rest of the porridge from the drawer she would carry in the smallest of the household cooking pots. Dougal could whittle her spirtles to stir her cauldron. She smiled. Perhaps he would have his uses after all. So far he seemed only to be a burden to her in her flight – apart from being a good companion and having at least some idea of the way they must take. One ladle she allowed herself and two horn spoons remembering how difficult it was to hold water or any liquid in her hands. Two flasks she would fill with milk at the start of their journey. Later they would be good for water carrying. Her knife went everywhere with her to gather edibles as she found them. Her mother's precious iron needle, with two of bone and several hanks of twine she added to the pile along with strips of linen with many uses. She would wash and dry those bound around Dougal's thigh tomorrow. The wound had healed well and provided he did not abuse his leg he should quickly regain his strength. He was fit and strong and had told her he had never been ill in his life.

She laid out her small collection of clothes and wondered what she could take with her. Her pride would not let her appear before Dougal's kin in her everyday garb. That would no doubt suffer greatly through the coming days tramping through bog and heather. If she wore her best clothes beneath her skirt and sark, tied her bundle on her back wrapped in her mother's fine shawl, as women carried small children, she could secure the whole with grandfather's belt from which hung the sporran. Then over the top she would throw her mother's plaid. Dougal would still need Morag's for warmth and shelter from the rain. The plaids would protect them from all but the heaviest downpour. She had helped her mother weave them from undyed sheep's wool to preserve the natural lanolin that shed water so well. She loved the black, white and shades of brown from her own small flock. She would miss them most of all. They had listened to her fears and problems since first her mother had taught her to milk. They stood not much taller than a big dog and were so used to her they would come at her call pushing their pink noses into her hand and butting her gently with their four or six-horned heads.

Dropping with exhaustion Morag went to her bed but once again her sleep was disturbed by dreams. She and Dougal were fleeing from the strath but they had crossed into a bog and her father and brothers were pursuing them, rapidly shortening the distance between them. The more she struggled to free herself and move forward the deeper into the mire she sank. 'Help me!' she cried to Dougal but he changed into Wille Bairn lifted her in his arms and carried her back to her father. Then she woke up.

When she reached the riverside next morning she found Dougal hopping about using his makeshift crutch.

'See how well I am doing,' he cried, just as the tip of the crutch sank into the sandy soil by the water and he had to abandon it and grab at a tree branch to stop himself falling in.

'Pride goes before a fall,' laughed Morag. But she watched his efforts with a sinking heart. If they were to flee undetected they must move by night or at least in the gloaming. It was hard enough to pick a path through the undergrowth for an able-bodied person but how was Dougal to manage it? She hid her fears and commended his progress. 'You've done well but don't push yourself too hard. You have at least today and tomorrow to get stronger. How is the pain?'

Dougal grimaced. ''If I don't think about it, it will go away'. My granny used to say that when she was an old, old woman. And 'pain, like the poor, is always with us'. That was another of her sayings. She was a wonderful woman and told the most amazing tales. She had stories going back two hundred years, and a memory as sharp as my *skean dhu*.'

'I look forward to meeting her,' said Morag.

Dougal shook his head. 'She died when I was away at the court. It saddened me I was not there at her end for they told me she asked for me. I arrived too late,' he said simply. 'She always said I would travel far yet stay near. I never really knew what she meant and now I suppose I never shall.'

'I am sorry for it. But I must get back. I shall bring my bundle here tomorrow with your food and leave it. If Willie Bairn doesn't come back I must get someone to tend my sheep. If they are not milked the poor beasts will suffer such pain. I can't let that happen. You continue to exercise gently and be ready to leave either tomorrow night or the day after. I daren't leave it any longer. Don't stray far from this spot or you could be seen. Remember it's not just your neck you would be risking,' she warned as she saw an objection in his eyes

Sobered then he nodded. 'I will stay close,' he promised.

On her way home Morag took a fine rabbit from the snare then uprooted the snare and, once back at the farm, added it to her escape pile. She emptied the drawer of old porridge cramming it into the sporran and small pot then spread the newly made mass into the drawer and slid it under its cover. That would keep father going until he organised his household. She filled the empty pot with water from the burn that ran behind the house threw in some wild garlic leaves and a small amount of rendered fat from the crock. Then she added the jointed rabbit and left it to cook. What else would she need?

She sorted through her treasures. The bag of pearls would hang by a thread around her neck. In it she would also put the gold pin her mother had worn on her cloak the day she was wed. She had promised it to her only daughter for her marriage day. For the first time in a long while Morag thought that perhaps that day might come. There was her horn comb and pins for her hair, three ribbons she had had from a Traveller woman, and the multi-coloured girdle she had woven from the finest of her sheep's wool. With beating heart Morag approached her father's sleeping place. She knew where he kept his box of coin. She would not take the golden pieces for such would be his rage he would chase her to the end of the earth to recover them. But she felt it her due to take small coins. 'The labourer is worthy of his hire', the minister had said. And that meant her hire too in Morag's eyes. All these years she had toiled for her father without thanks or even a kind word. In her more charitable moments she believed she reminded him too much of his dead wife. She could not recall him being so dour when her mother was alive. Had her death broken his heart? But then on other occasions Morag was convinced the man did not possess one to break. He owed her for the husbands who had been warned off and for the children she could have borne.

Next day Morag took her biggest bundle to leave with Dougal. 'Don't touch anything,' she warned. 'It is packed just so and ready for the road. How is your leg?'

'It ached last night but this morning once I had walked a bit it has eased.'

'Good. It is well you are young and fit. You have today and then tomorrow night we must be off. I feel my father's presence drawing closer.'

He looked to see if she was jesting but her face was serious and worried. 'Have you the sight?' he asked.

Morag shook her head. 'No, I thank God . . . at least, not as you mean it. That is a fearful gift to be given and a heavy burden to carry. But just sometimes, I feel as if someone has drawn back a veil and I can almost see beyond. It is a feeling,' she cried, 'not the sight. Not that!'

Clumsily he patted her arm. 'It's alright,' he said. 'I expect it is all the worry I have brought on you that makes you nervous. I am sorry for it and ready to do whatever you command.' He finished his promise with an impish grin that drew an answering smile from Morag as he had intended. 'I will be good,' he said.

Next day Willie Bairn appeared by Morag's side sure of his welcome. She didn't question where he had been. He seemed to have very little feeling of time passing and kept a different clock from the rest of the world. After she put food before him she set him some tasks to do and hurried down to Dougal. 'It is tomorrow,' she cried. 'If my kin were close enough to arrive today Willie Bairn would know and would have told me. Tomorrow I shall send him on an errand. I have a gift for my friend Ephie who is to marry. Willie shall deliver it and stay there the night. I will ask him to return for the following evening to keep me company. By then the sheep will need to be milked and he will be there to do it.'

'You and your sheep!' exclaimed Dougal. 'Is that all you can think of?'

'They are dear to me and I would not have any creature suffer unnecessarily – even you,' she retorted.

'I am sorry, but the nearer the time draws for departure the more I feel an urge to start.'

'I know. I feel the same. I must away. Be ready tomorrow at dusk.'

How Morag contained herself through the intervening hours she never could remember afterwards. All went according to plan. Willie carried her gift and good wishes to Ephie. Morag milked her sheep for the last time and filled the two flasks with the foaming warm liquid. She closed the sheep into the sheep cote for the night and drank the rest of the milk as she made final preparations. Just before she left she took a small flask and filled it with some of her father's jealously guarded *uisque'a bha* distilled in the strath. The fiery alcohol she would use as medicine to warm their bodies through winter chills.

The time had come. Walking with a curious rolling gait because of her double layer of clothing Morag fastened the house door and made her way down the strath. The die was cast. She would go North.

Mackay's Hotel, Sutherland 2010

Angus Mackay walked out of the hotel front door into the quiet of a September morning. In front of him the familiar sight of the three great hills lifted his heart. From left to right the skyline rose and dipped as it followed their crests, Foinavon, Arkle, and Stack. It was so good to be home. Far away to his right the top of Suilven rose above Lochinver. The sight of its sugar-loaf dome brought bitter-sweet memories of Brazil. Swiftly he turned his mind away from Luzia. She was lost to him as was the other one and homecoming had been hard without Dada here to welcome him. If only he could have come sooner, or Fate not struck Dada down until Angus could be at his mother's side.

His gaze swept across the magnificent view again. From the verdant green at sea level, colours and textures changed in stages through trees and bushes, rising to bracken and heather and then the bare rock of the peaks standing like cut-outs against a sky of unbroken blue. He crossed the gravel sweep in front of the house and walked over the few yards of level lawn to where it fell in a smooth slope to the road below. On the opposite side of the road, fields continued the descent to the edge of the loch. No ripple disturbed the smooth surface but in the distance he could hear the putt-putt of an outboard engine. As he watched, a small open boat appeared from behind the headland. Angus smiled. That was Hector, heading home after a night at sea. The boat's prow cut into the glassy stillness. Behind it formed chevrons widening out until they were lost in the water close to land where seaweed fringed the two-fingered shape pointing away from him towards the imposing edifice of Bervie Lodge three miles away at its head

He was not the master of all he surveyed. He grinned. That title belonged to Lady Annabelle Ross, the local laird, that autocratic old woman who lived in the Lodge and for whom he worked part-time as factor. And what on earth had possessed him to agree to that?

But this was his land, his homeland. His family had built the first dwelling on this broad shelf high above the water long, long ago before the first stone of Bervie Lodge was laid. Here he belonged. He turned his back on the familiar scene and returned indoors to be met by a familiar harassed figure.

'What's wrong, Kirstie?' he said.

'The English are coming.' Kirstie Morrison's voice was doom-laden. Rape and pillage must be on the doorstep. Angus's lips twitched with amusement.

'Aye, you can laugh Angus Mhor. But with Cissie away to Inverness and that wee besom Mhairi off her feet . . . I'll give her sprained ankle. There's no enough hands in this house to do the work the day. And a car's just over the bridge. How long are they staying? Surely Monday is a strange day to arrive?'

'They've booked four days for certain but may move on, may stay longer. It's lucky for us all we have the space for them after that cancellation. I'm sorry you feel our guests put you out, Kirstie,' he grinned. 'Would you like me to give you a hand?' He laughed at the scandalised expression his offer provoked.

'The day the Maister o' Mackay's does wimmen's work I'll be six feet under.' She glared at Angus, gave a snort of outrage and flounced off to the nether regions of the hotel. Sometimes Angus felt Kirstie was born in the wrong century. Master of Mackay's indeed. Didn't she remember the many times she'd scolded him when he was a child and then a thoughtless teenager? When she was giving him the edge of her tongue there'd been no talk of Master then. But of course that was before Dada died. Perhaps her new attitude was Kirstie's way of helping Angus into his new role. Big shoes to fill.

An opulent saloon came to rest before the front door of the hotel. Angus left thoughts of his childhood behind and went to greet his guests. The driver must be Mr Ernest Butler, a solid man, filling out his beautifully tailored country tweeds and with the air of a person used to giving commands and being obeyed. He shook Angus's proffered hand, then looked around in satisfaction and took a deep breath.

'Damn fine air you have here.' He breathed deeply again and exhaled noisily. 'Yes. Damn fine. Bracing.' He turned to his wife who was emerging from the car. 'Soon put some colour in Claire's cheeks, m'dear.' He moved round to the rear of the vehicle to give Fergus Beag instructions on how to unload the various pieces of luggage from its capacious boot.

The gardener-cum-porter had materialised at the front door when needed but it was the purr of the expensive engine that had attracted him. Fergus's ability to be invisible when needed to perform any task he disliked was legendary. However let there be the softest engine note humming through the air and Fergus appeared like the genie out of the lamp.

Mrs Butler briefly gave Angus her hand to shake then immediately returned her attention to the car. Her voice could be heard in the interior admonishing her niece to 'wrap up against the chill', and to be careful how she alighted onto the gravel.

Oh, Lord, thought Angus. That was all he needed. A spoilt brat and two doting relatives.

As Mrs Butler's well-upholstered form emerged backwards from the open car door Angus was treated to the sight of a dainty foot attached to a slim ankle. Things were looking up. No schoolgirl then. The rest of the newcomer's leg promised to fulfil its early promise but Mrs Butler's portly figure blocked his view. Angus moved forward to greet Miss Frobisher. Older than he had expected from her aunt's words, she was certainly no 'brat' and he felt sure no-one could be blamed for spoiling such a pretty girl. She shook his hand with an abstracted air and moved away across the grass as her aunt buttonholed Angus with a barrage of questions as to the exact fulfilling of their booking requests. Did the two rooms have en suite facilities, excellent views, and a quiet location? Was there a table reserved for them at dinner that evening?

Once he had satisfied her all demands had been understood and accommodated, Angus looked around for the younger woman of the party. She had moved to the edge of the lawn and seemed lost in the view. Angus was used to that. It was the way most people reacted on their first visit to Mackay's. He went to join her to answer any questions she might have. As he crossed the grass he heard her murmur.

'Aye, it's a bonnie place right enough.'

Angus smiled to himself. The English girl had obviously caught some of the Scottish way of speaking during her stay north of the Border. When he got closer he saw she was frowning.

'But where did all these people come from?' she asked.

He looked down to the water below and let his eyes range over its shores where advantage had been taken of the natural contours of the land. Croft houses nestled in sheltered hollows set in their own share of open land where sheep grazed undisturbed. Closer to the dwellings dry-stone dykes protected tended fields where hardy strains of wheat and barley struggled for existence in the salt-laden wind. But the former school house was now an excellent restaurant and here and there scattered among the old dwellings were several examples of how people had taken advantage of cheaper house and land prices in this beautiful northern spot to buy and build homes for retirement. At the head of the loch the chimneys of Bervie Lodge, the Big House, drew the eye. For a moment he wondered if she was experiencing a phenomenon he often saw. Especially at dusk, in the gloaming, it seemed to him looking from this spot that he saw the loch and its banks, not as they were today but in times long past, when there were no buildings, no roads, no sheep. From as long ago as he could remember this happened to him with no warning. As a child he had questioned his mother and worried his father that he might have 'the sight', but it wasn't so and he had learned to keep his observations to himself. So the answer he gave his guest was just the truth of today.

'Most of them have lived here all their lives,' he said, 'and their ancestors before them. The old saying "the apple doesn't fall far from the tree" is true enough round here. But there are incomers too, artists; some retired folk who crave the beauty of the hills; and, of course, the fishers. The deepening of our local harbour meant other boats, some foreign ones even, could come in with their fish and the place developed into a thriving port. Not so thriving these days I'm afraid.'

She turned to him with a frown. 'What? I beg your pardon?' she said. 'I've got such a headache.' She looked up at the house and frowned again. 'May we go inside?'

'Of course. You must be tired after your long journey.' As soon as the words were out of his mouth, he mentally kicked himself. Long journey? They'd only driven the few miles from Dornoch – so far as he was aware. An hour and a half? Two hours at the most? And in luxurious comfort. She'd think him an obsequious idiot. But her reply bore out his impression she was exhausted.

She agreed with his remark in a weary low voice. 'Aye. The road was long and hard. But we're here at last and here we'll stay.'

He took her arm to help her across the lawn where the high heels of her fashionable shoes dug into the springy turf.

'Not quite Gleneagles,' said Mrs Butler as her party mounted the shallow treads of the wide staircase following Kirsty's plump figure. 'What a lovely place that is. And I do wish we'd stayed at Skibo instead of going into Dornoch itself. I'm sure one of your cronies could have arranged it, Ernest. We'd have been so much more comfortable.'

'Wonderful place, wonderful,' remarked her husband. 'Old Carnegie knew what he was doing when he snapped it up, however derelict it may have been then.'

'Aye. A very fine place no doubt,' agreed Kirstie. She didn't see how her joining in the conversation produced expressions of surprise on both the Butlers' faces.

'But there was nothing wrong with our hotel, Cynthia,' continued Mr Butler. 'In fact I was pleasantly surprised. And the Dornoch Castle was a good deal less expensive than Skibo Castle would have been,' he chuckled. 'At least you can say you've stayed in a Scottish castle, so what difference does it make?'

'Don't be foolish, Ernest,' she said. 'There can't be any comparison.'

Claire Frobisher took no part in these exchanges. She trailed up the stairs in their wake, seeming almost unaware of her surroundings. In the hall, Angus stood and watched the ill-assorted group and wondered what the coming days might bring.

Kirstie arrived at the bedroom allocated to the Butlers and opened the door. She spoke as she preceded them into the room, then stood aside to watch their reactions. 'Skibo and the hotel in Dornoch might be very well,' she conceded, 'but for all his pennies, the Carnegie mannie couldn't buy a view like yon to put in the front of his castle.'

She had brought them to a halt in front of a window, which took up most of one wall. Although the glass was mounted in three stone frames, the effect was still to give an uninterrupted view of the landscape in front of them. From the waters of the loch below to the heights of the far hills, every detail was clearly etched in glowing colour.

Kirstie's mouth pursed in approval as she saw the visitors' reactions. For once, Mrs Butler was silent as she took in the majesty of the scene in front of her. 'No,' averred Kirstie, 'not even if he was a millionaire.'

'But he was a millionaire,' said Mr Butler.

'Be quiet, Ernest,' admonished his wife. 'That will be all, Kirstie.'

But Ernest Butler hadn't finished. 'Do you know the names of the mountains there, Kirstie?' He indicated the majestic hills whose granite tops were clearly outlined against the blue sky.

'I suppose they have some outlandish, unpronounceable Gaelic names,' his wife offered with plucked eyebrows raised in interrogation.

'No. They're easy enough and you'll have heard them at the horse-racing no doubt.' Kirstie pointed as she spoke. 'Yon's Foinavon, the middle one is Arkle and the one over there is Stack.'

Ernest Butler frowned. 'Foinavon? Arkle? They were horses. Racehorses.'

'Aye, sir, named for the hills. That's the Westminster Estate. They were the Duchess of West's horses and good ones too. We all made a few pennies when they ran,' she remembered with satisfaction.

'So did I,' agreed Ernest Butler rubbing his hands together, 'So did I.'

While the others had been admiring the view, Claire had slumped onto the bed, shoulders bowed in weary dejection, but at the shout of laughter from her uncle, she roused herself and joined them by the window. She stood drinking in the view then turned and threw herself on the bed once more, 'I don't know,' she cried. 'Why don't I know?'

'That will be all thank you, Kirstie,' said Cynthia Butler and hurried to take the sobbing girl in her arms. 'Come along my dear; let me help you into bed. You shall have a rest before dinner.'

Angus poured his guests their pre-dinner preference in alcohol; gin and tonic for Ernest Butler; sherry for his wife, and a soft drink for Claire Frobisher. Mentally he summed up the trio for the delectation of his employer next day. These days, Lady Ross may only accept a few invitations to dine or socialise with the local gentry, but her interest in their doings was as keen as ever. She demanded to be kept informed of everything that might concern her. As she considered the actions of all persons within a radius of twenty miles to be her business, this kept her staff always alert for any piece of news that might interest or entertain her. She was an autocratic and demanding boss, but a considerate and fair employer. Whenever Angus thought of her position in the community the title of 'benevolent despot' always sprang to mind.

Cynthia Butler was well into her praise of the famous hotel that had enjoyed her patronage on the journey north. 'Indeed, Gleneagles is a most superior establishment. There is nothing lacking. One could almost imagine oneself in London.'

Obviously she could think of no higher praise, thought Angus. 'Yes. It was one of the big station hotels,' he said.

Cynthia's face was a picture of indignation. 'No, no. I am speaking of Gleneagles.' She pronounced the name slowly as if she thought Angus might be a foreigner who couldn't understand English. He smiled down at her.

'When the railways reached popular destinations the big companies built wonderful hotels to accommodate the growing number of visitors. Gleneagles was one of them. And there's another in Dornoch. Did you see the big hotel with the marvellous views across the golf course to the sea? It's the Dornoch Hotel now but it used to be the Station Hotel. They thought nothing of having half a dozen Rolls Royces parked in the yard there. The rooms at the rear were for the valets, lady's maids and chauffeurs, but the principal rooms have superb views across the bay to Tarbet lighthouse. I suppose you could say the railways started the tourist boom.'

While Angus had been speaking Cynthia had listened in disbelief. Now she closed her mouth, which had opened in a most unattractive way, and moved to another topic. 'Of course, it's very pleasant here, too,' she condescended. She looked around the gracious drawing-room, which had another spectacular view, over the loch towards a skyline where Suilven reached its domed outline into the apricot blush of the evening sky. 'How long have you been here, Mr Mackay?'

Angus handed her the glass of very dry sherry she had requested and smiled. 'About five hundred years, Mrs Butler,' he said, and watched in amusement as her eyes grew round. Even her mouth opened again in shock as she took in the meaning of his words.

'You can trace your family back that far?'

'Indeed. My ancestor built the first house here on this ledge above the water. Over time the house has been changed, enlarged and beautified, but although I love it very much, it can never hold a candle to the view it commands. That is what makes Mackay's so special.'

He walked across the room to where Claire Frobisher sat on the window seat and held out her glass of fruit juice but she seemed unaware of his presence. As she gazed out of the window he noticed a small smile of contentment turned up the corners of her mouth in a most attractive fashion.

Next morning Angus greeted Claire Frobisher as she entered the dining room.

'Good morning,' he said. 'Did you sleep well?'

She smiled at him with shining eyes. 'Like a log. Such bliss. You have no idea. I feel marvellous today. It's being so far north. I knew I'd be better if we came on.'

She passed in front of Angus to follow the waitress to their table and didn't hear her aunt mutter to Mr Butler.

'She's said that at every stop we've made. Then a few days later it's the wrong place and we're on the move again.' She nodded to Angus, said they had both slept well and graciously added that their accommodation was quite satisfactory.

As he moved quietly about the room unobtrusively seeing none of his guests lacked anything for their comfort and enjoyment, Angus was hailed by Ernest Butler.

'He's the chap to ask,' Butler remarked to his companions. 'Now then tell me Mr Mackay, is there any good fishing round here?'

'Ernest, no. You promised,' said Cynthia Butler with a frown.

'Nonsense, m'dear. I agreed to do everything to make the holiday right for Claire. Well, I have. Look at her this morning. Just look. Bloomin'. Positively bloomin', aren't you m'dear?' He beamed at Claire Frobisher who smiled back with bright eyes and a happy face.

What a difference from the girl who had arrived only the day before. Angus looked again at Miss Frobisher. She looked up at him and gave the smallest wink.

'I feel fabulous,' she said. 'It must be this wonderful Highland air, not to mention my comfy bed and this nice breakfast. So do go off Uncle Ernest and slaughter a few fish if that will make you happy.' Her smile transferred to her aunt. 'Honestly Auntie Cyn, I feel fine. You don't need to nursemaid me today – promise.'

The older woman patted her hand. 'I must say, dear, it's some time since I've seen you looking so rested and content. Uncle Ernest can go and take the car. It's on hire so we might as well make use of it. You and I will enjoy a stroll around the grounds. We seem to be lucky with the weather. It's really quite warm. Perhaps you'd like to sit outdoors and read a book?'

While Claire thought for a moment Angus controlled the twitch of his lips at Claire's pet name for her aunt. Visions of a leather-clad Mrs Butler in six-inch stilettos and black mask brandishing a whip were firmly banished. The relatives awaited Claire's decision. 'Yes, I might. Good idea. But I certainly don't need to keep you by my side while I do it,' she laughed. 'You know me. Once I get into a story the roof could collapse for all the notice I'd take of it. So you'd be terribly bored. Why don't you go with Uncle Ernest? I'll mooch round the garden have a read and maybe snooze in a deckchair. I feel so comfortable here. I can really relax at last.'

Angus still stood patiently beside Ernest Butler's chair. He was quite prepared to discuss the best places to fish; the superiority of locally-tied flies over those purchased in a London store; and the enjoyment to be found on the banks or from a boat on the loch.

Once the breakfast stint was over Angus spent an hour in the office opening the post and attending to other paper work. After conferring with his mother on tasks for the day he went in search of Fergus Beag. The Butlers were descending the stairs as he crossed the hall. Claire Frobisher's exclamation of delight stopped Angus where he stood.

'Look! What a darling,' exclaimed Claire and hurried across the hall to where a large dog lay on the carpet in front of the huge fireplace where fragrant logs were burning. Ignoring her aunt's warning cry to be wary, Claire knelt beside him and began to caress his ears and scratch that awkward spot at the back of his head. In appreciation his tail thumped the ground and he half closed his eyes in pleasure. Claire looked round as she realised Angus was nearby. 'Does he belong to you? What's his name?' she demanded.

Angus laughed. 'I would say rather that we belong to him. He is Rex and definitely the king around here. As you can see he claims the warmest, most comfortable spot in front of the fire. But we let him get away with it as he is really quite an old gentleman and deserves a reward for many years of faithful service.'

'What is he? He looks like Lassie in the films.'

'I think he would prefer if you said Lassie looked like him,' said Angus 'You're right of course. They are both Rough Collies and both tricolour. You can get black and white or something they call grey but I prefer his black, tan and white markings.'

'So do I,' Claire agreed.

'You are obviously a dog person, Miss Frobisher. They always know.'

'Yes. Who wouldn't be? I had a dog . . . Lucky I called her. She was my fifth birthday present and I had to promise to feed and care for her and walk her and have her trained before I was allowed to have her. I had begged for what seemed like all my life,' she laughed. 'I'll never forget that moment. I was coming down stairs on my birthday morning and Father put this puppy on the floor in the hall. She was so sweet with a fat little tummy and she tried to climb up the stairs towards me. I just fell in love.'

'I know that feeling,' Angus agreed. 'What was she?'

'A cocker spaniel. Her long ears wiped away many of my childhood tears when I was in disgrace or upset about something.'

Cynthia Butler had been standing in the hall monitoring the conversation. Now she slung the coat she had been carrying around her shoulders and bent over Claire. 'We'll be off now, darling, if you're sure you really don't need my company.'

Claire got up and gave her aunt a peck on the cheek and a hug. 'No, no. Off you go and have fun. I'm going to be just fine. I've got that new book I bought in the shop in Dornoch. I haven't even opened it yet.' She accompanied her relatives through the open front door and onto the gravel where their car stood waiting. Fergus Beag gave it a last loving polish with the cloth in his hand and hurried to open the door for Mrs Butler. As they drove away Angus managed to collar Fergus and give him instructions for the day.

About half an hour later Angus walked round the side of the hotel and saw Claire Frobisher standing on the lawn, just where it fell down towards the loch. For a moment he hesitated then crossed the springy turf to her side.

She turned towards him. 'Isn't it beautiful? You are so lucky to live here. Have you been here all your life?'

He thought a moment. 'Yes. Yes. No.'

She laughed. 'Sorry! Uncle Ernest says my tongue runs on wheels. But you're saying you haven't been here all your life. I thought you told Auntie you'd been here for five hundred years? You should have a long grey beard.' Her eyes danced with amusement.

What a different kind of person she was from her staid and rather pompous kinfolk. How on earth had she escaped being brought up in their mould?

'My family have, yes. And I was born here, but I went adventuring in my youth.'

Her eyebrows rose. 'And that must have been a very long time ago. You're so ancient now, Mr Mackay,' she mocked.

He smiled. 'Some days I feel it.' His expression sobered as he remembered just why he had fled his home and travelled as far away as possible. Then he recalled how and why he had returned and frowned again.

'I'm sorry,' said Claire. 'I didn't mean to rake up bad memories.' It was Angus's turn to look surprised. 'You have a very expressive face, Mr Mackay. I think I touched an old wound,' she said quietly.

He shook off his dark thoughts and smiled at her. 'What's done is done, and thanks for the warning. I'll be sure not to play poker with you, and it's Angus.'

'And you know my name is Claire,' she said. 'If this was mine,' she opened wide her arms encompassing the total view, 'I'd never leave it. Never! It's the right place. The right place for me. I'm sure of it, and I've been looking so long.'

'What do you mean?'

For a moment she hesitated. Obviously her words had been more for her own benefit than a comment to Angus. 'Can I talk to you? I know that sounds silly. We've been talking. But I have so much bottled up inside me and I need to talk it through.' Her expression was anxious.

Angus thought a moment. Did he really want to get involved in some family crisis? What would he be letting himself in for? And yet she seemed troubled and his upbringing wouldn't let him abandon anyone in need. He smiled. 'Sure. It's often easier to unload on a stranger than to a close friend. Let's get a cup of coffee and bring it out here. The grass will be warm and dry enough to sit on and we won't be wasting the view.'

Once they were settled with their cups, he looked across at Claire. 'Fire away. What's bothering you?'

She turned her head away and looked up the loch. 'I don't know. And that's what's so frightening.'

Angus frowned. 'Frightening?'

She sighed then sat up straighter and looked back. 'I'd better start from the beginning. I'll try and keep it brief. My parents were both killed in a car accident.'

'I'm very sorry. How dreadful for you.'

'Yes, it was horrid. So sudden. One day making plans and the next – nothing.' She sat head bent lost in thought.

'Yes. I know,' Angus murmured.

For a little while there was silence, then Claire lifted her head and gazed at him with narrowed eyes. 'Yes. You do. Don't you?'

Angus nodded. 'But this isn't about me. Go on. Your parents died and then what?'

'For a while I was sort of lost. Beanie - that's my old Nanny - she'd been Mummy's maid years ago and then metamorphosed into a sort of housekeeper when I was too old for a Nanny - she kept things running at home. Uncle Ernest dealt with all the legal papers and things like that. I was told not to worry. There was enough money for me and to pay Beanie and the gardener. I stayed some of the time with my aunt and uncle and some of the time at home. That was better really once I'd got used to the emptiness, but then the dreams started.'

'Dreams? About the accident? About your parents?'

'No! At least I don't think so. You know what dreams are like. You wake up with a feeling, sometimes a brief memory, but mostly you just forget them.'

'Yes. But they can be upsetting.'

'I couldn't sleep properly and when I did I woke feeling tired and very sad.'

'Understandable.'

'Ye-es.' She didn't seem sure. 'But what made me sad?'

'You'd lost your folks. Of course you were sad.'

'I know. But it wasn't like that. Anyway Beanie called in Auntie Cyn and I was whisked off to their house. The doctor said it was delayed grieving and gave me some sleeping pills which are no use at all. When they work I wake up feeling even worse. But that was when the compulsion started.'

'Compulsion?'

'Yes.' She looked up into his eyes. 'I can't think of anything else to call it. Uncle Ernest thinks I've totally lost the plot. Poor old love. I think he was almost ready to take me to the funny-farm so he breathed a sigh of relief to see me looking bright-eyed and bushy-tailed this morning.'

'But why? After all, grief takes many forms. And it hasn't been that long – has it?'

'Just over a year. But if that was all it would be fine. Grief he could cope with, could understand - like when Lucky died. He really was so sweet to me then...even wanted to buy me another puppy but it was far too soon. And then only five weeks later Father and Mother...' she swallowed hard then raised tear-filled eyes to Angus, 'I lost everything – so suddenly - except for Beanie.'

'She's your stability.'

'Yes. You understand. That's grief but this new feeling,' she sighed. 'I've put them through it these past months. The problem is I don't know what I want or where I should be.' She looked out over the loch below. 'But I think I'm there.' She turned back to Angus. 'I feel at peace here. I feel I've come home.'

He nodded. 'Perhaps it's race memory. You must have some Scottish ancestors.'

She smiled at him. 'I wish. But it's not true. I asked Auntie Cyn. She's Mummy's cousin. Mummy was an 'only', so was Dad. That's why Ernest and Cynthia have been saddled with me. They feel it's family duty. Don't get me wrong. I'm not ungrateful. They've been marvellous but a bit . . .'

'Suffocating?'

She grinned. 'Yes. They have no children. I think I'm their surrogate child. Imagine that. A great lump like me.' She laughed. 'But when I started to fret, Ernest at least was seriously alarmed.'

'These dreams – you're looking for something?'

'Yes.'

'Don't you think it might be a - what do they call it – a manifestation of the way you feel after losing so much? I'm not qualified in this but commonsense would point to you wanting to find a new life, a new routine, a new way of living?'

'I see what you're getting at but what has that to do with Scotland and travelling north?'

'What were you fretting about?'

'I know it sounds silly but we went to the pictures. I think Auntie Cyn wanted to amuse me. We saw *Braveheart* and that's when it started. Of course they thought it was *Braveheart* I wanted - all that wild history and stirring loyalties - but it was nothing to *do* with that,' she said angrily. 'It was Scotland.' She turned again to look at him. 'Now it's your turn to think I've lost my marbles. But it called to me. I had to come. I had to,' she cried passionately rising to her knees.

'Many folk have found peace of mind and heart in the Highlands,' Angus said quietly. How he wished he could regain that peace himself.

Claire sank back onto the grass. 'That could be it, of course, but I don't know. There's something . . . something specific I'm looking for. There's something I have to do.'

'Is this about the dreams?'

'Yes. I think so. Since we left Edinburgh I've felt better and worse. As we travel North there's a feeling in my chest almost like excitement as though I'm going home or to a party. But everywhere we stop feels fine until I dream again. Then I know it's not right, and we move on. Uncle Ernest was mad when he found I'd been reading all sorts of books about Scotland ancient and modern.' She grinned at him. 'What a quarrelsome lot you were! You Mackays, and Macleods and the Sutherlands. Stealing other people's cattle and arguing about boundaries and kinships.'

Angus held up both hands palms towards her in mocking surrender. 'I think we've calmed down a bit since those days.'

'I know. But when we were in Dornoch we saw the place they burnt the last witch. Poor old woman. What a ghastly fate! There's a good museum down on The Meadows. Historylinks they call it. Isn't that nice? I spent ages in there. It was fascinating.'

'You certainly seem to be steeping yourself in our history and culture. Did you stay long in Dornoch?'

'About three weeks. I thought that was the place. It seemed to be the end of my journey. I loved it. I was actually thinking of buying a little house and settling there.'

Angus's eyebrows rose. 'Really? That was a bit extreme, wasn't it?'

'I might not have stayed there all year round. And I wouldn't be lonely. Lots of my friends would come to visit. A holiday in the North of Scotland would appeal to so many. Especially with the golf course there and everything.'

'So what changed your mind?'

She laughed. 'When I tentatively mentioned the house idea Uncle Ernest went ballistic. But that wasn't what did it. I dreamed again. Something pulled me on – farther north.'

'Well, I hope this is it for your sake. There's not much left really if you keep going north. Perhaps you'd have to cross over to Norway?' he teased.

'I hope it is too.' She nodded complacently. 'I know we've only been here twenty-four hours but I feel so settled here. I still don't know why.' She chuckled. 'Beanie didn't want me to come at all. She all but threatened to lock me in my room. Said Scotland was a backward heathen type of a place with no law and order and dreadful things could happen to me.'

'What?' Angus was shocked. 'Had she had a bad experience in Scotland?'

Claire laughed. 'Of course not. She's never been farther north than Birmingham. I really have no idea what got into her head.'

At that moment Angus's mobile rang. 'Excuse me. Hello . . . yes, Mam. I'll go right away. I have to go up the loch but I'll do that first.' He closed his phone and smiled at Claire. 'Duty calls. I have errands to run.' He hesitated a moment. 'What are your plans for the rest of the day?'

She shrugged. 'I have no idea. I told Auntie Cyn I would probably read and snooze but that was really to get rid of her. I don't feel like looking at a book when surrounded by all this fantastic grandeur and I was never farther from needing a snooze.'

'Would you like to come with me? As I said I have a few errands to run both up and down the loch. I could show you some of our more local scenery.'

Her eyes shone. 'Yes, please. I'd love that. Do I need a coat?'

Angus looked at the sky. 'Probably not, but bring a jacket, just in case.' He watched her run into the house. She seemed happier after their chat although he was sure nothing he had contributed to the conversation could have been of help in her situation. Grief could stay with you for years and took so many forms. Sometimes it could stay buried beneath the surface but ready to tear at you without warning. If coming about with him helped Claire to cope he was very willing to be of service. He carried the dirty coffee cups back to the kitchen and vowed to cheer up their young and very pretty guest. Maybe the cheering-up would go both ways.

By the time they got back to the hotel in time for a late lunch Claire had been taken over the brae and down the other side to Kinlochbervie's port - empty that day awaiting the return of the fishing boats to the quay-side market. In the small supermarket there she chose a bottle of malt whisky for Ernest while Angus filled his basket. She remarked in surprise at the size of the community tucked snugly into the fall of land, sheltered from the worst of the gales. Children ran and shouted in the school yard and on the football pitch, while gulls wheeled around the churchyard. When they retraced their steps and passed the hotel on their left she looked a query at Angus.

'We are off to my other workplace,' he smiled. 'I'm part-time factor to Lady Ross, our local laird.'

'Factor?' she frowned.

'I suppose you'd call me a land agent or estate manager. It's really the paperwork I do. So many of her people have been with her for generations, they don't need me to tell them how to go about their business. But it is useful for her occasionally to have me to settle some small dispute. And keep her right with the taxman,' he added.

'I thought a laird was a man?'

'While Sir Iain was alive I suppose he was looked on by some as the laird. But the estate belongs to Lady Ross. It's her ancestral home, passed down to her even before her brother died. He was the typical spoilt younger child - a bit of a black sheep by all accounts. After some particularly embarrassing *faux pas* the family sent him abroad and he ended up settling in Jamaica. He did eventually come home when his father died but he'd suffered from malaria on his travels - probably forgot to take his pills - and he was never really fit again. I remember him. He was what I suppose you'd call a loveable rogue. When we were kids he would sooner join in our ploys when he caught us near the Big House than turn us over to a keeper. He died about twenty years ago.'

'Poor Lady Ross! To lose father and, brother like that. Was she married by then? Does she have any children?'

'Yes, she was married but they had no children. She ran the estate. Even when he came home her brother, Malcolm, took no interest. Perhaps he felt quite rightly he would never really be master there. Sir Iain, her husband, was more interested in politics. He was a good man, but a bit remote. He did some fine work with the Crofters' Commission. I suppose you'd say he was respected rather than loved.'

'And Lady Ross? Is she loved.'

Angus grinned. 'Yes, indeed. As one loves an autocratic grandmother with a heart of gold. She cares for her people but never suffers fools. She's sharp as a tack. Nothing gets past her and her underground information service is so good she knows all the details about most things before the rest of us even hear anything has happened.'

'She sounds fearsome.'

'No. Not fearsome, admirable. Amusing – when in the mood; overpowering – if you let her; and crotchety when her arthritis is playing up. But I wouldn't change a hair of her head.'

By this time they had followed the shore of the loch, more or less, to where the road joined the main route from the south. Angus turned left onto it for just a hundred yards then right through large wrought iron gates. These stood permanently open in welcome if the greenery growing through their curlicues was any indication. Claire's head did the Wimbledon swivel as she tried to take in every detail beside the long driveway edged with rhododendrons interspersed with rose hedges. She caught glimpses of lawns and flower beds beyond.

'Auntie Cyn will want chapter and verse,' she explained, 'when I tell her I've been visiting a Lady.'

'Sorry,' said Angus. 'Lady Annabelle's away today. But I will certainly bring you back for a state visit,' he teased. 'She will want to inspect you. Be prepared to answer all her questions truthfully. She's a devil for picking up on any prevaricating.'

Claire laughed. 'Why would I want to tell fibs? I've nothing to hide.'

'Of course not, but you might feel some of her questions were impertinent.'

'Then I shall tell her so.'

'Brave girl. If you just hang on a minute I'll pop this through the letterbox and then we should get back for lunch. You must be starving.' He looked at her disappointed face. 'I promise I'll bring you back soon and you shall have the guided tour.'

For the next three mornings Angus found Claire waiting for him whenever he emerged from the hotel office after seeing to the post and whatever else needed his attention. He didn't mind her company. What man would? She was young, attractive and happy to fall in with whatever plan he had for the day. As often as possible he tried to take her with him when he had to leave the hotel, aware there were no other guests her age to keep her amused. And there was no opposition from Cyntha and Ernest Butler. They were genuinely both relieved and grateful Claire looked so well and seemed happy – at last. And, as Cynthia confided to Ernest, it wasn't as though Angus was a servant. His family owned the hotel and could trace their roots back for centuries.

Fiona Mackay also approved of Claire keeping Angus company. She heard his laughter more often than of late and watched with thankfulness his eyes crinkle with amusement and the smile on his face as he listened to the younger woman's chatter. Long may it last.

Each morning Claire danced into the dining room with glowing cheeks and shining eyes. She was always eager to know what her elders would be doing, making certain they would leave her to her own devices. She laughingly congratulated Ernest on his successful 'slaughter' of fish and was solicitous after Cynthia's continued enjoyment of relaxing time spent writing letters or reading one of the many books provided by the hotel for the enjoyment of their guests. Fiona marvelled at the change in Claire from the seemingly rather insipid girl who had arrived at Mackay's with her uncle and aunt to this vibrant young woman who greeted each day with sparkling eyes and an eager smile.

On Wednesday Angus needed to go down to Dornoch to see the Secretary of the Golf Club. Claire went with him. As he held the car door open for her she looked up with a glint of mischief in her eyes.

'Do you always wear a kilt or is this for my benefit – being an impressionable English girl?'

Angus settled her in her seat and slid behind the steering wheel adjusting his kilt as he did so. 'I only used to wear the kilt for special occasions and to church,' he said 'but my father wore his kilt as a matter of course. I never remember seeing him in a pair of trousers. When he died and I came home to help my mother I sort of took his place and took on the kilt too. I suppose it's a matter of respect. I only meant to wear it on duty at first, but I enjoyed it. It's so comfortable I rarely wear anything else now.'

'And you're always on duty anyway, aren't you?' said Claire. 'I like it. It suits you and I'm sure your Dad would approve.'

'I hope so,' said Angus as he guided the car out of the hotel gates. 'You say you love our scenery,' he went on, 'I think this is one of the most beautiful drives I have ever taken – and I have seen some amazing scenery in various parts of the world.'

They followed the route along the loch side to the main road then turned right to travel south overland between rock-strewn mounds holding secret pools rippled by errant breezes. When the sea came in sight again they swooped down a long brae to follow a river mouth inland where grass grew lusher and trees appeared, their wind-pruned barks bearing patches of lichen. From one part of the road to another Angus showed Claire how a string of lochs wove through the hills from the Laxford River to the dam on Loch Shin like jewels on a chain. She was enraptured by every vista as it unfolded before them and exclaimed in delight at the expanse of sea on one side and an area of mixed vegetation on the other when they eventually crossed over Loch Fleet by way of The Mound

'I suppose we came this way to Mackay's,' she said, 'but I didn't really look out of the window.'

Angus explained. 'Before the Mound was built in the early eighteen hundreds and the railways came, Loch Fleet was tidal right up to Pittentrail. We would have had to go by Bonar Bridge to get to Dornoch, so you can see how much time has been saved on any journey from the East to the Northwest.'

Before he went into the golf club office Angus settled Claire upstairs at the picture window overlooking the course and the Moray Firth. While he was gone she gazed out at the sandy beach and followed its line across the water to the town of Tain. She let her eyes travel the far coastline out to sea where Tarbet lighthouse guarded the far rocky promontory. She was reluctant to leave. 'Thank you so much for bringing me, Angus. When we stayed here we never came to the golf club. I think we walked on the beach once but the weather wasn't good like today and I was never this high up.'

'I'm glad you enjoyed it,' he said.

On the way back they stopped at Overscaig for coffee. In the lounge Claire looked across the water of Loch Shin to the hills beyond and sighed with contentment.

'Isn't this beautiful? Could you ever see a lovelier view than hills, water and heather all reaching up to the sky and not a high-rise or Underground station in sight?'

'I think you might pine for those familiar things if you were here on a driech February day,' Angus teased as he handed her a cup and saucer.

'Never. I have given my heart to the Highlands and am totally lost in love.' She took a sip of her drink. 'And this is exceedingly good coffee. Thank you.' Again she turned her attention to the view beyond the windows. 'What are those things on the water over there?' she asked.

Angus leaned across her to see where she pointed. 'Those will be the fish farm pens. The fish swim in the water of the loch but are contained in an enclosure. That allows free passage to the water so it is always fresh around them but keeps them in one spot for ease of feeding and capture.'

She pulled a face. 'Capture sounds horrible but I suppose they have to be able to get at them for market if it's a farm.' She laughed. 'What a funny thing to call it.'

'What would you call it?' he challenged. 'The fish are brought here small and fed to make them grow. Then they are harvested, so what name would you give that, my dear?' He smiled at her frowning face.

Claire thought for a moment. 'A hatchery?' she offered. 'I've heard of trout hatcheries down in England.'

Angus shook his head. 'No. They don't hatch them here. The fish are only brought to the farm later. You may not like the term but it is the truth of what happens.'

'Do they taste any different to wild salmon?'

'There's a fierce debate on that subject so don't get me started on it. But fish farming isn't only for salmon. There are trout, too, the rainbows and brown and even the big old sea trout that some people prefer to salmon. I keep hearing about different companies trying out new varieties and of course they do it for shellfish now as well. What's the matter?' he concluded as she studied him, head on one side, a serious expression on her face. 'Was I boring you? Sorry. I'm so used to answering guests' questions perhaps I gave you more information than you wanted?'

Claire shook her head. 'No, it's not that. I found it very interesting. How old are you, Angus?'

The question surprised him. 'Where did that come from? What has my age to do with fish farming?'

'Nothing, of course. But when you called me, 'my dear' you sounded positively avuncular. It could have been Ernest talking.'

Angus looked first startled, then alarmed. 'I'm not that old!' he exclaimed.

Claire giggled. 'I know. But sometimes your manner makes me feel you are a great deal older than I am and I don't think that's true. I'm twenty-one,' she offered, 'well nearly twenty-two actually.'

'Well I am a bit older than you. I shall be thirty on my next birthday.' For a moment he looked away across the loch, remembering. 'I was twenty–one when I left home,' he said at last. 'But it seems so much longer ago than eight years.'

'Where did you go?'

He forced a smile. 'Here, there, and everywhere my fancy took me,' he said. 'And did you have a marvellous twenty-first birthday? A ball perhaps?'

If Claire noticed his deft change of subject she gave no sign but simply shook her head. 'No. It was just after the accident. No-one felt like having a party, especially me.'

Angus reached across the table and gave her hand a sympathetic squeeze. 'I'm sorry to bring it back, like that.'

'It's alright. It does get easier remembering. I still miss them terribly even though I suppose you would call our family the most undemonstrative you ever met. It was Beanie who gave me all the cuddles children love. Mother was very busy with her charity work and the social round.'

'And you? How did you pass your time as you grew up? Pony club and tennis parties?'

She smiled. 'Pretty much. And then as I got older it was the usual. Father loved racing so it was Goodwood, Kempton Park, Aintree etcetera for him, and Wimbledon, Henley and Smith's Lawn for Mother. We skied at Aspen and sunbathed at St Tropez, although Mother always complained it was passé.' She frowned. 'What an idle creature you must think me. No, don't deny it. It's true. I was so bored, but what's a girl to do? I was never trained to do anything useful. I envy you. Your mother is wonderful, isn't she? She always has time for everyone, yet I've watched her and she works so hard, without seeming to. That must be an art. I wish I could do something - anything - but I'm useless,' she sighed.

'You're very decorative,' Angus smiled.

'Don't patronise me,' Claire hissed angrily. She looked over her shoulder to see if anyone had heard their exchange, but there was no-one else in the lounge. Those staying at Overscaig had either moved on or were out on the loch fishing.

'Hey! I'm sorry! Alright? I was only teasing. I'm sure there must be something you're good at. You say you spent time in the South of France. Do you speak French?'

Claire brightened. 'Yes, I do and rather well, though I say it myself. And Spanish, and German. I always loved languages at school and when we travel I try to speak the language of the country as much as possible.'

'Tres bien, mademoiselle,' applauded Angus. 'Voyons! Tu es formidable.'

'Don't worry. I won't take the huff again. I know you're teasing this time. But what use is it to speak three foreign languages in Scotland?'

'Tutt, tutt, the same use it is anywhere else. In the hotel business languages are invaluable. We get plenty of foreign visitors and although their English is usually good, some do need help and generally people appreciate being greeted in their own tongue. It's a kind of courtesy – if you can manage it.'

'I suppose it is. I never thought about using foreign languages for any real purpose - just to be able to speak them. But I could, couldn't I?'

Angus frowned. 'Could what?'

'Work at it. Do you need any help in the hotel?'

Angus shook his head. 'Not at the moment. The tourist season proper will wind down over the next few weeks. We do get walkers and some shooters and hardy fishers over the winter but we're not really busy – too far away from the slopes to attract skiers, even when there is decent snow in Scotland. I know sometimes my folks used to close for several months and go away in the winter or just enjoy their 'ain fire side', but latterly my mother has kept the place open. Sometimes I think it's just for the staff's benefit. Seasonal work carries little security, but our folk are loyal and apart from a couple of students we employ from the college in Dornoch, the rest have been with us for years.' He placed his cup and saucer on the table. 'If you've finished your coffee we must get on.'

Claire was quiet for most of the journey back to Mackay's. Angus wasn't sorry. He had his own thoughts to occupy his mind. But just as they crested the brae to turn into Mackay's she roused to question him with a frown. 'Angus, why does Kirstie call you Angus More? I thought you were a Mackay, or is that just the name of the hotel?'

Angus smiled. 'She calls me mohr,' he spelled it for her, 'because in Gaelic that means big. So she calls me Big Angus.'

'I see. So who is Little Angus?'

'He is, or was until he emigrated to Australia, one of my close friends from the first day I went to the school. He, Lachlan, and I fancied ourselves as the Three Musketeers – at least once we were old enough to read about them. And Fergus at the hotel is called Beag, which means small, so he is Wee Fergus just as Angus Sutherland was Wee Angus. Is that straight now?' he smiled.

'Absolutely,' Claire beamed. As she got out of the car and crossed the gravel forecourt Angus could hear her murmuring, 'Angus Mohr, Fergus Beag.'

He was still smiling as he entered the hall, but later his smile was absent as he questioned Fiona.

'Mam, am I a grumpy old man?' he asked her as they sat at the lunch table.

She was startled. 'What brought that on?'

'Claire called me avuncular this morning.'

Fiona shook her head, suppressing laughter. 'Well, you are a few years older than she is but surely not enough to be a grumpy old man? What made her say it?'

'She said it was how I talked to her and I patronised her. But I didn't mean to. It was a tease really but she took it the wrong way.'

'That was a pity. But I think I know what she means.' It was Angus's turn to look startled. 'For some years now you have had a position of authority, here, then in Switzerland and after in Brazil and also now with Lady Annabelle. When people are used to telling others what to do they assume a tone of command often without even knowing it. People in control are usually, but not always, older than those they are in charge of. Responsibility carries a certain weight which can make folks appear solemn or grave and if they don't have the habit of easy chat and laughter . . .' she hesitated, unwilling to wound her only son. 'I've been very happy to see you enjoying Claire's company, Angus. She seems a dear girl and sometimes I feel I've got my old Angus back again.' She blinked rapidly to push back the unwanted tears in her eyes.

Angus reached for her hand on the table cloth and squeezed it in his own. 'I'm sorry, Mam. I'm heart sorry to have grieved you so much, but . . . .' He bit his lip.

Fiona smiled. 'Nonsense, my dear one. Water under the bridge. We look forward now. Perhaps, instead of worrying, you should have laughed more with that young woman. They say it is the best medicine, don't they? We're really not too busy at the moment. If Lady Annabelle doesn't need you tomorrow why don't you take the day off? You could have a picnic - make the most of this warm spell. What do you say?'

Angus thought for a moment. There was nothing demanding his urgent attention - nothing that he couldn't deal with first thing tomorrow. And Mam was right. He hadn't had a break for ages. 'Okay,' he nodded. 'It's a deal, if you're sure you don't need me.'

'Get away with you. No-one's indispensable.'

'Where are we going?' demanded Claire as Angus swung the Landrover to the right out of the main entrance to Mackay's. 'Down to the harbour? Are we going out in a boat?'

'No. But if you'd like to I can arrange it for another day. Are you a good sailor?'

'Yes. I love it. But if we're not going out in a boat, where are we going?'

Angus tapped one finger against the side of his nose, 'Ask no questions . . . ,' he quoted.

Claire pouted in mock temper. 'Infuriating man,' she said. 'Don't worry, I shan't ask again. I'll just sit back and admire the view.'

It was certainly worth admiring. As they crested the hill behind Mackay's the open sea came into view beyond Kinlochbervie. Closer to hand sheep roamed among the rocks, bracken and heather of a landscape wild enough for any romantic heart. They swooped down the brae leaving the road to the school and church on their right, passed the War Memorial and the wee loch, and followed the road above the harbour. But, instead of turning left as they had the first day Claire had been this way with Angus, he took the right fork and soon left Kinlochbervie behind them. The road was narrow and the ground undulating. Claire could no longer see the sea but was fascinated by a landscape so different from any she had known before. Wide and wild with sheep dotted about and a few, very few, isolated dwellings, her eager eyes took in every detail, memorising them for telling that evening at dinner and for keeping in her heart.

After following this road for a mile or two Angus turned the Landrover left down another narrow road between two houses and over a cattle grid.

'Wow!' exclaimed Claire as the road seemed to take a sheer drop in front of them and the coast and sea lay below them as far as the eye could see. 'That's fantastic.'

Angus stopped the Landrover pleased at her reaction. 'This is one of my most favourite places in the whole world.'

'I'm not surprised. It's beautiful and savage, and gentle and wild, untouched and fresh.' Claire laughed at herself. 'I'm havering as you would say, but it's perfect Angus, perfect.'

He agreed. 'If you come here when the falling tide has washed the beach clean of any footsteps or rubbish people may have left before you, it is like Eden must have been. As you said; untouched; perfect. And then clumsy man comes in and stomps all over it,' he finished savagely and put the Landrover into low gear for the steep descent.

Claire frowned. She opened her mouth to speak, looked at Angus's glowering expression, then closed it again.

By the time he had negotiated the road to the bottom and parked in the small gravelled car park, Angus had managed to throw off whatever had been bothering him. He turned to Claire with a smile. 'There are toilets here if you need them. From here we go on foot.' They got out of the Landrover and Claire looked around.

'That wall there. Is that round the graveyard I saw on the way down? Is it an old one?'

'Aye. That's the graveyard.'

'Angus, don't think I'm morbid or anything like that but could we have a look? I love old churchyards. I like reading the inscriptions on the headstones. In some places they are really funny. One of my favourites I saw in Edinburgh on the way here. It said 'Stranger tread this ground with gravity. Dentist Brown is filling his last cavity'. Isn't that wonderful? If you don't want to come I'll go by myself if you don't mind waiting.'

Angus shook his head. 'No. I'll come. I should come more often to pay my respects I suppose. My ancestors are all buried here.'

'Really? That's wonderful. Imagine knowing where all your forefathers lie. That is amazing.'

They climbed the rutted path to the gate leading into the cemetery. Angus showed Claire the corner where the Mackays had been buried over the ages then encouraged her to wander at will. There was another grave he wished to visit, but alone. Finally he caught up with her. 'Well, have you had enough?'

She turned and smiled at him. 'Never. I could stay for hours.' She stood with one hand on the lichened stone nearest her and looked around. 'I should love to be buried here. To know that this will be your last resting place among your own kind must be very comforting. Isn't it?' As she spoke her hand gently stroked the weather-beaten stone.

Angus shrugged. 'To be honest I've never given it a thought in that way but now you come to mention it, aye, I suppose it is all part and parcel of belonging to a place.'

'Yes, that's right. Belonging. I don't feel that I belong anywhere.' She had little idea how desolate she sounded.

'Come on,' said Angus and put his arm around her shoulders. 'Can't have you getting upset. I'm getting hungry. Let's go and fetch the picnic out of the boot and move on.'

With the rucksack on his back Angus led the way up the steep path beside the graveyard wall offering his hand to Claire where the footing seemed to be difficult. Across the summit he stopped where a wooden flight of stairs descended at their feet so she could take in the view before them. The steps accessed one end of a long sweep of golden sand curving round the bay at the foot of steep dunes topped by marram grass holding back the sea from the short turf beyond. 'That's the machair,' said Angus pointing at it. 'It's a bit late now but from the Spring right through to early August it's just a carpet of changing colour.'

'What makes the colour?'

'Flowers; hundreds of thousands of tiny flowers. I'll show you another time but now I want my lunch. Come on. Grab the handrail. It's steep.' He bent to take off his shoes and socks and then set off. He had warned Claire to wear flat shoes and now she could see why. She followed his lead and slipped her bare feet out of her Indian sandals. The sand - wind-blown over some of the steps - felt cool to her skin. The wood was smooth, honed by sand and wind alike. She wriggled her toes and carefully made her way down to the beach behind Angus. At the bottom he struck off to the right ploughing through the deep soft sand in a slanting direction that would bring him to the hard-packed surface nearer the shoreline. Once they had reached its firm footing Claire ran to catch him up.

'This is lovely,' she cried as the breeze teased her blonde hair around her head. She pushed it back from her face. 'Thank you for bringing me. Where are we going for our picnic?'

Angus pointed. 'Just over there about half way round the bay. We'll make our way back up the beach and sit in the shelter of the dunes. It's a fine day but you may find this breeze chilly if you sit too long. I could make a fire but I really can't be bothered.'

For a moment Claire's face fell. 'A fire would have been fun, but you're right. You're on your holidays today and shouldn't do too much work,' she declared.

Angus laughed.

They did full justice to the contents of the rucksack and then lay back against the dune replete and lazy in enjoyment of the sun on their faces, the gentle breeze in their hair, the murmur of the outgoing tide and the cries of seabirds that were the only sounds to break the peaceful silence.

Claire turned her head towards Angus. 'Where's the church?' she asked.

'What church?'

'The church the graveyard belongs to? Has it been swept away by the sea or buried in the sand long ago?'

Angus smiled, 'Good heavens, no. Whatever made you think that?'

'Well, it's not there any more, is it? And I've been to places on the coast in England where whole villages have been buried beneath the sea.'

'Maybe so but this is Scotland and I can assure you our church is where it has always been.'

Claire scanned the horizon before her then craned her neck to look inland as much as she could see from their position. 'But where?' she demanded.

'In Manse Road at the end of the loch. You saw it when we passed today and I pointed it out when we went down to the shop.'

Claire frowned. 'But that's miles away,' she objected.

'Aye. It's a community church, always has been.' Angus sat up straighter and smiled. 'Take your head away from your tame English countryside, Claire. Imagine this land, no roads, no railways, no cars, no bicycles and very few horses, certainly none for the average working man. People lived near the sea where the soil was deeper and could possibly support a crop of bere or wheat.'

'Beer?' exclaimed Claire with a laugh, 'beer's not a crop.'

'B E R E is,' explained Angus. 'It's a hardy strain of barley that is still grown in places especially where there is salt in the air. Compared to what we have to eat their diet was pretty poor in those days. But they had food from the sea and what they could grow and gain from the land. Where you found a large enough area of reasonable soil there would grow up a small township maybe as many as six or eight families. But that was rare. Habitations were scattered but served by the one community church. Kinlochbervie didn't exist; the new housing estate didn't exist. There was nothing there.'

'But where did the people come from?'

'From all around. They walked, not the way the road winds now, but over the hill. They came from Rhiconich, that's up by Lady Annabelle's, and farther still from Achlyness, and from the other direction they walked in from Sheigra and Polin.' Angus laughed. 'I can see I'm speaking Greek to you. It doesn't mean a thing. I'll take you to these places in the Landrover and you'll see how far people came to church. They came for religion, of course, sometimes the services could go on for hours. But also it was a social occasion for meeting and greeting your neighbours, getting news and possibly making eyes at your future spouse,' he finished with a wink.

Claire had listened intently. 'Yes. If they were so scattered I suppose it wasn't too easy for young people to meet.'

'Where there's a will . . .' quoted Angus. 'and they were hardy. They wouldn't be put off their courting by having to tramp a few miles to see their sweethearts.'

'Just as well or the species would die out. Look! The sea's gone away. Can we get over those rocks to the island now?'

Angus looked to where she pointed. A grassy-topped piece of land stuck out into the sea. No bigger than half a dozen football pitches it looked as if someone had tilted an island so the seaward side showed a high cliff while the inland end rested on the rocks Claire spoke of. A tumble of them joined the edge of the island to the far corner of the beach on which they sat. 'Aye, no problem, so long as you take care not to turn your ankle. You may not be very big but I wouldn't fancy carrying you all the way back to the car,' he teased. Claire bent to pick up their belongings. 'No. Leave them,' said Angus. 'We'll get them on the way back.'

'Of course,' said Claire looking around, 'there's no-one to pinch them is there?'

When they reached the rocks the tide had quite gone out leaving enticing pools where sea anemones waved their tentacles and minute fish darted for shelter as the walkers' shadows crossed the surface of the water.

'Be careful,' Angus warned as they came to a place where all the rock was covered by glistening brown seaweed. 'It's very slippy. And so is that vivid green type over there. You need to try and find a purchase under the weed for your feet or keep your balance until you find a dry bit of rock.'

At last they had picked their way across the weedy rocks, left them behind and gained the surer footing of the grass. The climb to the summit was steep but well worth it for the panoramic view. From their vantage point they could see farther round the coast. The jagged rocks of islets and promontories broke through the water everywhere they looked. They sat on the short turf near the cliff edge and enjoyed the view. Not far away sea birds were diving into the waves.

'There'll be a shoal of fish over there,' said Angus pointing to the busy gulls. 'That's a sure sign, when the birds are feeding. And look, there's someone else wanting to share in the feast.'

A small boat nosed its way through the rocks farther along the shore-line making for the open sea. In companionable silence they watched its progress. It was so peaceful where they sat Angus felt himself drifting into a doze. He turned sleepy eyes towards Claire as she scrambled to her feet and came towards him. 'Do you remember the first time we came here?' she said. 'Iain was only three and you built him a boat made of sand over there on the shore.' Then she frowned and put her hand to her head.

Angus leapt to his feet and caught her as she swayed. Her head drooped. He held her close, his heart pounding. What was going on? What was she talking about? She hadn't even sounded like Claire. Was she dreaming and only seeming to be awake? Was *he* dreaming? As she stirred in his arms he loosed his hold and looked into her eyes. She was bewildered, frowning. 'Where are we?' she said.

'At Oldshoremore.'

She thought a moment. 'Oh! Of course. My head aches. Do you think we could go home now?'

He helped her down over the slippery grass and the treacherous rocks; held her hand as they walked over the sand to where their belongings lay, and watched her anxiously. At the top of the wooden staircase they stopped to catch their breath - it was a steep haul. Claire looked back at the beautiful deserted bay. 'So lovely,' she said. 'Thank you for bringing me.'

Once in the Landrover she immediately fell asleep and Angus had to rouse her when they got back to Mackay's. When she was fully awake she smiled at him. 'You are a pal, Angus. Thank you so much for taking me there and for the picnic and everything. It was great. I enjoyed every minute.' She scrambled down to the ground and slipped her feet into her Indian sandals. 'I can't remember when I had such a lovely day. Can we go out in that boat soon as you promised?'

'How's your head now?' he asked.

'My head? It's fine. What's the matter with it?'

'I thought you had a headache?'

Claire laughed. 'Not me, mate. I haven't had a headache since the day we arrived here. I feel fabulous.' She threw her arms wide, head back and spun round. 'In fact I've never felt better. See you at dinner. I've so much to tell Auntie Cyn.'

Angus watched her run into the hotel. She didn't seem to have a care in the world; didn't seem to remember that extraordinary scene at Oldshoremore. Had it happened or had he been dreaming? No. All the time he was helping her back to the Landrover she hadn't uttered a word. She had been like another person - or a sleepwalker - he thought; there and yet not there. What should he do? Should he tell her aunt and uncle? But what could he say? 'Your niece had a funny five minutes on the cliff top'? Of course not, but there was something strange here. He couldn't figure it out and now was not the time. He must shower and change to get on duty in the dining room. But the memory of the afternoon's events niggled in the back of his mind.

The following day Claire went with the Butlers to explore the coastline in the direction of Wick. They had a fancy to see the Castle of Mey and John o'Groats. It hadn't seemed so far on the map but by the time they returned it had been a long day out. All three went to their beds in good time that evening so Angus had little opportunity to speak to Claire. And what would he say? At breakfast she had been as bright and smiling as before, looking forward to seeing places she had read about in her many books on Scotland. Perhaps that was the problem? If it could be called a problem? She had immersed herself in tales of Scotland from present day to long ago. Were they taking over reality in her mind? Angus had first-hand knowledge of grief and the different ways people tried to deal with it - none better – but he couldn't remember ever having read or heard of this type of escapism.

'Are you busy, today? May I come with you?' Claire asked on Friday morning.

She looked cheerful and as sane as any person Angus knew. He pushed aside the nagging worries her strange behaviour had set up in his mind and answered readily. 'Aye, if you wish. I've to go up to the Big House again. I have more time today so I'll give you the guided tour I promised.'

'Brilliant! I'd better go and put on something more respectable if I'm to meet Lady Ross.' She looked down at her bright yellow cut-off jeans and tan T-shirt.

'Sorry! Don't bother to change. Lady Annabelle is away today.'

'What a shame. I'm longing to meet her. After your description I can't wait to see this fearsome old woman.'

Angus looked shocked. 'What have I said? That sounds a dreadful picture of the woman I know. She's . . . I don't know . . . I suppose she is old and she can be frightening - but only if you have a guilty conscience. How you described her sounds terrible. I didn't say that did I?'

'As good as. But you did say she could be your favourite grandmother too,' offered Claire with a grin.

Angus shook his head. 'Behave yourself and get into the Landrover. You'll just have to wait and see and judge for yourself next time.'

'Yeah. Third time lucky.'

Although Claire had been along this road five times now she still loved to see everything they passed. The view changed as they took bends and slopes. Angus pointed out Achlyness across the other side of the loch and Claire marvelled anew at the distance people had walked to church.

'They probably crossed over by boat and only walked the last part,' said Angus. 'I don't know.'

'It's still a trek.'

Angus led Claire in through the Big House kitchen this morning and introduced her to Eilidh Morrison. 'This is Eilidh, our Kirstie's cousin. She rules the Big House like Kirstie rules Mackay's,' he teased the plump, beaming little woman who barely reached up to his shoulder. 'If you are a good girl and ask nicely she might give you a cup of coffee while I finish up in the office. Then I'll show you round the place.'

'Get away with you, Angus Mhor. You'll be taking a cup yourself, no doubt?' As she spoke Eilidh bustled to good purpose producing a large mug of fragrant steaming coffee for Angus and a delicate china cup for Claire from a modern machine that looked quite out of place in the vast kitchen.

Angus disappeared through a doorway and, after thanking Eilidh, Claire wandered around the kitchen while she sipped the hot liquid. Two of the walls were lined with wooden cupboards glass-fronted in the top half with drawers and closed doors below. A huge range on a central island dominated the space but no heat came from it.

Eilidh watched the young woman with interest. 'Have you ever been in such a place before Miss Frobisher?'

Claire smiled. 'Only once and it wasn't quite like this. When we were staying at the Dornoch Castle Hotel we went to visit Dunrobin. I loved the nurseries and the kitchens best of all – complete with fire engine! But that was more of a museum. You actually live and cook here don't you?'

'Aye, we do indeed. But you'll be seeing the range is cold the day. Her Ladyship is from home and even when she is here on her own I use the wee gas stove.' She indicated a six burner gas cooker set against one wall. To Eilidh it must have been wee indeed beside the huge range but Claire was sure it would be more than adequate to feed a large family. She frowned trying to remember the cooker in her own home. She was sure it hadn't got so many burners and her kitchen was not exactly small.

'Do you ever use the whole kitchen?' she asked.

Eilidh sighed. 'Not these days. Time was, on high days and holy days I've seen this kitchen thronged with extra staff brought in and visitors' servants swelling the numbers in the Hall. Eh! It was grand. But since Maister Malcolm died and her ladyship's health has got worse she doesn't seem to have the heart to entertain these days. All these rooms, the sculleries, pantries, cold stores, flower rooms, all unused,' Eilidh shook her head. 'It's a crying shame so it is.'

'Are you ready then?' Angus's voice broke through Eilidh's sorrowful tones. 'Thank you for looking after her, Eilidh. I'll be back on Monday. Have a good weekend. When I've finished showing Claire around we'll go out by the front door. I'll pull it closed on the Yale.' He ushered Claire out through yet another door from the kitchen. This led into a smaller room Angus called a 'still room'. 'Here the dishes are finished off and made ready to take into the main dining room. See there are two doors there on the far wall. One goes one way and one another so the waiting staff don't bump into each other as they are carrying laden plates, two by two, to guests in the dining room. You'd be amazed how well it works. They can serve fifty people so quickly it almost seems instantaneous.' As he spoke he led her through one of those doors. The highly polished surface of a wide table seemed to disappear in the distance it was so long. Claire could well imagine fifty people sitting at it.

The walls of this room were covered in beautiful linen-fold panelling, above which ornate carving ran like a frieze all round the room. The only breaks in this were a vast fireplace on one side and the tall windows that took up the whole of the end wall.

Afterwards Claire had jumbled recollections of just what she had seen. There had been a secret door in the panelling beside the dining room hearth. That had led to a tiny telephone room with a slit window, built into the turret that rose between the dining room and the music room. Its opposite number on the other side gave onto a cupboard that in turn led to a staircase mounting to the roof.

'You've visited Dunrobin, haven't you?' asked Angus as they entered the main hall. 'Well the Sutherlands followed their example and, after a fire gutted the central part of the house they rebuilt it with concrete in about 1910. That is the walls and the staircase – it's called the canti-levered style,' he continued as he led the way up the graceful shallow steps. 'And we get the light here from the glass dome that covers the stairwell. There are three more of those, one in each wing.'

There had been withdrawing rooms, card rooms, games rooms and a gloomy library where the walls were covered in shelves holding more books than Claire had seen in her lifetime. Higher still were bedrooms and nurseries, and on each floor there was access to servants' corridors, narrower than the wide landings for the gentry, and carpeted with a plain drugget instead of the richly coloured Ship's Wilton of the main house.

'It's like another world,' exclaimed Claire as Angus showed her how servants could come and go around the house, up and down, to serve the unsuspecting guests. 'What a wonderful place to play hide and seek!'

Angus grinned. 'Yes it was. That's why I know the place so well.'

'Did you live here as a child then?'

'No, but whenever there were children staying at the Big House, I was summoned to keep them amused yet safe. Lady Annabelle is a wise old lady. She knew her wee guests wouldn't be able to resist exploring and she didn't want to spoil their fun. But she knew I'd not let them hurt themselves by falling off the roof or get into mischief interfering with the staff.'

'Why did she have so much faith in you?'

'She knew my father would skelp me if I didn't behave. My parents were regular guests at the Big House. Her Ladyship enjoyed my father's wit and fund of old stories. There was no-one could tell a story like my Dada,' Angus smiled nostalgically. 'And here,' he declaimed dramatically ushering her through yet another door, 'are the Sutherlands. The good, the bad, and the ugly, and one or two quite pretty ones as well,' he added with a grin. 'This is known as the Long Gallery. It joins the two side wings of the house, so the whole makes a square. The views from here down the loch are what you might call the back-to-front of our own. To my mind we have the best of it although this is quite good.' He drew her to a window from where they could see down the loch towards Mackays and the bend of the hills that hid the sea. To their left nestled the few houses of Rhiconich and beyond the main gate to the right the road started to climb up towards Durness.

'I see what you mean. I would certainly prefer your view of the big hills although to anyone who didn't know that, this would be fairly spectacular,' she conceded.

'My thoughts exactly. Now let me introduce you to Lady Annabelle's ancestors. Let's have some light on the subject.' Angus touched a switch on the wall and lights came on at intervals down the long room. Above some of the larger and more imposing portraits there were special lamps mounted to shine on the canvas below. 'We'll start at the beginning. This is Ruaridh Sutherland who, if history is to be believed, was not much more than a brigand. He claimed and held the land that now forms the Estate. After him came . . . .' he broke off as his mobile rang. 'Drat it! Sorry Claire, you go ahead and have a look. Most of the pictures have the names and dates under them. I'll take this next door. I know of old the signal to this room isn't very good.' He departed talking into his mobile and Claire was left to wander the length of the gallery following the fortunes of the Sutherland family as she did so. Only a few of the earlier portraits were women but later, perhaps as the family became more respectable, each head of the family was flanked by his wife. Here and there were family groups and it amused Claire to see the changing fashions in clothes for adults and children alike. The Army was well represented as was the

Church and then politics crept in along with titles. As she approached more modern times the number of children in the family dwindled. The last family group consisted of only four, Lord and Lady Sutherland and their children Annabelle who was obviously the elder, and Malcolm, a small boy with a mischievous expression on a face that was delicately made – almost pretty. His sister's arm was around his waist, her hand firmly clasping the material of his jacket. The artist had faithfully reproduced what he saw. Claire smiled. No doubt big sister had been told in no circumstances to let young Malcolm wriggle away. The penultimate picture was of Lady Annabelle and her husband. The last was a portrait - probably of Malcolm grown up - but Claire's attention was all on the young Lady Annabelle. It was a strong face, not pretty like her young brother. One could say almost beautiful. A very interesting face and belonging to a person Claire was more and more eager to meet.

'Holy Mother and all the saints!'

The voice startled Claire who had been lost in thought. She swung round only for a second thinking it might be Angus. But it was a woman's voice and she would surely have heard Angus approaching.

'Who's there?' she called and raised her hand to shade her eyes for the lamplight was falling full on her face. As she looked across the wide room she saw an old woman. Her face was lined and by her clothes she was one of those who worked in the Big House. But it was the look of horror on her face that made Claire frown. She looked behind her to see what had frightened the old soul but there was nothing except the wall with the pictures on it and surely she had seen that often enough? Claire turned back to question the newcomer but had no time. The old woman made the sign of the Cross on her brow and breast then another sign Claire didn't understand and then vanished. Claire blinked. What was going on? Then she laughed at herself. Of course! The woman was a servant and would know all the hidden routes.

By searching that part of the room where the disappearing act had taken place Claire found she was right. One of the discreet servants' doors led onto a narrow passage. She was tempted to follow the strange visitor but just then she heard Angus call and turned back into the gallery.

He laughed. 'If you were hoping to find me that way you'd have no luck. No-one uses that corridor these days. You'd probably get lost and no-one would hear from you ever again until your spectre moaned at night as it sought a way out.' He leered horribly at her but Claire wasn't in the mood for jokes. 'What's the matter? I didn't scare you did I? I was only fooling.'

'Yes. No. I know. It's not you.'

'Then who? There's no-one else here.'

'Not now. But there was.' Claire described the strange old woman.

Angus frowned. 'It sounds like Minty. Minty MacPhee. But what would she be doing here? She does the washing and ironing for Lady Annabelle and helps out at the hotel too. She's a funny old soul but I'm sure she wouldn't hurt a fly. What was it you said she did?'

Claire showed him. 'Like this. That's what Catholics do in church isn't it?' Angus nodded. 'And then like this.' Claire held her two arms forward with the first fingers of each hand crossing each other, the rest of her fingers curled close and her palms towards Angus. He raised his eyebrows, then frowned. 'What is it?' demanded Claire.

'Seems like she was making doubly sure of something,' he murmured. 'You know people cross themselves in church as part of their belief and also it's a kind of asking for protection in some cases.'

'And the other? What's that?'

'That's more of a pagan sign but means roughly the same thing. It's a sign to ward off evil.' He frowned again. 'Are you sure that's what Minty did?'

'Of course. She was only over there and there's nothing wrong with my eyesight. Besides how could I make that up? I've never seen it before.'

Angus shook his head. 'Don't worry about it. Minty's always been a bit strange. Some people say she's fey but I don't know. As long as she does her work and doesn't bother the guests at the hotel I've never really given her much thought. But I'll get Kirstie to have a word with her. She really can't be allowed to go round doing things like this. Now if you've had enough of Lady Ross's ancestors I'll take you home.'

No more was said of Minty or her strange behaviour on the way back to the hotel. Claire tried to put it out of her mind but Angus sought out Kirstie in the hotel garden and told her what had happened at the Big House. 'We don't want her starting to play those tricks here at Mackay's,' he said, 'so have a word in her ear, would you Kirstie? Just warn her I'll have none of it. If she doesn't heed you she'll be out of a job. Daft old besom,' he added as he strode away back towards the house. He wouldn't admit it but Minty's actions had disturbed Angus. What reason had she thought there could be for thinking Claire could possibly be evil? Was it something to do with Claire's strange behaviour?

The Butlers decided to extend their stay. As it was nearly the end of the season Mackay's was happy to accommodate them. The following day Ernest, Cynthia and Claire went off to Inverness, had dinner there and visited the Eden Court theatre in the evening. It was late when they returned to the hotel and none of them stayed up to have a drink in the bar or lounge.

At breakfast the following morning Claire was full of their visit. 'I brought the programme to show you, Angus,' she said. 'And do you know there's an ice show coming fairly soon? Imagine that! How on earth do they do it in the theatre?'

'I have no idea,' he said, ' but I've heard that however it is done it is a real spectacle. I'm afraid I have a heap of paperwork to wade through today so I won't be free to take you about.'

'Not to worry,' said Claire glancing towards the window. 'It looks as though the weather has broken anyway. I bought two new books in Inverness yesterday so I'm going to have a lazy day. Uncle Ernest reckons rain and fish are very compatible so he's off to slaughter a few more and Aunty Cyn is taking the car to some place on Loch Shin she has discovered that smokes salmon and venison. I think she wants to send presents to her pals. Saves lugging loads of stuff home and worrying over what to give to whom,' she grinned.

At teatime that afternoon Angus walked into the lounge. Already the cloudy day had turned into an early evening gloaming. He was so familiar with the layout of the room he didn't bother turning on the lights but made straight for the hearth to build up the fire. He stooped and lifted three peats from the basket and dropped them into the centre of the glowing mass of ash. Immediately flames leapt up as the heat burned off the peat 'whiskers' and Angus got the shock of his life as a voice cried out behind him.

'The flames. The flames. They're burning the cathedral.'

'What on earth?' he cried and whirled to see Claire start up from where she had been lying dozing on the settee. Her eyes were wide open as she stared into the fire.

'God help us all. They are destroying His house,' she cried.

Angus stepped up to the settee and sat beside her. He took her by the shoulders and gently shook her. 'Claire, Claire,' he said. 'Come on. You're having a bad dream. Wake up.' As he held her and looked into her face she blinked twice and her eyes began to focus.

'It was terrible,' she whimpered. 'Those poor folk. Trapped, then betrayed. Murdered.'

'It was a dream,' said Angus. 'Just a bad dream.'

'But I saw them,' she said. 'I saw the flames. I smelled the smoke. The whole town was burning.'

'That was the peats. They often flare up at first. See. The flames have died down now. I had no idea anyone was in here or I would have put on a light. Stay here.' He reached across and switched on the table lamp at the end of the settee then went round the room lighting the other lamps until the whole place was bathed in a warm glow.

Claire wrapped her arms round herself and shivered. She looked up as Angus came back to stand in front of her. 'It was so real,' she said. 'It was horrible.'

Angus frowned. 'I think you must have a vivid imagination. It's time to get ready for dinner.' He stepped forward to help her rise and as he did so kicked something on the floor by the settee. 'What's this?' He picked up the book that lay by his foot and scanned the cover. 'Ah ha! Mystery solved I think,' he smiled. 'Were you reading this before you fell asleep? Researching more of my bloodthirsty ancestors?'

Colour came back into Claire's cheeks as she admitted she had been devouring one of her new purchases, yet another book on Dornoch and the burning of the cathedral. 'I suppose you're right. I must have been dozing, thinking about the book when you made the fire blaze up. But it was horridly real at the time.'

'I'm sure it was, but don't dwell on it and there'll be no harm done. Your aunt will be chasing you to get cleaned up for dinner if you don't hurry. Mr and Mrs Butler came in half an hour ago and went straight upstairs,' said Angus. He watched her from the hall as she hurried up to her room. Perhaps it would be better for all concerned if Miss Claire were to reduce her interest in Sutherland's turbulent past?

'I'se telling you, Kirstie, she has to go!'

Claire heard the unfamiliar voice coming from the kitchen as she walked down the passage towards Angus's office. She couldn't for the life of her think why, but somehow she knew the speaker was talking about *her*. She stopped where she was and listened.

'Wheesht, Minty. What nonsense is this you're talking now. Miss Frobisher is a very nice young lady. I'm sure she wouldn't hurt a soul.'

'She's trouble,' warned the voice – obviously the speaker was Minty Macphee, the old woman Claire had seen at The Big House. 'She is trouble and she'll bring shame and disgrace on more house than this.'

'Stop that now,' Kirstie's voice was sharp as she reprimanded the older woman. 'You don't know what you're saying. Miss Frobisher is here just for a few days with her relatives and will soon be leaving. Don't let Mistress Mackay or Angus Mhor hear you talk like this. We will not have you upsetting the guests. You may be let off your nonsense by us, but these English folk will certainly complain of you if they hear you - especially Mistress Butler. And then it's you will be down the road with no character. Lady Ross will no be taking kindly to your behaviour either.'

'My poor lady, my poor lady. She mustn't see her. Keep her away, Kirstie. Keep her away. She'll bring harm and disgrace with her painted face and her bottled hair.'

'Is that what all this is about? Just because a young lady uses a bit make-up and likes to have her hair tinted? You're all about in the head, Minty. You've seen other guests, aye and with far more make-up than the Frobisher lassie wears, an' all, without causing all this pother. Away now to your work and let's hear no more of your havering.'

Claire heard footsteps approaching the open door and quickly retraced her steps to be out of sight when Kirstie or Minty emerged into the corridor. Instead of seeking out Angus she went up to her bedroom and looked in the mirror. What had the old woman seen that was so offensive?

The reflection looking back at her wouldn't turn the milk sour. She might not be the most beautiful woman on the planet but she'd never had any complaints before. She leaned closer to inspect her face. Perhaps she could wear less make-up? After all this wasn't London where it was necessary to protect her skin against pollution and cover up the pallor of city life. Here the air was fresh and clean, a bit too fresh perhaps to leave off her creams altogether? But her face was now lightly tanned by the sun and her cheeks wore a soft flush of attractive pink. Since she had been sleeping so well each night the dark circles under her eyes had disappeared. She nodded her head at her reflection and smiled. 'You don't look too bad, you know.' Then she leaned closer still and parted her hair with her fingers. How many days was it since she had been to a beauty salon? Along the length of her parting her natural darker colour was beginning to show. Was this such a bad thing? She'd felt it right to go blonde in Town but up here she suddenly wanted to revert to nature; to get rid of the artifice she associated with her old life. And there was no time like the present.

'Mrs Mackay, can you recommend a good hairdresser in the area?'

Fiona Mackay smiled at her. 'It depends what you want. There is a young woman who goes around the houses. I think she is reasonable for what most folks here need. But if it's for yourself I think you'd be better going to Inverness. I'm not saying there aren't good hairdressers nearer, in Dornoch or Lairg maybe, but to tell you the truth when I need my hair done myself I like to make a day out of it, give myself a wee treat you know?'

Claire smiled back. 'Yes, I do know what you mean.' She looked down at her hands. 'Perhaps I should do the same. My nails are a disgrace. I usually have them done at least once a fortnight but I can't remember when they last had professional attention. It just doesn't seem to matter so much here.' She bit her lip. 'That sounded so rude. I'm sorry. I didn't mean it that way - really.'

Fiona laughed. 'Don't fret. I know exactly what you mean. I think it's the hills that do it.'

Claire frowned. 'The hills?'

'Yes. We see them from nearly every window of the house. They are so majestic and eternal. When I have worries I gaze at them for hours until my petty concerns don't weigh so heavy and somehow I find a way of carrying on.'

'It's hard to imagine you with worries,' said Claire in admiration. 'You are always so serene.'

'Thank you, my dear,' smiled Fiona. Her eyes twinkled. 'Perhaps I should have been an actress if I can fool the world so well?' Then her face became serious. 'But I've not had troubles to seek. I lost my husband, too young and too suddenly. And for a while I believed I'd lost my son also,' she added half to herself then smiled again at Claire. 'But you have been like a breath of fresh air to us all. I am so glad you decided to extend your stay. It is a pleasure having your pretty face in the house.'

'Thank you. Tell me, please, do you think I wear too much makeup?'

If Fiona was taken aback by this question she gave no sign but looked at the serious young face in front of her in a considering fashion. 'You do your makeup very well. There is nothing garish or blatantly false about it. Perhaps it is a little heavier than we are used to seeing round here but no more than that. It would certainly be unremarked in London, I'm sure, or even in Inverness.' Suddenly she frowned. 'Has someone been making impolite remarks?'

Claire hastened to reassure her. 'No, not at all. I suppose it's just that I have started noticing things again.' She didn't elaborate on this remark which may have sounded strange to her listener's ear. But Fiona Mackay was well aware of the bereavement Claire had suffered and had also personal experience of that state. To Fiona it was perfectly understandable that Claire was able only now, after a complete year, to revert to her interests and habits from before the death of her parents. Claire gave Fiona a brilliant smile. 'I think I'm going to follow up your idea and have a pampering day in Inverness. Is there a phonebook I can use – with a Yellow Pages?'

'Come through to the office. You can use the telephone there without interruption.'

Two days later Angus waved off the big car holding Claire with Cynthia and Ernest Butler as they departed for Inverness. Fiona crossed the hall as he turned back to go to the office.

'They're off then?' she said with a satisfied smile.

Angus grinned. 'Yes, at last, after at least three false starts, turning back for reading glasses, field glasses – in case they spot a golden eagle – which will probably turnout to be a buzzard,' he smiled, 'and an extra sweater in case of a haar coming in. I wish I'd never opened my big mouth on the subject,' he went on bitterly. 'I thought it might amuse them to hear about the day I went into Inverness wearing shorts. Remember, Mam? We were sweltering in a heat-wave here. But when I got down to Inverness the whole town was swathed in a cold thick clammy haar and I must have looked like a right eejit shivering in my shorts. I know it was ages ago and I can laugh at myself now but then I was so young my pride was hurt. Every day since Mrs Butler has asked me did I not think it was the kind of weather we might expect a haar? But what's going on Mam?'

'What do you mean?'

'You're grinning like the Cheshire Cat and Claire looked as though she was up to some kind of mischief. I haven't forgotten your birthday, have I?' he asked in sudden alarm.

'No, darling. You know my birthday is in April.'

'Yes. Of course. That's good. But what is it?'

'I can't think what you mean,' said Fiona with a bland expression and barely concealed amusement. 'I must get on. See you later, dear.' Once she had reached the shelter of the linen cupboard she stifled her laughter in a shelf of spare pillows and wondered just how much of a transformation Claire was intending to make to her appearance. It was doing her too-serious son good to have the company of a pretty, self-assured young woman again. For a moment a shadow crossed Fiona's face as she thought of happier times when Angus's laughter had rung throughout the hotel and his step had been eager to greet each day and each new experience. Then she shook away sad thoughts and began to check the laundry.

Angus's first view of the 'new' Claire was from above. He was descending the main staircase as the Inverness party entered the hallway laden down with carrier bags. At sight of them he checked thinking for a moment that Cynthia and Ernest had encountered a friend and brought her back to tea. When Claire turned, he frowned and groped for a name in his memory then she smiled and he realised who it was. She saw him on the stairs, came to their foot and stopped to look up at him.

'Hello, Angus. Have you had a good day?'

They were the very words he was about to ask her and he smiled at the thought then stopped and frowned. This was Claire, but different. What was it? Of course the hair . . . so much darker . . . but that wasn't it. When he had first seen her turn around there had been something or someone else in his mind. She was Claire and not Claire. He frowned harder trying to place her or rather the person she reminded him of but it was no use.

Claire saw his frown and misinterpreted it. She lifted her chin. 'What's the matter? Don't you like my new hair do? It's not new, really, just a return to my own colour, or nearly. I couldn't let that grow back while the rest stayed so fair. It would have looked ghastly.'

Angus considered the picture she made. 'I like it fine. It suits you. But are you sure you haven't got any Scottish blood in you? Now you have changed your hair . . .'

'Changed it *back*,' she interrupted him.

'Changed it back,' he repeated, 'you have a real Scottish look about you.'

She laughed. 'No way. Although I would like that. The Frobishers sailed with Walter Raleigh – or was it Francis Drake – I can never remember, and Mother was Althea Forrester. I tell you, you can't get more English than us. I must go and put away all my goodies before dinner. See you later, Angus.'

He watched her mount the staircase with the Butlers and idly thought how strange it was that of all the millions of people in the world, everyone was unique, or almost. There were identical twins of course but they carried the same genes and then he had heard that somewhere everyone has a double. But he had never come across his own and doubted it was true.

'Tea with Lady Ross,' exulted Claire next day as she sat beside Angus in the car. He had got the Mondeo out of the garage in honour of the occasion. This was also to prevent any stray wisps of hay, mud, sand, or animal feed marking her pretty dress, a hazard always present when travelling in the Land Rover - that useful work-horse. 'Third time lucky.'

Angus smiled at her excitement. 'I don't know what you're expecting,' he said. 'She's a grand old lady who can be either irascible or charming depending on her mood and the degree of pain her arthritis is giving her on any one day. She doesn't suffer fools gladly and will prefer you to speak up for yourself. But she does appreciate good manners so you'll be alright.'

'I'm not frightened of her. I think she sounds wonderful, like the kind of grandmother I would have liked.'

'Do you not have any grandparents?'

'No, that is, not living'. She threw him a cheeky grin. 'I assure you, sir, we are very respectable and I have photos of my grandparents to prove it – they were married too,' she added with a gurgle of laughter.

He grinned. 'You're very full of yourself this afternoon, aren't you?'

She agreed. 'You are such a delight to tease, Angus. You always rise you know.'

'Do I?' He pondered on this for a minute as they swept up the drive of The Big House. Had he really got so staid and dull? Ishbel used not to think so. But then far too much water had gone under the bridge of his life since those days.

'Here we are,' cried Claire. 'My goodness! Are we going in the front door? Now I am really honoured,' she mocked as he helped her out of the car and drew her up the steps to the massive oak door set deep in a pillared and carved stone surround, the whole protected from wind and weather by a stone portico.

Angus rang the bell then opened the door and led her into the main hallway she had already seen on her tour. Eilidh Morrison came bustling from the nether regions.

'Welcome, Miss Frobisher, welcome,' she beamed but faltered as she took in Claire's new appearance. For a moment she hesitated then recovered herself and went on. 'Her ladyship is just ready for you. If you go into the Blue Sitting Room, Angus, Lady Annabelle will join you directly.'

He led the way and Claire followed, taking in her surroundings in more detail than on her last visit. The Sitting Room was aptly named having walls of softest blue. The same colour was repeated in the silk upholstery of the two settees that faced each other across a marble fireplace. Between them stood a low square wooden table. Its sides were deeply carved and Claire could see carving on the top also beneath a sheet of protective glass. On it stood a large bowl filled with fragrant pot pourri, besides several silver ashtrays and small ornaments in the shape of animals. There were silver photograph frames on the grand piano standing in the bay window through which the late summer sun streamed brightly. The walls held gilt-framed paintings of various sizes. Fragile-looking chairs with spindle legs were dotted about the room. Delicately hand-painted vases and table lamps, together with the embroidered cushions on the settees and plump armchairs, completed the décor of a charming and very feminine room.

'Take a seat,' said Angus, but he remained standing as Claire chose the settee that faced the door. Soon they heard a whining noise and she looked in enquiry towards Angus. 'That's the lift,' he explained. 'It was first installed for Malcolm during his last illness. He sickened, then weakened and finally seemed just to fade away. It was really sad. He was Lady Annabelle's younger brother, the only family she had left. Shhh! Here she is.'

They heard the tap of a cane or walking stick across the parquet of the hall, then she appeared, the Mistress of the Big House, its land and its people. Claire took in every detail of the woman who had captured her imagination and was not disappointed. She could still make out the younger woman in the picture she had seen in the gallery, but Lady Annabelle's face was now criss-crossed with the wrinkles time and grief had etched there. Her snow-white hair was dressed high on her head, fixed with tortoiseshell combs. She wore a modern afternoon dress but the high ruffles of the neckline and her autocratic posture as she stood in the doorway, head held high, reminded Claire of pictures she had seen of Queen Alexandra. Automatically she rose to her feet as Lady Annabelle came forward to greet her.

'Welcome to my home,' she said as they shook hands. 'I hope Angus has been looking after you.' She walked forward again a few paces to tap him affectionately on the cheek with her free hand. With amusement, Claire turned to watch him submit. In doing so she faced the window for the first time. 'How are you enjoying your stay in Scotland, Miss Frobisher? I believe it is your first visit?' Lady Annabelle looked across to Claire as she spoke, then gripped Angus fiercely by the arm as she swayed. Her face went white and Claire was afraid the old lady would faint. She moved forward to help Angus but Lady Annabelle shook her head, leaned heavily on her stick and bade Angus help her to a chair. 'Forgive me,' she said, at last. 'Angus, will you ring for tea, please? Miss Frobisher please come over here and sit beside my chair.'

Claire exchanged her original settee for the one on the other side of the coffee table facing the window. 'Are you alright, Lady Ross? Can I get you anything? A glass of water perhaps?'

'No, thank you. I am perfectly well, now. Tell me about your family, Miss Frobisher. Angus says you are here with your aunt and uncle?'

'Yes. They are very good to me and brought me to Scotland to pander to my whim really.' Claire felt she should 'sing for her supper' and entertain her hostess with more than a 'yes' or 'no'. She remembered Angus saying how Lady Ross liked to know all the details of the people around her, whoever they might be.

The old lady's eyebrows rose. 'A whim? You came here on a whim?' She seemed to be very interested. 'What kind of whim? A gut feeling, or fulfilling a long-held ambition?'

'More a gut feeling I suppose. I certainly haven't spent my whole life longing for Scotland,' smiled Claire, 'although now I am here I feel I don't ever want to leave.'

Lady Annabelle nodded as she watched the animated face of the young woman in front of her. 'Yes,' she said. 'Yes.'

'Here we are then m'lady,' said Eilidh as she pushed a laden trolley into the room. On the top shelf were wafer thin porcelain teacups, saucers and plates, two tea pots, milk jug, sugar basin and a bowl containing lemon slices, also a silver kettle on a beautifully ornate stand, below which burned the blue flame of a spirit lamp. The two lower shelves held plates of dainty triangular crust-less sandwiches, scones, fancy cakes, jam and clotted cream.

'Thank you Eilidh. I will pour and Angus will pass the plates.'

Eilidh nodded and left the room without once looking at Claire.

'Do you prefer Indian or China, Miss Frobisher?'

'Indian, please.'

For a moment conversation lapsed as Lady Ross busied herself with the makings of the tea and Angus passed cups, plates and food until everyone was served. Then Lady Ross continued her questions. 'And where were you born, Miss Frobisher?'

'In the Lake District. Apparently my mother didn't have an easy pregnancy so Father took her to the Lakes, far away from, as he put it, 'the racket of Town'. She must have thrived there - no doubt the country air suited her - for I was born with no fuss at all, slipping into the world before he could even get her to the hospital.'

Lady Ross's eyes narrowed. 'And how old are you?'

Angus interrupted, 'Really, Lady Annabelle!'

She quelled him with a look. 'Well, Miss Frobisher?'

Claire smiled. 'I don't mind, Angus,' she said. 'I am twenty-one Lady Ross. I shall have my twenty-second birthday this year.'

'In or about November, I should think.'

At the older woman's words Claire looked amazed. 'Yes. The twelfth of November actually. How on earth did you know that?'

'Have you brothers or sisters?'

'No. I'm an only child . . . as were my parents,' Claire added before her inquisitor could ask.

Lady Annabelle frowned. 'But then who are your relatives? You spoke of an uncle and aunt.'

'They are what you might call courtesy titles. In fact Aunt Cynthia is my mother's cousin. So really it is very good of them to bother with me at all. Particularly as we hardly saw them before my parents died. I didn't even know Uncle Ernest was an executor of Father's Will.'

For a moment the old lady remained silent gazing into space with eyes that saw only her thoughts. Then she looked at each of them in turn. 'Have you had sufficient to eat?' For herself, she had barely touched the food on her plate. 'Come with me.' She allowed Angus to assist her to rise then waited while he withdrew his supporting arm. Together the three of them left the Blue Sitting Room and crossed the hall. 'I will take the lift. You young people meet me upstairs.'

As they turned and mounted the staircase Claire looked at Angus. 'What's going on, Angus? What happens now? Is she always so abrupt?'

'Abrupt? Yes, she can be. But I don't know what she is playing at today. I've never seen her like this.'

They waited until Lady Annabelle had exited the lift and then accompanied her slowly along the corridor until they reached the entrance to the Picture Gallery. As before Angus touched the switches and lights sprang up the length of the long room. Looking neither to left nor right her ladyship led the way and the others followed the full length until they reached the last group of pictures. It was on the spot from which Claire had seen Minty MacPhee that Lady Annabelle paused. 'Come child,' she beckoned to Claire, 'go over there and turn to face me.' She pointed to a spot near the wall.

Intrigued, Claire smiled and did as she had been bidden. As she turned, she heard Angus catch his breath.

'Ah!' The old lady was triumphant. 'You see it too?'

'My god, yes. But how? *That's* who she reminded me of when she came back from Inverness.'

'Excuse me,' cried Claire. 'I *am* here, you know. Will you please not talk about me as though I couldn't hear. What's going on?'

Angus came forward and taking her by the shoulders turned her to face the wall. Just beside her was the portrait of Malcolm Sutherland, the one she had not looked at closely on her last visit. 'Do you look in your mirror properly each day, Claire? What do you see?'

Claire frowned. She had no idea what Angus was talking about. Her mirror? What had that to do with anything? She looked at the portrait of Lady Annabelle's brother, first with indifferent eyes and then with a shock of recognition. She took a step closer and examined the painting more closely but it was in oils on canvas so she stepped back and got a better effect. There was no doubt about it. Replace Malcolm's curls with their hint of red, with her straight locks of lighter brown and the portrait could have been painted from a photograph of herself. She turned and smiled at the other two. 'Wow! That's amazing. Well, they do say everyone has a double somewhere in the world don't they? I suppose it doesn't necessarily have to be a person of the same sex. I think that's lovely. I do hope you don't mind my purloining your brother's looks?' she asked Lady Annabelle with a laugh.

'It's funny you should say that,' said Angus. 'I was only thinking about doubles and likenesses yesterday and here we are. Talk about coincidence.'

'This was painted for his twenty-first,' said Lady Annabelle. 'He would never sit for another. He said he'd rather stay young and good-looking. And he was,' she added with a gentleness in her voice Angus had seldom heard. 'Come. Let us go back to the sitting room. I have a story to tell.'

Once settled comfortably back in the Blue Sitting Room from whence the tea trolley had disappeared, no doubt due to the efficiency of Eilidh, the two guests looked expectantly at Lady Annabelle. For a while she seemed to study the pattern of the carpet at her feet then raised her head and addressed herself to Claire.

'My brother, Malcolm, was fifteen years my junior. There had been another boy in between us who had died in infancy, so I suppose, when he was born, Malcolm became the hope of the Sutherlands – our branch at least. He was absurdly spoiled but it was all too easy to do. He was an enchanting child, good-looking as you have seen, with the smile of a fallen angel and a nature as sunny and loving as anyone could wish. Our mother could not bear to part with him to send him to school so he had a tutor at home. My brother never knew what opposition meant. Fortunately, or perhaps not as it turned out, he was bright and passed the entrance to university with flying colours.' Here Lady Annabelle paused as if gathering her thoughts or her courage for what came next.

'At the 'Varsity he fell in with a wild crowd. He was friendly and wealthy and no judge of character. At first it was just a question of more money to bail him out of his gambling debts. Then the university authorities took the unusual step of writing to warn our parents their son was using drugs to a degree that could not be ignored.

'A family friend, a medical man, went to see Malcolm and was palmed off with promises to rein in his behaviour and get his head down to studying. For a while we heard nothing more. Then came the news Malcolm had been rushed into hospital with a drug overdose.' Again she paused, her lips pressed together in remembered grief.

Claire looked across at Angus and raised her eyebrows. Why was Lady Ross relating what were obviously painful facts that happened so long ago? He returned her look, shook his head slightly, and shrugged, having no more idea than she.

'When Malcolm had recovered our father brought him home. He seemed happier and was having treatment for his addiction. He was, as always, universally popular. But then things began to change. Hints were dropped that Malcolm's behaviour was unacceptable. Mothers of marriageable young girls so far from encouraging his inclusion in all invitations began to bar him from their homes. Irate fathers stormed up our drive to interviews with our father. At last he really blotted his copybook. I was never made privy to the full details, being considered a female, and so needing to be sheltered from the rougher aspects of life.' Here Lady Annabelle hooted in derision. Claire smothered a giggle and even Angus turned a laugh into a cough.

'The upshot was that Malcolm was banished to manage our estates in Jamaica. Of course there was a resident overseer so his lack of experience couldn't do any harm. In truth he was bored and fed up. He hated the heat and longed for home. He wrote me heartbreaking letters begging me to intercede with our father for his return. I tried. But it was useless. One day Malcolm disappeared from the Jamaican estate, together with a large sum of money. He went off on his travels, 'trying to find himself' he told me in the rare letters he sent me from outlandish places. His style of living ruined his health. Then he caught malaria, for which he probably had no adequate treatment. I know it recurred for the rest of his life and used to leave him prostrate and more weakened than before, after each bout.

'It was only after our father's death that he returned. The estate should have come to him but it wasn't entailed and my father had no thought of bringing Malcolm back from exile, so I had been running it for a while. My husband was very busy in politics and I relished being in charge here,' said Lady Annabelle with a challenging glint in her eye. 'When Malcolm came home he had no desire to usurp my rule,' she concluded.

'I remember him coming back,' said Angus. 'As a child he fascinated me because he had yellow skin.'

Lady Annabelle gave a snort of laughter. 'Indeed he did. He was recovering from some kind of fever and looked quite dreadful. But he did improve in looks, though never regaining the handsome face of his youth.'

'He was always kind to us,' said Angus. 'He came fishing with Lachlan and me and Angus Beag. Lachlan is the doctor's son,' he explained to Claire, 'and my great mate. We were inseparable but we always loved Malcolm to keep us company. He told the most fantastic stories and had endless patience with a trio of bairns. I was eight years old when he died and I missed him sorely. So did Lachy.'

'We all did,' said Lady Annabelle. 'No matter how often he broke your heart you would always forgive him. Everyone loved him. Not always to their advantage,' she added, looking directly at Claire.

'About twenty-one years ago we had a maid in the house, a bonnie girl, bright and honest. She was called Senga. That is a form of Agnes and means pure and chaste, as I am sure she was when she came to us. I grew quite fond of her. Indeed her lovely smile and pleasant personality were a delight in a house that lacked the light-hearted joy of children. But that was something I couldn't provide,' she said with a painful honesty, 'and Malcolm showed no inclination to find a bride and settle down. Perhaps he knew, even then, he wouldn't make old bones.

'One day Senga disappeared. She had been looking unhappy for a while. Even I had noticed it and questioned her. But beyond bursting into tears she gave no indication of her troubles. I had enquiries made all around the area. I wanted to trace her to help her if I could, but it was soft-hearted Malcolm's reaction that amazed me. His attitude was that if she no longer wanted to be with us then it was her affair. We should not hound her.

'I was very indignant at that. I had no intention of hounding anyone. She was traced as far as Inverness having hitched a lift with a local farmer. But after that there was nothing. Time passed and other matters took my attention, but I never forgot Senga.

'Then came the awful days when Malcolm slipped into his last illness. It started with a recurrence of the malaria and despite modern medicine, he just seemed to have no strength to fight it. He was sometimes delirious and spoke wildly of Senga, of how he must find her. When he was in his right mind again, he realised just how ill he was. He asked to see a lawyer and made his Will, a thing he had always put off, declaring with a laugh that he intended to live for many more years until he had a long grey beard,' she recalled with a sad smile. 'A few days before he died he confided in me that Senga had run away because she carried his child.'

'Good heavens,' cried Angus.

'How sad for her,' said Claire.

'Sad indeed for all of us,' said Lady Annabelle. 'If he had known, he would have looked after her. I'm not saying he would have married her. Although I believe he had known for some time he hadn't long to live, so perhaps he might have married her to give the child his name.'

'What do you mean, if he had known?' said Angus. 'I thought you said he told you? So he must have known.'

'Apparently not - until some time after.'

'How did he find out if the girl was gone?' queried Claire.

'Senga had a great friend who also worked in the house. I told you Senga was a good-hearted girl and she helped and looked after another who was more simple-minded. Apparently Minty MacPhee had helped Senga on the day she left the house. She had carried some of Senga's possessions she couldn't otherwise manage and followed her to Inverness travelling separately.'

'Minty!' exclaimed Angus.

'The old woman,' cried Claire.

'What is it? What about Minty?' demanded Lady Annabelle.

Angus explained what had happened in the Picture Gallery the day he had brought Claire on her tour of the house.

'And she wanted Kirstie to get rid of me,' added Claire and told what she had overheard at the hotel. 'But why?'

Lady Annabelle turned to Angus. 'Pour me a dram of the Macallan will you, dear boy?' she said. 'And one for yourself. Will you have a drink?' she asked Claire. 'I think we are all going to need one.'

Claire shook her head. 'No thank you. I don't usually drink in the afternoon.'

Angus ignored her and poured three measures into the heavy crystal glasses on the silver tray that had appeared on the sideboard in their absence. 'Look at the clock,' he said.

Claire was amazed to see it was after five o'clock. Where had the time gone?

Lady Annabelle took a sip of her whisky and with a hand that trembled placed the glass on the table beside her. She went on with her tale. 'Senga's absence must have bothered Malcolm in spite of his seeming not to care. He remembered her kindness to Minty and one day got the truth out of her. Senga had been pregnant . . . pregnant with his child . . . and had gone away rather than disgrace him and herself. She was a very brave and gallant soul,' she added quietly.

'But what happened to her?' asked Claire.

'Malcolm knew I had used every avenue possible to trace her when she first left. Although he was sad she had gone he had not concerned himself too much. That wasn't his way. But now there was the question of a child it nagged at his conscience. He promised himself he would do something about it but it wasn't in his nature. So virtually on his death bed he told me somewhere in the world I had a niece.'

'A niece?' said Angus. 'How did you know it was a girl?'

'Minty told him it was so.'

'But then Minty must have been in touch with Senga after she left and after the birth?'

'I thought so and questioned Minty exhaustively but she had been away tending her sick aunt in Glasgow not long after Senga's disappearance and no matter how we questioned her she simply said she had 'heard' these things. Eventually I hired a firm of private detectives. They managed to trace Senga's movements to England. It appears she boarded a ship for Canada and there was no mention of a child with her. I thought the infant had died,' said Lady Annabelle, 'until now.'

Angus frowned.

Claire looked enquiringly at Lady Ross. 'Have you had more news then? How exciting,' she said. 'So the story is going to have a happy ending after all, is it?'

'I hope so. I do hope so,' said the older woman and took a large gulp of her whisky.

Angus was quicker than Claire to catch her ladyship's drift. 'You can't mean it? But she has family?'

'Does she? A cousin only turning up after the death of her 'parents'. Who was around at the time of her birth? No-one to tell tales apparently? Don't be so naïve, Angus. It's happened before often enough.'

Claire looked from one to the other puzzled and anxious. 'What are you talking about? Who are you talking about? I don't understand.'

Angus stood up. 'We're leaving.'

'But why? I don't understand. What's happened?'

'Stay,' commanded Lady Annabelle.

'No.' said Angus. 'You can't do this, ma'am. You're playing God. You have no right.'

'She has the right to know her family, her ancestors, her father,' she flashed back at him.

'And if you're wrong? What harm have you done?'

'I'm not wrong,' she cried. 'I know her in my bones. I'm not wrong. You think me arrogant and I confess it, but this time, Angus, blood calls to blood. If I were wrong what harm have I done? Just a poor old woman raving and out of her mind.'

Despite himself Angus's lips twitched with amusement at Lady Annabelle's description of herself. Had anyone else dared to use such words . . . the mind boggled.

'Will someone please explain to me what is going on,' cried Claire. 'The two of you are talking in riddles about a 'she' that I think means me. But I don't understand.'

Angus was still on his feet. He looked down from Lady Annabelle to Claire then said gently 'Lady Annabelle believes you are her lost niece, the child of Senga and her brother Malcolm Sutherland.'

'What? But that's ridiculous.'

'Is it?' demanded Annabelle Ross. 'You say you were born in the Lake District. Whereabouts?'

'I'm not sure. Someone spilt wine on my Birth Certificate at my christening and it's smudged. But I have – had – a father and mother all my life until their deaths. What are you trying to say?'

'I believe Senga went away and had her baby and somehow, we don't yet know how, your parents adopted you, that baby, and she went to Canada alone.'

'But that's crazy! I'm sorry if that's rude, but it is.'

'You said your father took your mother away during her pregnancy because she wasn't well. A most extraordinary step to take. It would be far more likely she would be kept near her own practitioner in London if that were the case. Do you have the long or short form of Birth Certificate?'

'The short.'

'Ah! Yes. That would fit. And there was no-one else to recount the story of your birth. How convenient.'

'But you're wrong. Of course there was someone else.'

Lady Ross looked taken aback.

'Beanie was there.' cried Claire triumphantly.

Angus opened his mouth to speak then closed it again.

'Who is this 'Beanie'?' demanded Lady Ross.

'My present housekeeper, who was my Nannie, and before that my mother's maid. She was there in the Lakes with them. They'd been on a cruise and then went straight up to the Lakes.'

'I thought you said Beanie had never been farther North than Birmingham?' queried Angus. 'She didn't want you to come to Scotland, did she?'

'No, but . . . that was just Beanie being silly because I was leaving her behind. She still thinks I need looking after.'

Lady Ross was triumphant. 'Or she was afraid you might find the truth.'

Claire put her hand to her head. 'It's not true. You're confusing me. I don't know why you're doing it. I am Claire Frobisher. I always have been. Please Angus, can we go home? I have such a headache.' She gathered up her handbag and almost rushed from the room. At the door good manners made her stop. She turned but would not look directly at her hostess. 'Thank you for your hospitality,' she muttered then fled along the hall towards the front door.

Angus looked down to where Lady Annabelle's hands gripped her whisky glass and shook his head. 'What have you done?' he said.

She looked up at him with defiance in every line of her body. 'I am right,' she said.

The next day Claire managed to avoid Angus. He spent the morning attending to his other guests' needs. Mr and Mrs Henderson wanted a route planned for the following day and Mrs Marchmont and her middle-aged daughter wanted him to book seats at Eden Court. In the afternoon Angus was on Lady Ross's business about the estate.

To Ernest Butler's delight Claire professed an interest in learning how to fish. With Cynthia in tow the two spent the day by the water. Poor Ernest with inexhaustible patience exhorted his niece to pay attention and follow his instructions. Never had Claire been so clumsy or so stupid. Time after time he demonstrated and she half-heartedly tried to follow him. But his words were drowned by the questions that rang through her head. Why did Lady Annabelle believe Claire was her niece? On a chance likeness to her dead brother? Why hadn't Beanie wanted her to come to Scotland? She had been amazingly insistent. But she hadn't cared that they would visit the Lake District? Why had the old woman, Minty MacPhee, wanted her got rid of? What shame was she going to bring?

By the end of the day Ernest was sure Claire had had enough and was surprised she insisted on repeating the lessons next day.

'I'm sorry, Uncle Ernest. I will try harder. You are so good to me,' she said with a lump in her throat and gratified Ernest with a rare kiss on the cheek.

On the third morning Angus kept watch on the staircase and managed to waylay Claire on her way to breakfast. 'Are you alright?' he asked.

'Fine thank you,' she replied briefly and tried to pass by but he took her gently by the arm, drew her to one side and held her at the door.

'You don't look as if you slept well,' he said with such kindness she felt the tears well up into her eyes. 'Please don't let this business bother you. I don't know what got into Her Ladyship. Normally I would have said she was the sanest person I know, but this . . .'

'Please! I don't want to talk about it.'

'Of course. I understand, but remember I'm here for you. Don't throw out the baby with the bathwater,' he said with a smile. 'If you fancy another picnic or a jaunt in the car, just say, and I promise *you* will set the conversation. I've missed your company,' he finished.

She smiled, nodded her head and scurried into the dining room. He was so kind. Why was it that people's kindness could reduce her to tears when bitchiness rolled off her back like water off the proverbial duck's?

That day she did try harder at her fishing and once or twice achieved a reasonable cast. But as they packed up the rods she had to agree at last with Ernest that her heart wasn't really in it and she would probably never make a fisherwoman.

'Just as well you're not set on it, as I do think it's about time we were thinking of going home,' he said. 'The roses are back in your cheeks but you've been quiet the last couple of days. Don't take it to heart you can't manage the fishing, my dear. I know it's not everyone's cup of tea.

At talk of home, Claire's heart leapt. Yes. They would go home and she could put all this nonsense behind her. But as fast as the thought came it was chased by others. Did she want to? And where was home? She had never felt so 'in the right place' as she had here since they arrived at Mackay's Hotel. And if she went away would the questions stop? On the way back to the hotel the possibilities raced round her brain. How could she make it all stop?

That evening after dinner she collared Angus and asked for a few minutes private conversation

'Just give me half an hour to tidy up things here and I'll meet you in the hall. We can go out in the garden or even for a run if you like, where we can't be overheard.'

She was grateful for his understanding and watched the clock hands move around as she drank her coffee and gave random replies to Ernest and Cynthia's conversation. At last it was time. She stood up. 'I think I'll go and have a chat with Angus. I haven't seen him for a couple of days.'

Cynthia smiled. 'That would be nice, dear. Yes, you run along. I think that's one young man who is going to miss you very much,' she added with a knowing look.

Claire gave a weak smile in reply and hurried out into the hall where Angus was waiting. He put a light jacket round her shoulders and ushered her out of the front door. 'Mam won't mind you borrowing this. It's starting to get chilly in the evenings now. If we're lucky we'll get a burst of Indian summer and then it will be winter with a vengeance. Are you wanting to walk or sit?'

'Sit, please. I can't sort my head out while I'm walking.'

He led her round the corner of the house and down the path through a shrubbery to a clearing in which stood a small summerhouse commanding a view of the loch below. 'The breeze is in just the right direction. If we sit facing the loch we'll be sheltered from it.'

'How lovely. I didn't even know this was here,' cried Claire as she watched the rising moon throw a silver pathway across the rippling waters. 'It's so peaceful here. I'd just like to stay forever and not have to bother about anything.'

Angus said nothing. He had promised her she could choose any topic of conversation and he intended to keep his word. For a while they sat in companionable silence drinking in the beauty of the night. Then Claire sighed.

'This afternoon Uncle Ernest was talking about us going home soon.'

Angus waited.

'At first I thought yes, this would solve everything. Back in England I'd just get on with my life as it was before. And then I realised I'd just be taking my worries to another place.' She turned to look at Angus. 'You can't run away, can you? Not from yourself and thoughts that won't be shut out.'

Angus was shaken. How had he given himself away? Then he realised she was talking about herself. The question was purely rhetorical. He heaved a sigh of relief and replied rather too firmly. 'No. Never. They always catch up with you . . . in the end. No matter how far you go or whatever you do, they are always with you.'

For a moment Claire looked at him curiously then her own problems took over her mind. 'You do understand. So what shall I do? How can I get any peace?'

'What do you want? What will give you peace?'

'Answers. I don't really believe what Lady Ross said. But the likeness is strange and very strong. I want proof,' she cried passionately. 'But how do you question the dead? Mother and Father . . . if that's who they really are . . . are the only ones who could tell me. So what do I do now?'

'I don't think they are the only ones,' said Angus slowly. 'Your Beanie must know what happened in the Lakes. She could put your mind at rest. And I believe Minty knows more than she ever told Lady Annabelle'

'If she wouldn't tell Lady Ross I doubt anyone else could get the truth out of Minty,' cried Claire. 'Her Ladyship could put the fear of God into anyone I imagine if she so wished.'

'Indeed she could,' Angus smiled, 'but have you never heard the saying that you catch more flies with honey that with vinegar?'

'Yes. So what?'

'I believe my mother could get at the truth if she set her mind to it.'

'Mrs Mackay?' Claire looked distressed. 'But I didn't want anyone else to know.'

'I promise you, Mam is as close as the grave. She would never go blabbing about your private business. But if we confided in her I know she would help you.'

'I'm sorry. I didn't mean to be rude about your mother. I think she's lovely. It's just that the more people know about it the more possible it seems. And it's not. It's not! I'm Claire Frobisher. And if I'm not, then who am I?'

'That's the question isn't it? And if you want to find the answers I think you have to be brave and ask the right people the awkward questions.'

'I suppose so. It's the only thing to do, isn't it?'

She sat with shoulders slumped in an attitude of such dejection Angus was full of pity for her. Then she shivered. He stood up and gave her his hand, 'Come on. You're getting cold. Catching a chill won't solve anything. Remember. I'm here whenever you need me. And Mam will help too - if you want her.'

'Thank you. I'll think about it.'

Claire did think about it, all night long. When morning came she was heavy eyed and tired. Her head ached but she had made up her mind. At breakfast she tackled Ernest and Cynthia. 'Could you please come upstairs after we've finished, both of you? There's something I want to tell you, and ask you.'

Cynthia Butler's mouth opened in an 'o' of surprise. 'My dear! Have you got exciting news for us? Are you sure? Holiday romances can be very beguiling but they don't always last you know. Not but what he seems a delightful young man, not too young either, so has his head screwed on alright.'

Claire looked bewildered. 'What on earth are you talking about, Aunty Cyn?'

Ernest took one look at Claire's face and harrumphed with laughter. 'Barking up the wrong tree there, old girl.'

Cynthia ignored him, pursed her lips and finished her piece of toast. 'Well, if you will spend all your time in one man's pocket what do you expect people to think?' She didn't speak to either of them for the rest of the meal, which suited Claire perfectly.

Upstairs she followed them into her aunt and uncle's large bedroom . . . but of course they weren't really, they were cousins. But were they? Were they any kin of hers at all? Claire stood as the questions went round and round.

'Well? What is it? What have you to tell us,' demanded Cynthia who was still upset she had made a fool of herself, jumping to conclusions.

Claire looked from one to the other as they stood in front of her. 'Am I adopted?' she said.

Both of them opened their mouths, no doubt to refute the suggestion but instead replied with a question. 'What on earth made you ask that?' cried Cynthia.

'Why do you want to know?' said Ernest at the same time.

Neither question was what Claire wanted to hear. 'What's going on?' she said. 'What do you know?'

'Nothing. Nothing at all, m'dear,' assured Ernest belatedly. 'The suggestion's preposterous.'

'But it wasn't a suggestion,' said Claire. 'It was a question. And I saw how you two looked at each other before either of you answered. So tell me. What's going on?'

'There's nothing going on,' soothed Cynthia. 'It was just a misunderstanding when you were born.'

'What misunderstanding?'

'It just seemed a bit odd, that's all. Your parents went off on a cruise and then straight up to Scotland for the grouse shooting. We hadn't seen them for a while. You know your uncle used to work for de Beers. I was with him on a business trip to South Africa at the time you were born but if Althea had been pregnant I'm sure we would have heard. It was common knowledge they'd given up trying. In fact there was a story going round that your father, Edwin, was impotent. So you can imagine everyone's surprise when they turned up after Christmas with you. Of course we were all delighted for them and you were an absolute poppet, very healthy and well-developed for an early baby.' Despite herself Cynthia's old suspicions were showing now. 'Apparently you arrived nearly a month too soon. But there's not much difference between a three month old and a two month old child so it was all forgotten about. Althea explained they hadn't told anyone in case something went wrong. After all she wasn't that young and bad things do happen. It was understandable they didn't want to get their hopes up too much.'

Claire had listened in silence to Cynthia's rambling. Now she looked at Ernest. 'And what did you think Uncle Ernest?'

'You know me, m'dear, I leave the infantry and all that kind of thing to the women. I was just pleased for your father. He was a fine man and your arrival certainly stopped the stupid stories.'

Claire bit her lip. This was not what she wanted to hear. Now there was Senga's missing baby and the appearance of an unexpected baby somewhere else.

'What made you ask, Claire,' queried Ernest. 'You've never questioned your birth before. Why now?'

'I can't tell you at the moment. I need to speak to Beanie but I promise I'll tell you as soon as I know myself.' With that rather garbled answer she left them and went in search of Fiona Mackay.

'Can you please help me, Mrs Mackay?'

Fiona smiled at Claire. 'Certainly, my dear. If I can, I will. Not another visit to the beauty parlour I trust? I don't think Angus could stand the shock if you turned into a redhead.' Her mild joke fell on such stony ground Fiona was concerned. She noted the dark circles under Claire's eyes and took her gently by the arm. 'Come into the office. We can be private there. Would you like a coffee?'

Claire shook her head. 'No, thank you. What has Angus told you?'

'Angus? Told me about what?'

'About me?'

Fiona was at a loss. 'I'm sorry. I think you mean something specific and not just what a lovely girl he thinks you are. But he hasn't said a word of any note. What is all this about? He hasn't upset you has he?'

'No. Oh, no. He's been so kind but he said you would help and I thought he might have . . . but he said he wouldn't . . . so I should have believed him.'

'Let's sit down and start from the beginning, shall we?'

'Yes. Of course. You must think I'm going bonkers.' She took a deep breath and told Fiona the whole story from the visit to Lady Ross's - the first time she had seen Minty - to the overheard words at the hotel, through the tea party and finally what her aunt had told her. 'Do you think I'm paranoid? Or is there really something behind all this?'

Fiona weighed up what she had been told. 'I think there are enough odd facts and unexplained happenings to make you very uneasy. I do think you will have to try and find the truth of it all before you can be at peace with yourself again. It may turn out to be nothing and disappear like snow off a dyke when it is investigated. But to be sure you must try and find out the facts.'

Claire nodded. 'When you say it so simply like that, of course I see you're right. I feel as though a great weight has been lifted from me. I think it was just not being able to make a decision on how to go forward but you will help me, won't you?'

'Me? But how? Of course I would if I could. But I never really knew Senga. She worked mainly at the Big House. She did give us a hand occasionally when we were very busy here but I was busy too and had a small boy to keep from under my feet all day,' she smiled.

'But Angus said you could get the truth out of Minty.'

'Minty MacPhee?' Fiona nodded. 'She's a rare one. Fiercely loyal to those who are good to her but sometimes it is difficult to know what makes her tick. I will try and see if she'll open up to me but I still think your best bet will be your old nurse. If she can be persuaded to tell the truth - whatever it may be - then we will know.'

'If my mother was pregnant as she said and kept it quiet and I was born a month early then we'll know I am truly Claire Frobisher. But Lady Ross still won't know where her niece is, or indeed if she is still alive.'

Fiona nodded. 'That's true, but let's not borrow trouble 'til it's here. You phone your Beanie and I'll tackle Minty.'

Sutherland 1570

Morag sat back on her heels and looked around their resting place. A natural clearing surrounded by scrub and low wind-pruned trees provided concealment. There was a wide cleft in the sheer height of rock at their back which gave shelter from the wind and rain. Somehow up above, where the rock became solid again, a clump of heather had managed to root in a crevice giving an overhang into which any trace of their fire-smoke disappeared. It was a fine stopping place for the moment but what would happen when the winter came? Already the nights were so cold they had taken to cuddling together under her plaid, with cut bracken and Dougal's plaid beneath them to keep off the chill.

She estimated it had been nearly three weeks since they had abandoned the wee boat and struck off on foot. By now they should be much further on their way. But Dougal's wound had been reopened by his exertions on the night of their escape. He had hidden the damage and pain from her as long as possible, but when the wound became infected he had, at last, collapsed. Fortunately it happened just as they had found this hidden spot and here they had stayed while she nursed him back to health. Even when he swore he was mended and fit to move on she forced him to rest. She fed him well, from food she had been able to provide with her snares and, on one occasion, a visit to the river, to supplement the dwindling provisions she had brought with her. Then as his strength increased, she had bidden him exercise the injured leg carefully until now he had convinced her he was as good as new. They could move on. But where?

Before the first harsh frosts and storms of winter they should have met up with some of Dougal's kin, but they were far away to the north and east. Morag still felt surrounded by danger. Dornoch was only a boat ride and one day's hard march away for a determined man like her father. If his need of her services didn't enrage him enough to follow her, the loss of her dowry would enflame him. He would feel he'd been made a fool of. He couldn't fail to notice she had taken her pearls and her mother's brooch. He would know there was a man involved - no doubt thought she had managed to go courting under his nose. He would hate that. He could never bear to be crossed, to lose control of any situation. He would never forgive her and, though it take him to the end of time, he would never give up. Morag shivered. She didn't want his forgiveness, just to be free of him, forever. She prayed, if he followed her, he would seek her southward. Surely it wouldn't occur to him she would make her way north into unknown, enemy territory?

Ruaridh Murray might not have worked it out right, but there *was* a new man in Morag's life. She smiled. If man you could call him. Times he was as heedless as young Robbie, always needing care and restraint. But at others he did play the man, pushing her behind him when there seemed to be danger ahead - even though the danger turned out to be only one of the wild goats that roamed at will on the crags above her head. She smiled again at the memory. Indeed, had it not been for the dread of pursuit, these past three weeks would rank among the happiest of her life. The weather was kind, food plentiful and her companion full of light-hearted fun and stories to make her eyes widen, until he collapsed in a fit of laughter at her gullibility. Then she would pummel him and tickle him until he cried for mercy. So who was the child? She shrugged. What harm did it do? Since Mother had died there had been precious little laughter heard on the farm. Gradually Dougal was teaching her how to be young again.

But happiness didn't solve their problem. They must find shelter for the winter, and as far away from here as possible. Tomorrow they would move on. As soon as Dougal brought back whatever he had found in the way of food, she would cook it and stow it away in their packs. Now Dougal was fit he could carry his fair share of their goods.

In his enforced idleness he had not wasted his time. They now had birchbark beakers and containers to add to their chattels. His hands were skilled with a knife and she enjoyed watching him whittle her a new spirtle to stir the tasty broths she made, or a wooden spoon. If only they could find somewhere to bide for the winter they could, between them, make it snug and lack for little comfort.

'Make up the fire, Morag,' cried Dougal as he made his way into the small clearing. 'I've got a fine hare,' he boasted.

'Good heavens! A hare! But how?'

'I climbed to the top of the cliffs yesterday and found a 'dancing ground'.' He saw her puzzled frown and explained. 'Have you never seen one? It's where the hares go mad in the Spring, but even at this time of year you can often find one or two not far away. I set a good strong snare and just hoped. And look!' He held up the body of the hare by its back legs. It was a fine big beast with plenty meat on it and a coat already thickened against the winter cold.

Morag clapped her hands. 'It's beautiful, Dougal. Quite beautiful. If only we could stay and get some more, I'd make you a jerkin even your fine courtiers wouldn't turn their noses up at.' She took the hare and pulled out her knife. Swiftly she gutted the carcase, dropping the entrails onto the fire. It wouldn't do to attract predatory animals or leave such evidence of their presence behind for anyone to find. Carefully she skinned the hare, marvelling at the thick soft pelt. After she had quartered the body she thrust it into their cauldron. The rabbit Dougal had also brought she dealt with in the same way, then added a handful of sorrel leaves, juniper berries she had gathered on their way, and a small amount of water. 'Watch the pot,' she bade Dougal as she covered the top with a wooden lid he had made. 'See it doesn't boil dry. Keep checking,' she added with a smile, then gathered up the two skins and headed for the river bank.

Dougal opened his mouth to protest, but she had disappeared into the scrub. He shook his head. She didn't have to go on about it. It was only once he had neglected to keep a careful watch and their precious food had burned. Knowing nothing about cooking, he hadn't realised water disappeared when it was boiled. But he was learning fast.

Morag smiled as she made her way down to the water. It wasn't fair to tease him so, but just retaliation for his tall tales. And bless him for bringing the hare. Maybe they would be lucky enough to get more later in the year. It was true she now had a good stock of rabbit skins, but the work was tedious to sew them together. Where the seams were there was always less warmth than in the main fur, so a fine big hare made much warmer clothing. And they were going to need it.

Morag approached the river with care, always watchful for the presence of other people in the area. So far they had been lucky. She found her favourite strip of sandy shingle below the river bank and knelt to her task. First with her knife and then with a smooth stone and handfuls of sand she cleaned the skins of blood, sinew and flesh. Then she spread the skins with more sand and rubbed with the stone until they were smooth and soft to the touch. As she worked she wished she had the bark, leaves, water and time to treat them properly and the lanolin from her sheep's wool to make supple leather, but cheered herself with the knowledge her present treatment would at least make them serviceable, if not as comfortable as she was capable of doing.

As her hands moved in the familiar task, her mind was free to wander. Dougal had said he would present her to his kin, but what would happen then? How would she be received? Who was she? No longer Morag Murray of the Strath, respected and with a family at her back. She was homeless and had foolishly cut herself off from everything dear and familiar. Was she mad? Bewitched? What had possessed her to act that way? Possession? No. Don't be foolish. If it was mad to want freedom to lead a happy life, then she would be mad. If she was possessed it was only with the longing to know more of the world than that bounded by the steading and a very occasional trip into Dornoch. At the farm her life was no better than a bonded servant, so she had made her decision; had cast in her lot with Dougal; and she would face whatever happened with the high courage of the Murrays.

Once her task was completed to her satisfaction she brushed off any remaining sand and rolled the skins together. The next step would be up to Dougal. She grinned as she remembered his reaction to her first request for his services. He had blushed like a young girl.

'Me! Piss on the skins? You're jesting!'

She had hidden her desire to howl in merriment and preserved a grave face. 'No indeed. It is necessary. At home I kept a vat and there I put water, bark, leaves and piss. Horse piss is the best.' She bit her lip to keep her face straight. 'But we must make do with what we have.'

'No! I won't! I can't! You *must* be jesting!'

'I'm not. I need to preserve the skins until we are settled somewhere and I hope to work them to suppleness for wearing. If only we had sheep,' she mourned. 'The natural oil in their fleeces is wonderful for treating the skins to keep them soft and stop them drying out and cracking. Come on, Dougal,' she said more sharply. 'Stop being a baby. You can take them away and get on with it. Spread them on the ground. Piss on the inside, not the fur, then roll them together and bring them back to me. I don't intend for my work to be wasted just because you're not man enough to do what is necessary.'

Of course he had complied. She hadn't perfected her knowledge of men's pride and weaknesses on three brothers not to be able to handle one young stranger. The second time she had asked him there had been no demur. Now they made a good team.

They completed their preparations for the journey and settled for the night, but sleep was long in coming to Morag. What did the future hold? She was quiet as they set off next day heading west by north, trying to follow the rapidly dwindling river back to its source in the high hills, then they would be able to strike out to the east..

Two weeks later they had covered many wearisome miles. The going was hard. Sometimes for a rest they had followed the river bank, but this was courting danger. One day a small child appeared ahead of them, stopped with rounded eyes and stared, its thumb firmly fixed in its mouth. The surprise was equal on each side. Dougal and Morag also stopped, prepared to retreat and run, but before they could make up their minds a woman called for the bairn. The child didn't move. Its eyes grew rounder as it took in these strangers. Its mother came from a clump of trees to the right. Alarm flashed into her eyes as she saw Dougal and Morag. She swooped upon the bairn, scooped it up in her arms and stepped back warily.

Morag pushed Dougal in the back, urging him forward. She plastered a smile on her face. 'Good morning, Mistress,' she called as she walked past the staring woman. 'A good day to you and your fine son.' She nodded towards the child and carried on walking. Her heart thumped in her chest. She prayed the mother had strayed far from her smoke, perhaps seeking berries for a meal. If her dwelling was ahead, or even nearby she could call for help and there would be questions to answer, at the very least.

Behind was silence. Morag breathed more easily and, as soon as they were out of sight of the woman, they turned sharply away from the river and once more had to force their way through thick scrub and deep heather. How she regretted the impulse to choose an easier path. They wouldn't make that mistake again. And instead of make their resting place before evening, they must push on for as long as possible to make sure the woman's kin didn't investigate their presence.

As the early darkness fell, the chill wind rose and numbed their hands and faces. It had been hours since Morag could feel her bare feet. Even if she stubbed her toes, or bruised her foot on a rock, she wouldn't know anything of it until she could thaw out. At least the wind kept the clouds moving above them. They could see the stars and keep a rough check on the direction they were headed. That night they slept where they fell from sheer exhaustion, simply rolling themselves together in the two plaids and huddling under the lee of a rock.

Next morning it was hard to creep from the covers. The sun shone brightly, but frost sparkled in the morning light wherever they looked. Morag was still anxious about their encounter of the previous day and so they ate their cold meats as they walked along. Perhaps this was one of those occasional early frosts that occurred even before an Indian summer, giving warning of what was to come? Indeed as they walked they got warmer until they were almost too hot in their motley assortment of clothes. But they made good progress and Morag was agreeable to stopping in time to gather kindling and make a fire in a sheltered spot as the shortening day drew to a close.

Next day they met the pig.

It was another cold, sunny morning. The sunshine lifted their spirits and the glimpse they had, from the top of a steep rise, of a body of water ahead, convinced Dougal they were nearly through the strath. The river they had been following had reduced from a stream to a burn which they had followed to higher ground eastward of north. Then they had lost it in the undergrowth. Dougal was sure the water ahead was a big loch, that stretched for miles. He had heard tell of it. They could follow it to its end then turn to head east towards the coast and his homeland or strike off before then if he could only find the way.

He had just finished explaining all this to Morag when a noise ahead on the animal track they were following made them pause, listening. A strange noise, grunting and whuffling. What or who could it be? Dougal stepped in front of Morag and loosed his dirk from his belt. She stooped and armed herself with a good throwing stone. They waited. Then Dougal burst out laughing as a large, extremely fat sow sauntered into view, her snout rootling to each side of the path as she came.

'I think we shall have to leave her in peace,' he said. 'Even with your cooking skills and way of dealing with dead animals, she would be much too big to carry away.'

Morag smiled. 'Don't be foolish, Dougal,' she said, even as the saliva rushed into her mouth at the memory of hams baked in clay in an open pit. She walked towards the enormous beast.

Dougal jumped into her path. 'Stay,' he warned. 'Wild swine can be dangerous. She looks harmless enough but my father always said their great bulk hid impressive speed.'

Gently Morag pushed him aside. 'She's no wild beast,' she said. 'See how our presence doesn't perturb her in the least.' She moved forward. The pig stopped and looked up at her, its snout waving to get her scent. Dougal held his breath. Morag held out her hand. The pig moved forward, still scenting with her snout, then stopped at Morag's feet and lowered her head.

Morag laughed as she leaned forward and scratched the huge animal along its back. 'See,' she said. 'I told you she was tame. She's someone's beloved companion, obviously used to human touch. Bur what is she doing here I wonder?'

Dougal came forward and walked all around the beast which was blissfully rolling its shoulders under Morag's ministrations. 'It's been tethered and broken free,' he remarked. 'See, here's the remains of a rope trailing from its back leg.'

'Well, now,' said Morag, 'what are we going to do with you, my bonnie?' she addressed the pig.

'What do you mean,' said Dougal, 'What should we do but leave it and go on?'

'We can't do that. This animal is very valuable and, if I'm not mistaken, soon about to farrow. Someone must be desperate if they've missed her. Think about it. To lose the beast is bad enough, but to lose the litter, too? Winter food or coin for future use. It could mean the difference between life and death to the owner.'

Dougal hesitated. 'But it's not our problem. What do you want us to do? You ken fine we must keep away from smokes. Are you intending to walk bang into the middle of one and shout, 'who's is this fine pig'?'

Morag smiled. 'Of course not. But we can turn it around in the direction it came from. That is on our way and we may meet the owner seeking it.'

'Oh! Very well.'

The deed was easier said than done. Their large charge had no intention of returning home. However the track was narrow and the humans determined. With the aid of a stout stick in Dougal's hand to guide the pig along, and a hard shorter one for Morag to continue scratching its back, they got it turned round and the odd trio proceeded along the path. There was much laughter, stopping and starting as each new whim took the sow and the humans persuaded her out of it.

Onto this merry scene came an anxious old woman. With one hand she held the shawl about her head. In the other she carried a stout stick, similar to the one wielded by Dougal. Her first glance was one of delight at the sight of her precious sow, then she looked warily from one to the other of its companions. Morag read the expressions flitting across the old woman's lined, weathered face - delight, fear, curiosity followed each other in swift succession.

'Good day to you, Mistress,' she called with a smile to ease the cailleach's fears. 'Have we found your runaway?'

'Indeed, child, and a wicked, ungrateful beast it is. Fed on the fat of the land, housed in a byre as dry and warm as any could wish and this is the thanks I get.' She looked with sharp eyes from one to the other of her animal's rescuers. 'But you are not from these parts I think?'

Dougal stepped forward. 'Indeed, Mistress, we are on our way home. I am Dougal Mackay and this is my sister Morag. We have been visiting kinfolk by Beauly and must return before the winter.'

'Mackay kin at Beauly,' murmured the old one, then nodded. 'I am Elspeth Sutherland. My late husband was a Robertson from Forres, but when he died I returned to my own place.' She looked around. 'The day draws in. You must come and eat with me. Bide the night before continuing your journey the morn's morn.'

Dougal and Morag exchanged a quick glance. Morag longed to spend a night under a proper roof within the shelter of four strong walls, perhaps even to lie on a real bed. She was so tempted. Dougal too thought longingly of food eaten from a bowl or platter, instead of from the cauldron with his fingers. In the safety of a strong building he could relax his guard against the unseen perils of the night. Lately he had heard wolves calling, in the distance certainly but too close nonetheless. However both runaways were aware that accepting hospitality involved answering questions.

Could they pull the wool over the cailleach's eyes? It was customary to offer shelter and food to any traveller who passed by your dwelling. Would a refusal arouse more suspicion? Their thoughts and unspoken communication had taken but a moment. Morag smiled. 'Thank you, we shall be glad of your kind hospitality,' she said. And the die was cast.

Mistress Sutherland had brought with her a handful of the sow's favourite roots so the pace of their journey increased. The animal track they followed joined a wider path trodden by human feet and at last they spied a smoke ahead of them. It was made up of one sturdy dwelling house and a good sized barn placed at right angles. Chickens scratched in the churned earth between the two buildings and Morag heard the plaintive bleat of sheep from an enclosure forming the third side of the steading. Dougal helped the cailleach trap the sow in a corner and guarded her while Mistress Sutherland opened the wooden door to the byre attached to the house. Once her precious beast was provided with food and water and Dougal had laid large stones against the bottom of the door for extra strength to prevent another escape, the hostess turned to the needs of her guests.

They were a puzzle to her. As she stirred the peats and swung the pot on its iron hook over the heat to prepare a meal, Elspeth Sutherland, wondered at the story behind their appearance. That they were brother and sister she didn't believe for one moment. Although they were easy in each other's company and seemed to be able to communicate without words, they were so unalike to look at they would surely have different sires if indeed there was a relationship. They weren't local that was certain. She knew everyone for miles around. Her first thought was a pair of runaway lovers, but as she watched them discreetly she soon banished that idea. There was nothing of the lover in the young man's treatment of the young woman, nor of the beloved in hers. Although, as the hours passed, she became aware there was a definite fondness between them.

The girl was bone weary. Elspeth knew that feeling. You just kept going and going because there was no other choice, but once you let yourself relax and rest, it was almost impossible to get up and move on. Well they could rest here. She was a pretty shrewd judge of folk and felt no threat from her visitors.

The following morning after the most wonderful sleep either of them had had in weeks, to her dismay, Morag found she couldn't move. Try as she might her body would not obey her. Tears of helplessness sprang to her eyes. She gazed at Dougal who stood over her in bewilderment.

'What is it, Morag? Are you injured?'

She shook her head. Fear added to her distress. Why couldn't she move? Was she bewitched? She looked across the fire to where Elspeth Sutherland was stirring a pot. 'Why can't I move?' she begged.

'Because you are worn out, child,' the old woman answered. There was sympathy in her eyes as she went on, 'your body is claiming its rest, having served you to the last ounce of its strength. It knows you are safe here and here it will keep you while it mends and regains its powers.'

'Safe!' exclaimed Dougal, his whole stance wary, 'that is a strange word to use, Mistress.'

Elspeth smiled. 'To a body, safety is warmth, comfort, and good food,' she replied. 'Your . . . sister must build up her strength before you continue your journey . . . home. Come, eat now. We will talk later.'

Every pause she made in that speech let her listeners know she was suspicious of their story, but the accompanying smile and invitation to eat reassured them somewhat. Morag knew if her father himself stood at the door, she wouldn't have the strength to rise and run. For the first time since the beginning of this mad journey she would have to let their fate rest with someone other than herself and her own endeavours. As soon as she had taken a bowl of broth, her eyes closed and she slept again.

For the next three days Elspeth Sutherland asked no questions while Morag ate and slept. They were a contented household. Elspeth enjoyed the company disrupting her solitary life. Dougal helped her with the chores and she came to be fond of the good-looking lad with the merry eyes. Once the work of the day was done, the night fallen and the fire made up, Elspeth entertained her guests with the old stories. She told them of the ugly witch Alison Gross, and of the sad tale of the wife of Ushers Well and her two sons. Then Dougal, not to be outdone, related the story of the pipers Farquhar Grant and Thomas Cumming of Tullochgorum who travelled to Inverness and were tricked into playing for the faeries under Tomnahurich hill.

Elspeth clapped her hands. 'I haven't heard that tale in many a long day. And where did you hear it, laddie?'

Dougal smiled. 'My uncle, my father's brother, brought it with him from one of his travels,' he said.

'And is this uncle a regular travelling man? Is he also a piper, perhaps?'

'He can blow up his pipes for a reel or two when there's none by who can play better,' Dougal replied, 'but without a merry company, the noise he makes would scare the beasts. His strength is in his brain, mistress and the news he can carry from the great lords to Her Majesty's Court.' Too late he saw Morag's warning frown, and cursed his own ready tongue and open manner.

But Elspeth made no comment. She took note of Morag's unease and held it in her mind for later pondering, but turned the conversation to Dougal's skill at whittling. 'I see you often take a bit wood in your hand, laddie. Do you enjoy making things?'

'Aye. It's something I've always done. Usually when I should have been tending to my books,' he continued with a laugh.

Morag sighed in despair and shook her head. It was no use, Dougal could no more keep his tongue still in his head when addressed in friendly fashion than she could have left Elspeth's sow to run far from her mistress. It was their nature. And anyway, now she was feeling so much better they could be on their way. Surely no harm had been done?

The following day Morag took Dougal to set snares away from the house. 'We'll catch a good few rabbits and leave some with the cailleach to repay her for her hospitality,' she said. 'She can smoke the meat and keep it against a hard winter. And we shall take our share and hurry as fast as we can to find some of your kin with whom to spend the cold weather. Or perhaps they will lend us horses so we might arrive at your home before the snows come in?'

As usual Dougal wasn't worrying about the future. 'Aye. They will surely do that,' he answered, 'when we can find them.'

Elspeth frowned. 'How far would it be to your nearest kin's smokes?'

Dougal shrugged. 'I have no idea,' he said cheerfully. 'We simply need to find our way to Strath Vagastie and follow it to Loch Naver. All the folk round Altnaharra are our kin. It can't be that far now.'

Once again Morag wondered with impatience how she could have entrusted her future to such a careless loon. Would his promises of a fair welcome in his father's house turn out to be just as insubstantial as his knowledge of the way home?

When they got back to the crofthouse all thoughts of Dougal's faults were banished from her mind. Elspeth's sow was farrowing and not having an easy time. The sow was huge and heavy. Elspeth was old and, though fit for her age, hadn't the strength to help the suffering animal. She knelt beside the bulk of her precious beast and wrung her hands. 'What can I do? What can I do? Hamish Mhor, who would help her, is away to Muir of Ord with his cattle.' She rocked back and forth on her heels. 'To lose the litter will be hard but to lose my wee Vhairi . . ..' She wailed in grief as though the pig were already dead. 'Many's the cold winter night she's kept me warm. And I have only her for company now my man has gone.'

Morag knelt beside Elspeth and put her hands on the sow's huge belly, pressing down with her palms and feeling with her fingers. 'She's ready right enough. And there's plenty movement there, but something is certainly wrong.' She shifted her position and went to the sow's rear. 'Aye, she should be pushing them out like stripping ripe berries off the bush.' She turned to Elspeth. 'Do you have fat, goose grease or something like?'

'Aye, but why?'

'Get me some and I think I can help her,' promised Morag.

The cailleach rose, hurried into the house room and came back with an open-neck earthenware jar. Morag took it and dug out a handful of the grease it contained. She smothered it over her right hand and arm and knelt again by the sow's rear. Gently she pushed her hand into the huge body. 'Aye, my bonnie one. I'll help you,' she murmured. 'We'll do it together. Ah! I have it. Naughty wee thing. Would you try to come out the wrong way round then? Shame on you, giving your mother such grief.' As Morag talked in a low soothing voice, Elspeth went to the sow's head and rubbed the hairy cheeks in sympathy. Dougal looked on in amazement as Morag's arm slowly disappeared inside the sow. 'Come on, now, behave,' said Morag and shoved her arm strongly farther into the sow. 'That's it. Turn round now will you and do things right for all our sakes.' As she spoke she gently withdrew her arm. Once it was clear of Vhairi, the sow's flank gave three huge heaves and the first piglet slid into the cold light of day. Others followed smoothly and with ease. Once the cross-lain rogue had been turned, the rest came as they should. Morag smiled as she wiped her forearm on a handful of the sweet heather with which a doting Elspeth had made a bed for the mother-to-be. 'She'll do fine now,' she said.

'Aye, so she will,' echoed Elspeth, 'and it's grateful I am, child, for what you've done this day. At your age I maybe had the strength to do the same, but then I hadn't the knowledge. How does one so young get to be so wise?'

Morag shrugged. 'I've always liked the beasts. I watch what others do and I remember.' Pleased though she was with the outcome of her help, she had no intention of telling Elspeth how, ever since her mother's death, she had been in charge of all women's work on the farm.

Almost as though she followed Morag's train of thought, Elspeth went on, 'Your mother must be so proud of you and she'll be missing you sorely I have no doubt.'

'Morag's mother is dead,' said Dougal, 'that's why she knows so much. And thinks she knows even more,' he added with a grin, remembering the many times she had scolded him for transgressions or ignorance since their mad flight began.

Morag closed her eyes in resignation. Would he never learn? But there was no query from the cailleach who was at the new mother's head crooning words of praise for the seven bonnie piglets who were already wriggling towards the swollen teats. Perhaps she hadn't heard Dougal's careless talk?

Next day the snares they had set were all full. Dougal shouted with glee at the sight of eight good-sized rabbits. 'We'll feast like kings,' he gloated.

'No, we won't,' said Morag. 'We'll tell Elspeth we are leaving, cook this lot to take with us and set the snares again to get some food we can leave with her.'

'Of course,' agreed Dougal. 'I'd forgotten.'

'Don't go,' begged Elspeth, when they told her their news. 'The weather is cold and your journey is long. Bide here with me until the Spring. I fear the early snows will catch you before you reach the shelter of your home.'

'We have kin all along the way,' Dougal reassured her.

'Hmm,' was the only reply. But the look on Elspeth's face made Morag's lips twitch. If only they could trust the old woman. To be constantly on guard like this was horrid and, although she had taken care not to actually tell any lies, she felt uncomfortable at hiding the truth from one who had only given help and comfort without question or reserve.

'We have to go,' she said gently, taking the cailleach's worn old hands in her strong young ones, 'but we do thank you and we'll never forget your goodness to us.'

'Nonsense. 'Tis I should thank you and I do, for the life of my Vhairi and yon bonnie weans. So you'll really go?'

'Aye. The morn's morn. We'll get the catch from the snares for you at the dawn and go straight after we've broken our fast.' She would have liked to ask the old one how to avoid the dwelling of that Hamish Mhor

Elspeth had spoken of and also the big smoke called Laorig. It was almost a township she had told them and was the nearest to the croft though still two hours away. But she didn't want to raise any more suspicion, so bit her tongue and instead kissed the sunken cheek so close to her, then stepped away and spoke with deliberate briskness to cover the moment of emotion. 'I must cook this meat if we're to take it on our journey tomorrow.'

By nightfall all their preparations were made. No-one found anything to say as they sat round the fire after their last meal. It wasn't long before Elspeth covered the embers with damp peats and all three settled to seek elusive sleep.

Their thoughts had kept them awake so long, the younger pair slept heavily and later the next day than they had intended. Morag roused to hot breath on her face and whiskers tickling her nose. She shook her head and put up her hand to push away whoever was crowding her. Her fingers met solid bulk and as she woke fully she found herself face to face with Vhairi. Morag laughed and sat up, shoving the questing snout away. 'Off with you girl. Whatever are you doing here?'

Her voice roused Dougal who sat up and rubbed a hand over his face. 'What's happening? Why's the pig no in the byre?'

That was indeed the question. What had seemed amusing at first became a worry. Morag pushed aside her plaid, fastened her girdle round her waist and hurried across the room to the entrance to the byre. The wooden door lay pushed aside by Vhairi's passing into the house. Inside the adjoining building Elspeth lay moaning on the ground. Morag rushed to help her. 'What is it? What's wrong? What happened?' she cried. 'Dougal, come quickly.'

As Dougal came running, Elspeth opened her eyes. 'So stupid,' she said weakly, 'so stupid. I came to feed Vhairi and tripped on the piglets. Oh! My ankle,' she moaned as Morag ran exploratory fingers over Elspeth's body and legs.

'Take her in your arms, Dougal,' ordered Morag. 'Be careful how you lift her.' As he obeyed, Morag ran ahead and smoothed the cailleach's bed. 'Lay her down here. Gently, gently. There now,' she addressed Elspeth, 'don't fret, everything will be alright. I am going to bind your foot and ankle in linen and you shall rest here until it's well again.'

'But . . .,' began Dougal.

She quieted him with a look. 'Go see to Vhairi,' she commanded, 'and then you can go and empty the snares.' While he was gone she reassured the old one they would not abandon her. They would stay until her ankle was well and she could manage on her own again.

'What else could I say?' she demanded of Dougal who was ready to argue when he heard the news. 'Could you go off and leave her to starve? And Vhairi,' she added with a smile, for she had heard him talking to the sow as he watched the pretty piglets guzzling at her teats.

'I suppose not,' he agreed. 'But you know this probably means we're stuck here for the winter? There'll be no travelling once the snows come down.'

'Aye, that's right. But if we can't travel, then neither can anyone else,' she added with a grin. 'We'll be safe here, Dougal, safe, warm and well-fed – we'll see to that – and we can bide the winter and be fit and strong and ready for the road when the spring comes. I'm not sorry we have to stay. You seem unworried about anything, but I've thought with dread where we would pass the winter months if we couldn't reach your kin.' She had the satisfaction of watching his face as her words painted an unwelcome picture in his mind.

'Aye. You're right,' he said. 'We'll be fine here, snug and warm and we'll care for the cailleach too.'

Morag smiled agreement, happier now than she had been since they left the farm. They had food, shelter, safety and a new friend.

Mackay's Hotel 2010

Claire took a deep breath as the ringing telephone was answered at the other end, far away in England.

'Hello, is that you Beanie?'

She laughed. She was so nervous. Of course it would be Beanie. Who else would be answering the phone at home? She listened to her old companion's voice, acknowledged news from home and hurried on to the purpose of her call before she lost her nerve.

'I'm glad everything is going well at home, Beanie, and I miss you too. You should have come with us . . . you know you were invited. I'm sure the house wouldn't have fallen down if you'd left it for a week or two . . . I'm not sure when we're coming back. I had thought it would be soon but something's happened . . . No! I'm not hurt and yes, Aunty Cyn and Uncle Ernest are alright too.'

Claire clenched her hand even harder on the telephone receiver until her knuckles shone white. She bit her lip. Here goes, she thought and crossed the fingers of her free hand.

'What happened when I was born, Beanie? . . . I mean, what doctor attended Mother and which hospital did she go to after the birth, to make sure she we were both well? . . . But I do want to bother my head about it . . . in fact there is so much bother going on in my head I can't think straight. Tell me the truth. You owe me the truth after all these years . . . No! It *is* my business! Who else's? . . . I'm going to put the phone down now and leave you to think about it. If you won't tell me the whole truth when I phone you tomorrow I want you to pack your bags and leave my house before I come back . . . But, Beanie, I would never be able to trust you again so there would be no point in you remaining . . . I'll call you tomorrow evening about quarter to seven. Goodnight. Please do this for me . . . No. I know exactly what I'm doing. I love you, but don't think I don't mean what I say.'

Claire put down the receiver with tears in her eyes. Whatever happened she thought she would never forget the sound of Beanie's despairing cry of 'Miss Claire' as she severed the connection.

There was a tap at the door of the office where she'd made the call. In her bedroom there was too much of a chance she would be interrupted by Cynthia. Fiona had been more than willing to allow her the privacy of the office and now it was her voice that called gently. 'Claire? Have you finished, dear? May I come in?'

Claire wiped away her tears and blew her nose then walked over and opened the door to Fiona. 'Quite finished, thank you, Mrs Mackay'

Fiona took in the damp eyes and woebegone expression. 'Oh! Dear. Didn't it go as well as you'd hoped?'

Claire shook her head. 'Beanie tried to tell me there was nothing. But I know her too well. Her very indignation and emphasis that everything was straightforward told me she was lying. And she didn't want to - or probably couldn't - tell me the doctor's name or the hospital involved. Said it wasn't my business.' She shook her head in disbelief. 'How ridiculous is that? She didn't want me to bother my head about things that happened long ago. Doesn't that tell you there's something fishy?'

'It certainly seems as if she doesn't want to discuss it. If the facts are what we believe then it may be you were never legally adopted. Beanie might be still protecting your mother . . . that is, the mother you have always known.'

'You're probably right. She's been with the Frobisher family just about all her life. She came as a young girl and was trained as my mother's maid, then became my nanny and now I'm grown up she rules the whole house with a rod of iron,' Claire smiled. 'She's the one permanent fixture in my life.' Then her expression became grave, 'but maybe not for too much longer.'

'Whatever do you mean?'

'I've given her an ultimatum. Don't you see,' Claire burst out passionately, 'if she won't tell me the truth how can we carry on? Beanie, in the house knowing secrets about my past of which I'm ignorant. It just wouldn't work. So I told her to 'fess up or move out.' She bit her lip in distress.

By now Fiona knew a little of what her old nanny meant to Claire. 'That was a very brave thing to do,' she said. 'Do you think it will work?'

Claire shrugged. She felt so weary. 'I don't know. But if it doesn't I don't know where to go from here. And I meant what I said to her,' she finished and folded her lips to shut out the hurt of Beanie's non-cooperation.

Fiona saw a new side to the young girl she'd come to like so much. Behind the lovely face and pretty manners there was a strength of character she could only admire. She just hoped Claire's ultimatum would bring about the desired result. In the mean time she must try and prise the truth out of Minty MacPhee. She looked at the clock. About this time she should find Minty at her work but what on earth she could say to get the truth from the strange old woman she had no idea.

When breakfast service was ended Fiona arranged with Angus that he should bid the two parties of departing guests farewell while she put a plan into action. She walked into the laundry carrying two mugs of tea. Minty was taking the sheets from the dryer and feeding them into the rotary iron.

'Good morning, Minty. I've brought you a cuppa. It's nearly lunchtime but it's thirsty work heaving those sheets about, isn't it?' Fiona didn't wait for a reply but placed one of the mugs on the windowsill close to where Minty worked, then walked over to the other side of the room. She put down her own mug and began to count the linen waiting to be washed. 'Stock-taking is so tedious,' she complained, 'and I never seem to have enough time to do it all at once. If I don't complete the job once started then everything is in the wrong place – a bit like some people.'

Minty looked across the room at Fiona with blank eyes. Fiona knew that look. It meant Minty had something on her mind but wasn't sure what it was all about. 'Thank you for the tea, Mistress Mackay,' she said and went on ironing sheets as though there had been no interruption.

'It used to seem much easier,' went on Fiona, 'but of course that's when we could call on extra staff from Lady Ross. Who was that young friend of yours, Minty, the pretty girl who was always smiling and so obliging?'

It seemed Minty wasn't going to answer and then, 'Senga,' she muttered.

'That's the one. You know I keep thinking of her lately. I wonder where she is? You were very close, weren't you? Do you know what happened to her? She left so suddenly - such a shame - she was a lovely person. Right, that's ten pairs of doubles and now I can start on the singles.' She didn't look directly at Minty but was aware the woman had picked up her mug of tea and wrapped both hands around it. She stared at the surface of the liquid and began to rock her body back and forth.

'Shame. Shame,' muttered Minty. 'Such shame. Only thing to do. Best for m'lady, best for her, best for him, aye and the bairn. The shame - but all gone now. All gone.' She lifted her head and gazed directly at Fiona. Her eyes were bright and hard. 'She shouldn't have come back,' Minty said viciously. 'Make her go away. She shan't hurt my lady. She's wicked. Wicked it is to bring that face from the grave and cause trouble. Beautiful he was and no-one could deny him, but bad, bad, bad all through. Such a worry to m'lady but all gone now. All gone.' She nodded. 'Minty saw to that,' she said, a smile of satisfaction on her face. 'Minty saw to that. Made it all better. There, there, my dearie. Don't fret.'

Fiona abandoned the pretence of sorting linen and moved across to stand by Minty. 'Of course you did,' she said gently. 'You wanted to protect your mistress, didn't you?'

Minty nodded. 'Had to do it - had to do it - sad. Minty was sad. Senga her friend, but bad girl. Not bad – weak – loved him - but that's not right. He was gentry.'

'Poor Senga,' said Fiona quietly.

'Poor Minty. All alone.'

'Where did you leave her, Minty?'

'In the digs.'

'Which digs?'

'The ones in Glasgow – where the woman was. Not the big ones. That's where I took the baby. But that was after. Then Senga went away.' She shook her head. 'Poor Minty, all alone.'

'Where did you take the baby, Minty?'

'Poor Minty. All alone'

'Who took the baby, Minty?'

'Poor Minty. All alone.'

And that was all Fiona could get out of her. As long as she believed Fiona had known about Senga leaving Minty's words seemed to flow. But once she was questioned further the information dried up. Fiona tried cajoling and even bribing with chocolate cake, one of Minty's great weaknesses, but it was no use. She couldn't get any more answers. It was so frustrating. She hoped Beanie would solve the mystery the next evening.

Claire sat at her bedroom window and gazed into the moonlit garden. Her chaotic thoughts wouldn't let her sleep. Who was she? If she wasn't Claire Frobisher as she had always believed then who? Lady Ross seemed to think Claire might be her long lost niece the daughter of her dead brother Malcolm and the maid Senga. What would she feel about that? It just seemed so weird like a Mills and Boon. But perhaps the other way round? Didn't it turn out the peasant girl became a princess? Or was that a Barbara Cartland? She leaned her hot forehead against the cool glass of the window.

What if it was true and Lady Ross was really her aunt? What difference would it make? Would she just go back to England and carry on as before? Could she? Would the house she'd always called home still belong to her as it said in Father's Will? If she hadn't been adopted had she any right to it? Had she any rights at all? Illegitimate. That's what she'd be. People said it didn't matter so much these days if your parents weren't married, but in the circles in which she moved it mattered rather a lot – especially if there was inequality of birth and no-one really knew much about your mother. And of course once it got out - as it surely would, this kind of thing always did – would people look at her differently? Would her old friends drop her?

She gave an impatient shake of her shoulders. Would she care?

Strange, she mused, how she didn't really have the kind of friends other people talked about - long-term confidantes who shared secrets and swapped stories of boyfriends and parental tyranny. Even at school, although she had been popular and always had plenty of company, there was no-one truly close. If you had a tennis court in your garden and belonged to the local Sports Club where you could take guests to swim she supposed you would never be short of people to play with.

Her parents – if they were her parents – had a circle of bridge and golf playing friends with whom they spent their leisure. These friends had children Claire's age and naturally the young people got together for dances, parties and all the other pastimes approved of by their elders. The Frobishers had already begun to invite eligible young men to tennis parties and to dinner although Claire had assured them she had no intention or desire to get married yet. Mother had the guest list ready for the ball they had intended to give for her twenty-first. She had discussed it with Claire on several occasions, changing the names as engagements were announced in The Times.

Tears pricked Claire's eyes. She sniffed and bit her lip. They were so good to her. Had there ever been anything she might have felt or noticed to give her a clue she was different? Father was usually busy, spending long hours in his study when he wasn't in London. She had no idea where he worked in Town, had never visited his office, never even thought about it. Father was sort of aloof. But then he was a man. Weren't all men like that? Uncle Ernest didn't fuss over her, or over Cynthia his wife, so probably Father was just normal. Mother wasn't a demonstrative parent either but no less so than the parents of most of Claire's friends and acquaintances. There were Nannies to take care of the younger children and when they were older they were expected to be able to amuse themselves or behave in a grown-up fashion when allowed to help their parents entertain. So why did she feel, on looking back, as though there had always been something missing?

It was Angus. Or more correctly, Angus and Fiona, and even Angus and Lady Ross. There was a connection between them when they were together. It showed in the tone of voice, the look in their eyes and the little things - like Angus making sure there was a cushion at Lady Ross's back when she sat down. Or Fiona Mackay putting an affectionate hand on Angus's arm as they talked together. Claire sat up straight on the window-seat. That was it. Affection. All her life she had been tended to, her bodily and mental needs met but there had been no true, warm affection. Wrong, she thought. There had been affection - from Beanie. But Beanie was not a parent and Claire hadn't the knowledge or experience to compare behaviour. She had simply accepted that Beanie treated her one way and her parents another. So really she had lacked for nothing. It was just that her needs were met by the wrong people. No. That wasn't right.

Claire shook her aching head. What did she mean? She tried to think it through. It was great that Beanie loved her and that was as it should be. She loved Beanie. But surely her parents could have, should have, loved her too. Their child. Their only child. If she was?

Having worried her thoughts full circle Claire crept into bed and laid her aching head on the cool linen of her pillow. The faint scent of lavender soothed her jangled nerves and finally she slept.

Next day Claire refused all offers of company from Cynthia, Ernest, Fiona and Angus. She couldn't be still. She didn't want to have to make conversation especially with well-meaning friends and relations – if they were. Always her thoughts came back to her parentage. She took a book to the secluded summerhouse Angus had shown her. In its shelter she was protected from the usual errant breeze that came off the hill and could relish the warmth of the sun. She tried to read but the words jumbled on the page. Scenes played themselves out in her mind as she struggled to find some clue to her status in the past behaviour of the people with whom she had spent her whole life. But it was no use. Everything had been just normal. She'd never thought of or looked for anything different – then. It all seemed so natural - as it had been. That *was* her life. And there'd been nothing wrong with it she thought angrily until Mother and Father had died. If only . . .. But you can't ever go back. She rubbed her eyes to discourage the gathering tears and went into the hotel to look for lunch.

The hall was cool and quiet. The only guests left beside themselves were four fishermen who spent every daylight hour on the loch or river. Claire hesitated then turned into the bar. She smiled at the barman, Hamish who was polishing glasses. 'Is it possible to have just a sandwich here?'

'Of course, Miss Frobisher. What would you like in it?'

She hesitated. Even that decision seemed too great a burden in her present mood. But if she said 'you choose' to the friendly barman he would think she was crazy. 'Have you got smoked salmon, perhaps? A round of that on brown and maybe just a plain tomato on white too? Plenty of pepper and salt.'

'No problem,' Hamish assured her. 'Would you like something to drink with it? A nice cool lager perhaps? We're surely having a real touch of Indian Summer this week.'

'That would be lovely. Thank you. I'll sit over by the window if you could bring it to me.' She settled herself beside one of the low tables and looked out at the view. It was just as Hamish had said, a glorious day with the sun glinting on the waters of the loch below and only one or two puffy white clouds hovering above the crest of Foinaven. She had had no idea. Here she was missing out on enjoying the best weather they'd had since their arrival. Perhaps Angus would have taken her back to Oldshoremore? Claire frowned. But perhaps not. What had happened there to make him look at her so strangely afterwards? Oh well, she had other things to think of now.

The afternoon passed slowly. Back at the summerhouse Claire watched the waters of the loch. From time to time a small boat would putter inland mostly on the far side from the hotel, but she could make out the colours of the boat and the number of occupants. Her thoughts wandered. Who were they and what business were they about? What a beautiful place this was to live and work. But probably in winter it could be cold and miserable with rain sweeping horizontally across the water and chill winds biting. What would it really be like to live here all year round? The heat made her sleepy and the buzzing of the busy bees seeking the last nectar of the year lulled her into a drowsy state of suspended animation.

At last it was time to go indoors and change for dinner. Although the simple sundress she wore would have been acceptable in the hotel dining room Claire was glad of Cynthia's old fashioned habit of 'dressing for dinner', even at home. It gave her something more to do to fill in the time until she could ring Beanie.

She stood under the shower and let the water stream down on her upturned face. How she wished it could wash all her troubles away, like Old Man River, the song she had loved as a child. She hummed the melody and remembered the deep chocolate smooth voice of the singer. Somehow it was soothing. At last regretfully she switched off the shower, stepped out and prepared to face what the evening might bring.

'I don't understand it.' Claire frowned at the receiver in her hand. 'What time is it?'

Fiona looked at her watch. 'My watch says ten to seven but I know it's a couple of minutes fast and you've been holding on for at least four already. Even after you redialled,' she said.

'I can't believe Beanie wouldn't have been hanging about waiting for my call so I thought I'd misdialled,' explained Claire. 'And I certainly got it right the second time. I was doubly careful. Why doesn't she answer? She must realise I'll get the truth out of her in the end. There's no point in putting it off.'

'You definitely said this evening?'

'Yes. At a quarter to seven.' Claire's eyes grew huge in her pale face as she said, 'You don't think she's gone do you? Remember I told you I'd said she must leave if she wouldn't tell me what happened when I was born? But she wouldn't go. Would she?'

Quickly Fiona soothed her. 'No, my dear. From what you say I'm sure she would never do such a thing. It seems to me you are her family, her child, her whole life. She would never desert you like that.' Fiona was glad Claire had asked her to wait with her while she phoned Beanie. It was supposed to have been for moral support when the news was told – whatever that might be - but this situation was even more upsetting. No news and no Beanie, it seemed. 'Why don't you leave it now and try again at quarter to eight? Come and have a coffee, maybe put a drop of brandy in it? Glaring at that receiver won't make it be answered any faster.'

Claire nodded and put the receiver down. 'I guess you're right. Okay. I'll try again in an hour. I just don't know where she can be?'

'Can you hear the telephone all over the house? Could she be up in a loft or somewhere maybe searching for old records, letters? You know the kind of thing.'

Claire's smile was brighter and relieved. 'Of course. That's what it'll be. Although we have telephone extensions all over the place at home, there are none in the attics or the old maids' bedrooms we mostly use for storage nowadays. Although I can't think why she couldn't have done her searching earlier,' she grumbled. 'She's had all day.' She allowed Fiona to lead her into the lounge where Cynthia and Ernest were already sipping liqueurs with their coffee. Apart from them the lounge was empty. The four fishermen had removed to the bar straight after dinner.

During the course of the evening Claire tried three times more to get in touch with Beanie. By quarter to ten she was quietly frantic, convinced she had driven away the one person in her life who truly loved her. Her companions had run out of reassuring ideas and the five of them sat round one of the larger occasional tables in the lounge. Seeing the comfort the presence of the Mackays, mother and son, brought to Claire, Cynthia and Ernest Butler had closed their lips on any protest at strangers knowing their business. It appeared to them the Mackays knew more about this possible family scandal than they did themselves.

When loud voices were heard in the hall a quick glance from Fiona sent Angus rising quietly to deal with the disturbance. He appeared to have everything under control as the noise died down.

Claire sat gazing at the curtained window in despair. What was she to do now? The older group looked helplessly at each other. They felt so useless. They gave Angus's return to the lounge scant attention until Fiona realised he wasn't alone. There was a stranger with him. As hostess she rose to greet the new arrival.

Angus stayed her with a gesture and a slight shake of the head. 'Claire,' he called softly, 'there's someone here to see you.'

Claire turned listlessly in answer to his summons then her mouth and eyes opened wide with shock. She hurtled out of her chair and threw herself into the arms of the woman who stood next to Angus. 'Beanie! Beanie! Where have you been? I was so worried. I thought you'd left me,' she cried and burst into tears.

'There, there, lovey,' said Beanie patting her on the back. 'Your old Beanie'd never leave you, silly girl. There, there. Come on now, dry your eyes and let's all calm down.' She produced a snowy white handkerchief from a large black leather handbag and offered it to Claire. 'Have a good blow, lovey, and you'll feel better.'

With a hiccough of laughter Claire took the hanky and did as she was bidden. 'That's what you always used to say when I was upset, Beanie.'

'And it usually worked. Now then, I've had a long journey and I'd appreciate a cup of good strong tea, if that's available.' She looked round the assembled company.

'Of course, Miss . . .' Fiona couldn't bring herself to address her new guest as Beanie.

Angus came to her rescue. 'This is Miss Benton, Mother. My mother, Mrs Mackay, Miss Benton. She will arrange a room for you. Perhaps you'd like something to eat with your tea? A sandwich or a bowl of broth?'

'No, thank you, young man. I had my dinner in Inverness but I would like my tea as soon as possible

'Right away, Miss Benton,' said Fiona and went to see to her arrangements.

'But how did you get here, Beanie?' said Claire. 'I don't understand.'

'I came by train of course. Train to Inverness, then Lairg and from there I had to take a taxi that this young man paid for. I didn't have enough cash on me.'

'Don't worry about that,' said Claire and Angus together.

'Angus'll put it on the bill,' explained Claire. 'But I still don't know why you're here. You knew I was going to phone you tonight. I've been out of my mind with worry, imagining all sorts of things; you fallen down somewhere, helpless and listening to the phone ringing and ringing, and then I thought . . .' her voice broke.

'Now then that's enough of that,' said Beanie. 'I'm here safe and sound if thirsty and tired. Ah! Here comes my tea.' She wouldn't say another word until she had finished her first cup and poured a second. She also ate a piece of the delicious shortbread Fiona had ordered to be put on the tray. Then she looked at Claire gravely. 'I thought long and hard after your call yesterday. Everything was fine as it was and no need for change. If your parents had lived life would have gone on as they intended. But now they're gone and you're asking questions. Questions I never thought to hear.' She shook her head and bit her lip. 'I would have taken the knowledge I have to my grave believing it hurt no-one but now perhaps I have to speak. First tell me why you suddenly want to know about all this?'

In detail Claire told her the whole tale of her suspected relationship to Lady Ross. 'And Minty

MacPhee knows something, we're sure, but she won't tell,' she finished.

Beanie nodded. 'Ah yes. Minty MacPhee. Extraordinary name. Not easy to forget. She was the one who brought you to us all those years ago.'

In spite of mulling over the possibility for the past few days the truth was still a shock to Claire. Her heart banged in her chest. 'So it's true?' she stammered, 'I'm not their daughter?'

Beanie reached for Claire's hand and patted it reassuringly. 'You are their daughter in every way that counts. Your mother, God bless her, didn't give you birth but you were in her arms from the time you were seven days old. She treasured you, lovey, and you must never forget that.' Beanie pursed her lips. 'It wasn't easy for her to show affection. Your grandfather – he died before you were born – was a cold man. He'd been in the Army and ran his household like a General on parade. Your grandmother took refuge in invalidism and left her children to their nannies and maids. So you see my Althea had never known what it was for a child to be loved so much by its parent they had to just squeeze it to death until it giggled, or to nuzzle into its soft sweet-smelling skin. She just didn't know,' she concluded sadly and watched the tears gather in Claire's eyes. 'But she did love you in her fashion.'

Claire nodded. 'Yes. I know she did. I never questioned our relationship until I saw real love shown.' She turned to look up at Angus. 'You are so lucky you know, having a mother like yours.'

He smiled and took Fiona's hand in his. 'Yes. I do know,' he said and gave the hand a gentle squeeze.

Fiona released herself and fished a tissue out of her pocket. She blew her nose in a businesslike manner and sniffed back the tears that had pricked her eyes when she heard her beloved son's words. 'Well now should we leave you to talk to Miss Benton, Claire? I'm sure you have a thousand questions for her.'

Cynthia Butler nodded her approval of this suggestion. After all it was a family affair.

But Claire would have none of it. 'No. Please, if you can spare the time would you and Angus stay and listen? You know as much as I do at the moment. And it's your story too – in a way. You knew Senga – my mother – and perhaps there'll be gaps you can fill in. Please stay. I really would like you to hear the truth.'

'Of course we will if you wish it.'

'I do. I really do.'

Cynthia disapproved wholeheartedly but against Claire's determination she could do nothing. She shrugged her shoulders and settled herself more comfortably. Now she would find out the answers to questions that had flitted through her mind so long ago. This should be very enlightening.

Beanie finished the last of the tea in her cup and moved the cushions on her chair to suit her. Then she paused. All eyes were fixed on her face. At last she sighed and began. 'It's quite difficult to know where to start. They always say start at the beginning but how do you know what *is* the beginning. One action brings about another.

'When your parents got married it was understood as a matter of course they would have children. It was what one *did,* sometimes to carry on the name of a proud old family; sometimes to inherit and carry on a business. It was never discussed but always expected. But time passed and your mother never conceived. Eventually there were visits to the doctor but all was well – with her. It seems the problem lay with your father who had had mumps when in his teens. It was thought he was one of the unfortunate few who had been rendered unable to father a child. It was a shocking blow and for a while your mother was in a terrible state, not only for herself but for him. As time had passed there had been gossip in the clubs.' Beanie shook her head. 'Men are such children. They wouldn't stop to think of the effect of sly jokes and innuendos on a man in your father's position.' She tutted and paused in her tale, her eyes seeing scenes from the past.

'So what happened?' prompted Claire.

'Eh? What? Oh.' Beanie blinked and dragged herself back to the present. 'They decided to go on a cruise and forget about the malicious whispers. I went along to 'maid' your mother. It was all very glamorous I suppose for them. But I was sick as a dog in the Bay of Biscay,' she remembered with a shudder.

Claire smiled. 'Poor Beanie. Then what happened when you got back to England?'

'We'd sailed from Liverpool so returned there. Your father'd left his car garaged near the docks. I thought we'd go home but instead we set out for the Lake District. Your mother told me they'd decided to buy a house and spend most of their time in future out of London. I wasn't even consulted,' she sniffed, 'but of course your mother knew I'd go anywhere she did.'

'Of course she did,' smiled Claire. She was sitting on the settee beside Beanie and took one of her hands. 'Lucky Mother.'

'She knew she would always have me,' agreed Beanie, 'but she didn't have a confidante. She had no close woman friend of her own class to share her troubles with. I suppose that's why she opened up to Mrs Freestone.'

At the new name her listeners exchanged puzzled looks. Who was this Mrs Freestone? And how did she come into the equation?

'She ran the guesthouse we stayed in,' explained Beanie. She saw Claire's raised eyebrows and smiled.

'Yes. It was a change from the usual luxury hotel but a very comfortable place indeed nonetheless. Mrs Freestone was a widow left alone without children in a large beautiful old house. I have no idea how your parents heard of The Grange but that's where we stayed. Gradually your mother and Mrs Freestone became friends. I suppose the question of children arose. It usually does when people are getting to know each other and those two had that in common. No children.'

'All this is very interesting no doubt,' interrupted Cynthia, 'but what does a Lakeland landlady have to do with Claire's birth?'

'I'm coming to that but you needed to know the background.'

Claire could see Beanie was tired. She was no longer young and had had a long, fatiguing journey. Claire glared at Cynthia and patted Beanie's hand. 'Of course we do, darling, you just tell it in your own way. Or would you rather leave it until the morning after you've had a rest?' The last thing she wanted was for Beanie to agree. If the truth didn't come out tonight she knew there would be no sleep for her.

'I've started, so I'll finish. Isn't that what that man on the telly says?' smiled Beanie. 'But I'll make it short. We can fill in the details later. Apparently Mrs Freestone's cousin also catered for guests but not in the same class as The Grange. She gave 'digs' in her Glasgow house to theatrical people and I suppose anyone who needed cheap lodgings. In spite of their different life-styles the two women were fond of each other and spoke at least once a week on the telephone. The cousin – I never did know her name – told Mrs Freestone about the young woman who had moved in to await the birth of her baby. No husband, no job and no way of keeping the child. Mrs Freestone told your mother and so a plot was hatched to bring the child down to the Lakes as soon as it was born. Your father registered the birth in Carlisle I believe.'

'Just like that?' Claire was stunned. 'No plans? No preparations? Were they mad?'

'And what about the authorities?' put in Cynthia. 'Did it never occur to them to regulate the situation? I would have thought if they were going to adopt they would want a son?'

'Couldn't do that m'dear,' said Ernest shaking his head. 'Had to be a girl. Must have seemed like Providence when a female child was available.'

'Why?' said Claire. 'Why couldn't it be a boy?'

'Wouldn't do, m'dear. Very upright man your father. Knew you'd get married and all that so didn't matter if you weren't of the blood. But couldn't have a b . . . b . . . love-child foisted on Society to carry on the Frobisher name. Wouldn't do at all.'

'Be quite, Ernest,' said Cynthia. 'Carry on, Beanie.'

'Thank you, madam,' said Beanie with a glare at Ernest. 'No-one asked questions and we came back to London three weeks later once we'd gathered all you need for a new-born, and your mother and I had worked out how to look after you, dear,' she laughed. 'And quite a comical time it was too. Talk about the blind leading the blind.'

'And it was Minty who brought the baby to the Lakes?' queried Fiona.

'Yes. I don't think the birth mother could bear to hand the child over to strangers. I suppose if her friend took the baby it would almost seem as if she were just looking after it for a while. Minty stayed for only two days. I think to reassure herself we were good people and to be able to tell Claire's mother what we were like.'

'But I don't think she did,' put in Fiona. 'I think when she got back to Glasgow, Senga had gone.'

'How sad,' said Beanie.

'How brave,' said Angus.

Claire frowned. 'Brave?'

'Don't you see? If she'd stayed and waited for Minty she would have had the opportunity to change her mind. Minty could have shown her where you were and she could have taken you back. But she knew she could never care for you properly and so she did the brave thing and disappeared.'

Fiona nodded. 'Yes. I think Angus is right. Poor little Senga.' She smiled at Claire. 'She would be so proud to see how you've turned out and so glad she gave you to your new mother. You've had all the advantages in life she couldn't give you. And now,' she continued getting up from her chair. 'I don't know about anyone else but it's my bedtime. Angus and I have work to do in the morning. If you would like me to show you to your room, Miss Benton, I'll take you up now?'

'I'll come with you,' declared Claire, 'and help you settle in.'

The party broke up and they went their separate ways but Claire wasn't the only person to lie awake through the long night digesting Beanie's story and wondering what it would mean in the future.

Sutherland 1570 – Winter

Morag snuggled deeper under the covers and listened to the wind moan and hoot around the house. She could fancy it a wild beast determined to batter down their shelter, pierce them to the heart and shred their bodies with its icy talons. Sternly she told herself she was a woman grown and mustn't let tales of boggarts and wind devils frighten her as though she were a bairn. But she thanked God for the strength of the stone walls that shielded them from the storm.

She thanked Him also for Dougal's happy idea of making a type of net to throw over the roof and weigh it down with stones as he had seen done along the coast where he stayed. It had been a pure pleasure to watch him work. Since he had completely recovered from his wound, he seemed to have grown taller, his shoulders broader. Sometimes Morag's hands itched to smooth the muscles over them and down his back She smiled and reminded herself she had got as much pleasure from watching the garrons pull the plough. But they hadn't made her hands twitch. Only Dougal did that. By the sweat of his body he had unearthed huge rocks and fastened them by ropes to the roof covering. Else she was sure the wind would have ripped the turfs away and left gaping holes to let in the weather.

From where she lay she could hear the cailleach snoring. Elspeth's leg was almost as good as new and she could get about now without the aid of the crutch Dougal had fashioned for her. But she left it to the young folk to go down to the river in search of fish, to set and clear traps for any hardy rabbit or hare that might venture abroad from its burrow, to herd the small family of piglets to find fodder now they were almost weaned and to measure out the precious food for the sheep kept secure in the cote at right angles to the house.

The heat rising from the pigs in the byre, built as always slightly lower than the rest of the dwelling, kept the large house room cosy even in the depths of the winter. The fire never went out and Dougal made sure each day there were enough peats brought in so Elspeth need not face the cold which she complained set her leg to aching.

How lucky they were, thought Morag, to have found Elspeth, or rather to have found her sow. In the darkness she smiled, remembering that day. Of the seven piglets born afterwards only three remained. Elspeth had traded the other four, as it seemed was her habit each time Vhairi farrowed. It was the farmer Hamish Mhor who had concluded the bargain with Elspeth.

There'd been dread in Morag as the huge shadow had fallen across the doorsill. Her heart near choked her, it beat so hard at the back of her throat. For an instance she believed it was Ruaridh Murray come to drag her home, but Elspeth had greeted the visitor with pleasure.

"Hamish Mhor, it does my heart good to see you, neighbour. Come away in and take some broth."

Morag shrank back into the shadows at the end of the room. Had she been near the door to the byre she could have slipped through and away before being seen. But he arrived as she sat at Elspeth's loom, weaving the fine wool the *cailleach* had spun from her sheep clipping.

"Morag, child, come and met my good friend Hamish Sutherland, son of my late mother's mother's sister's child. Since I have been widowed he has been as good to me as a brother. This is my young friend, Morag, Hamish, here for a visit with her brother Dougal. And glad I am they happened to be here just now." With this she launched into a long and detailed description of Vhairi's adventures, followed by her own misfortunes. If Hamish Mhor realised she was distracting him from enquiring further into her visitors' kin he gave no sign but listened, at first with enjoyment and then with concern, to the unfolding tale. By the time Dougal arrived with two rabbits for the pot Hamish was expressing his heartfelt thanks for the aid the visitors had rendered to his kinswoman.

"I would have come up sooner had I known you needed help," he assured Elspeth, "but I expected to see you in the kirk at Samhain – for All Saints prayers," he assured his new listeners.

Morag hid a smile. Was their visitor worried she might think he still kept the old pagan feast? With a pang she remembered that if Samhain was past then Ephie would be already married, and she had missed the wedding. Perhaps even now her friend carried a child under her heart? She shook off old regrets and returned her attention to the conversation.

"I'll keep the cattle until the spring for you and bring them up at Beltane. I have hides on my garron and sacks of oats. What else was it you asked me to get you?"

"Stop your teasing," scolded Elspeth, "you know fine it was a new peat iron I was needing."

"And you know fine I told you I would cut your peats in future so there was no call for you to get a new one."

"But you did."

"Aye. I'd not be wanting my ear skelped," he told the young folk with a grin. "The cailleach's gey fierce when the mood's on her."

"Get away with you now. Dougal will help you take the sacks to the barn." When the menfolk had gone out to unload the garron, Elspeth went to the wooden dresser Morag had so admired from the first day she arrived. It stood on carved legs with two drawers. One, Morag knew was for the porridge, but in the other Elspeth kept some treasured mementos of her marriage, a few precious sheets of paper and some quill pens with an ink block. Morag could read simple words, but Elspeth could write them and had promised to show Morag how it was done in the long dark winter days. On the top of the dresser, and the three shelves above it, stood beakers, bowls and platters. There was an earthenware jug and a leather covered bottle. Elspeth set out three beakers and a fine drinking horn rimmed with chased silver.

"It was my man's," she explained to Morag when she saw the admiration in the young woman's eyes. "I only offer it to very special people." As Hamish Mhor and Dougal came back into the house she poured four measures from the bottle and handed round the drinks. Hamish Mhor received the drinking horn with a nod.

"This'll keep the cold from my belly on my return journey," he said. "Slainte," he lifted the horn to toast the company and then drank deep. "Aye, Elspeth. That's food for the gods you have there."

Morag took a good drink from her beaker and nearly choked. She'd been expecting some of the heather wine Elspeth had the secret of making. But this was *uisge beatha* and it burned its way down her throat setting her insides glowing like the peats on the fire. She sat contented now to listen to Elspeth and Hamish Mhor exchanging news of people she had never heard of. When Dornoch was mentioned, Morag blinked awake from the pleasant doze into which she'd fallen. Hamish was recounting tales of his trip to the cattle fair at Muir of Ord.

"Aye," he sighed and shook his head. "We live in desperate times, Elspeth. Those who had withstood the siege of the cathedral for over a week at last negotiated hostages and came down."

"What does that mean?" demanded Morag.

"It's usual in warfare," put in Dougal, anxious to show in this he knew more than she. "The losing side give hostages to the winners as troth for their future good behaviour. Is that no right," he enquired of Hamish.

"Aye, that's the way of it. It is the rules of warfare you might say. In as much as there is any rule in it, the giving of hostages is well recognised as a means to stop the fighting."

"That's good then, isn't it?" said Morag happily.

Hamish shook his head. "With honourable men that's true. But the Earl is a hard and bitter man. He reneged on the promise of hostage taking and commanded his son, John, Master of Caithness, to behead them."

There was an audible drawing-in of breath as his listeners contemplated the treachery.

"But the Master would have none of it," continued Hamish, "nor the Mackays who had stood with him in the battle."

Morag cast a quick glance across the fire to where Dougal sat, his head strained forward not to miss one word of Hamish's recital. With all her strength she willed him to stay quiet, not demand further details and perhaps give away his own part in the story.

"So where are they now, these hostages," asked Elspeth. "Taken to Dunrobin no doubt?"

Hamish shook his head again. "Dead," he said, "all three. When not the Master, nor the Mackays, would do the deed, the Earl commanded Duffus. Now the Murrays had ravaged Duffus's land and he was hot to obey. He saw to the beheadings himself. But much good did it do him. Soon after he took sick and died. They say he was haunted to his grave by his foul deed. Be that as it may, the Murray fighting men are gone to join Earl Alexander and so the wheel will turn again until deaths can be avenged."

There was silence as they all gazed into the fire thinking on the events Hamish had related. Where was her father? wondered Morag. She was sure he had survived the battle and returned to the farm, but had he left it again? Surely the strath was far enough from Dornoch for him and her brothers to stay – if they had the sense to keep their heads down and no-one betrayed them as fighting men? She had little affection for any of them except her dear Robbie, but she wished them no ill. She dared not question Hamish further. Who knew where his loyalties lay?

Elspeth rose and poured each a second good dram from the bottle. "Away with gloomy thoughts," she said. "Here we have good company and can be thankful we are not gentry to be moithered by politics and power struggles. Slainte."

They returned the salute and then talk was of the coming winter, discussing the possibility of harsh frosts and deep snow.

She had been glad when Hamish Mhor left, thought Morag. He had brought a gust of harsh reality into the cosy world they had made, shaking them out of the gentle rhythm of life they had adopted, since arriving at the haven of Elspeth's hearth. She couldn't stop her thoughts revolving around the fate of her family back in the strath. Had her menfolk gone with the others to join Earl Alexander out of reach, at least for a while, of that other cruel earl who ruled so harshly? Had the women and children stayed behind, or the whole strath fled to safety? Had Duffus and his like ravaged the land left defenceless? If only she could find out. Dougal too was mad to know what had happened after the battle. Were his kin still around Dornoch or returned to Strathnaver? They talked in whispers away from the house wondering what to do and how to get more news.

"The only news we'll have will be from Hamish," said Morag. "He seems to be her only visitor."

"What about when she attends the kirk? There'll be news exchanged aplenty after the service."

"Aye, but we'll no be showing our faces there," she reminded him. "And we'll need to have a good excuse not to."

All their feverish whispering brought no good council. Everyday chores and small concerns took over their lives again and gradually their anxieties subsided. The weather grew colder. Dougal had made the roof cover. Elspeth had bidden Morag cut more heather and bracken to lay on her bed and Morag had been surprised and amused to see the cailleach's bed was made of woodies - ropes of heather - stretched over a wooden frame.

"It's gey comfortable for old bones, better than your mattress on the ground, but the draughts creep along the floor underneath when the wind's from the east and then I need plenty heather between them and me".

Morag smiled remembering the huge armfuls she had carried in until Elspeth was satisfied. Then there had been more to bring for her own bed and Dougal's. Now each had a fine thick layer of springy heather and bracken on which to lay their coverings.

When a peat fell in the fire a lick of flame gave light to caress the shining black of the soot-covered rafters. Here and there it glowed on the eyes of the roosting hens as they raised their heads to check on the disturbance. The quiet clucking of their complaints was a familiar and comforting sound. Just as Morag decided she really should crawl out from her warm nest to mend the fire, she saw Dougal's shadow on the wall as he arranged fresh peats to guard the warmth till morning. She snuggled down again.

It was so good to have a friend; one who pulled his weight and shared her adventures. Of course if it hadn't been for his wound, she wouldn't be here at all. Would she ever have left the farm? Over her father's dead body! And perhaps that might have come to pass if she'd stayed. But what then? Her brothers would have inherited the farm and she would simply become a drudge for their wives. When Dougal had said 'Come with me' it had opened up the possibility of a new life, a future free of constraint, but she had had no idea how it would end. She still didn't. Was she mad? And Dougal himself was changing. For no reason he seemed to take offence and then, when questioned, he would slam out of the house and not return for hours. She had caught him watching her. Was he regretting asking her to come with him? Did he think she would be a burden when they reached his kin?

He'd said his kin would welcome her; said she would find a good husband; said he would get them there. Just before their arrival at Elspeth's home Morag had begun to doubt that. She was pretty sure he had no idea where they were or how far it was to Strathnaver even, and his family stayed beyond there. But over the past weeks he seemed to have grown and matured. He thought things through more before hotly stating an ill-considered opinion. He'd taken on all the heavy work of the farm even asking how, when he was not sure. That in Morag's eyes was a definite sign of improvement and self-confidence. He was no longer the irresponsible loon with whom she had escaped from Dornoch's battleground, but an assured and capable man. One in whom she would now more easily put her trust when they moved on. If they moved on together? Morag knew fine Elspeth would love to have the younger woman bide with her, would like to have them both stay, but Dougal was mad to get back to his kin, and for Morag, the cailleach's home was too close to Dornoch and the strath.

Hogmanay came and went. They feasted and drank, both Elspeth's wine and more *uisge beatha* until they fell asleep on their beds without even loosening their clothing. They told tales and sang songs. Elspeth still had a sweet strong voice and Morag felt tears in her eyes as the cailleach sang of long ago loves and heroes lost in battle. She seemed to remember Dougal had even danced for them at one point, or was that the *uisge beatha* playing tricks with her memory?

From the turn of the year they looked for better weather, a lengthening of the days. But January passed in ice and snow. The days were short. The nights were long and cold. Tempers frayed. Dougal was irritable and Morag had a yearning she couldn't put down simply to hunger. Was she homesick for her own kind? No-one ventured out except for the most urgent and pressing of reasons, mostly to tend the sheep in the cote.
"You need a door to the cote from here," grumbled Dougal as he shook snow from his plaid.
"Aye," agreed Elspeth, "that would be fine and handy. But the cote is round the corner and higher. Maybe we'd lose our heat from the byre?"
"There's more from the midden there this day," laughed Dougal. And it was true that since they had all partaken of some dried berries plumped out with water and stewed, they'd paid numerous visits to the byre to shit. Dougal had fashioned some wooden plattens to keep their feet out of the muck when they needed to go in, and for daily wear Morag had sewn some of her precious rabbit skins into shoes for all their feet. The fur kept them warm, but the skins were not hard-

wearing so they only put them on in the house when the outside chores were complete and they could sit and blether. That was when Elspeth began to teach Morag how to write. They drew the bench up to the table and worked by the light of the oil in a cruisie lamp or the flame of a precious fir-candle. Morag made the shapes as small as she could to save the precious paper, but her hand was clumsy and she hesitated to practise, knowing how hard it would be for the cailleach to come by more.

One day Dougal came back from his chores, stamped the snow off his feet at the door and handed two stones to Morag. "Here, try this," he said. "I found it down by the burn. I've seen bairns at court taught with just such a piece, but better fashioned and held in a wooden frame."

Morag turned the stones over in her hands. One was large and flat with a fairly smooth surface. The other was rounded at one end and sharper at the other. She shrugged and looked at Dougal. "What do you want me to do with them?"

"Practice your letters," he said with a grin. He showed her how with the smaller stone she could make marks on the big flatter one and how these could be rubbed off with the corner of her plaid.

Morag's face lit up. "Thank you, thank you, Dougal. See, Elspeth, what Dougal has brought me. Now I can practice all day and not waste your precious paper with my terrible shapes."

Elspeth nodded. "They're getting better. You study well," she smiled, "but yon's a gey handy idea. Bless the boy."

So with songs and stories, study and chores, the days and weeks passed in warmth and good company. Dougal and Morag did their best to hide their feelings when the black dog rode their shoulders. They wouldn't allow their discomfort to upset their hostess.

The weather was harsh, and prudent Elspeth eked out their supplies. Days passed when, if they were bound to the house by storms, they ate only a bowl of thin porridge with a handful of soaked berries. At last these were finished and the porridge became more like gruel each day. Elspeth fretted for her beasts' welfare and prayed for the winter to pass.

Morag lay still, her ears pricked. What was that sound? There it was again. Oh, no! It was a drip, slow but regular, somewhere close by water was dripping. Inwardly she groaned. Surely they had come so far through the harsh weather without any major disaster, except the shortage of food. But that was usual in the dark months before Spring arrived. The gnawing ache of hunger in the belly was a fact of life. Now it seemed their luck had run out. Should she get up and try to deal with it herself or wake Dougal?

"Morag," came a whisper through the gloom. "Morag, can you hear that? Isn't it wonderful?"

Wonderful, thought Morag. Has the boy lost his wits? "Wonderful?" she whispered back. "What's so wonderful about a leak?"

Dougal laughed softly. "Wheesht, lassie. Can ye no' tell the difference atween a leak and a thaw?"

"Thaw?" Morag sat up, her face alight with joy. "Really, Dougal? Are you sure?"

"Let's go see," he answered. "Don't wake the cailleach. She needs her rest."

"Aye, she may," came Elspeth's voice, "but small chance she has of it with you two roaring like stags in the rut."

Morag giggled as she wriggled out from under her covers, tightened her waist and pulled her plaid over her shoulders. Dougal was already by the fire, placing more peats to heat the room before Elspeth got up from her bed. Together they went to the door and gazed out.

Where yesterday there had been deep snow, sculpted by the wind into drifts and shapes from wildest imaginings, now the whole landscape was rounded as the thaw smoothed points and edges in every direction. Morag fetched a bucket and put it beneath the eaves where the melting snow could fall and fill it - one chore less. The snow was still too deep to reach the burn in comfort, even if it had begun to run again, and snow took so long to melt and heat it was pure joy to stand and watch the bucket fill with clear water.

In the east the sky was already lighter promising a bright day ahead. Morag set the door wide and let the fresh air into the house. It reached Vhairi in the byre. She raised her head and grunted, demanding freedom. The piglets caught the excitement and squealed in chorus with her.

"No yet, mo gradh," called Elspeth. "You'd get a chill out there after the warmth of your cosy byre. Wait until the snow is gone."

"That won't take long at this rate," said Dougal, as he unearthed peats from the pile at the door. "And not before time. These lower ones are fine and dry. I'll shake the snow from the top of the pile. We don't want it melting into the peats even if I've thatched them with heather."

Dougal's prediction proved right. The thaw continued all that day, through the night and the following day. A weak sun shone from ten in the morning until four in the afternoon when the darkness fell and the temperature dropped like a stone, but never to the point of freezing so hard again. Dougal and Morag exulted that Winter was over and Spring had come.

Elspeth, more cautious, waited to rejoice until all danger of frost was past. But at last, when all the snow was gone and the heather and grassland were pushing tender shoots, Morag and Dougal returned one day from herding the pigs and sheep to feed on the new bounty, to find delicious smells emanating from the house. Elspeth had killed one of her hens, declaring 'the useless craitur was never a good layer' and had prepared to welcome the new season. She baked the bird in clay in the middle of the peats, then pulled spare flesh off it to make a thick cock a' leekie with barley she had hidden against that day or severe starvation. Morag was able to contribute the first leaves of new wild garlic she had picked as they made their way home.

It was a feast fit for a king. The only jarring note came when Dougal declared he would not eat better at his own father's hearth. This brought a silence and realisation for all three they couldn't continue along the path they had trodden during the winter. With fair weather would come ease of travel and visitors. Perhaps some of the welcome ones would ask questions of Elspeth's guests. Perhaps others would be less welcome.

Morag shivered. Elspeth's heart grew heavy. Dougal looked from one to another to see what ailed them before he recalled his words and wondered when he would once again feast with his kin?

Elspeth shook off her sadness and covered the moment by producing the precious *uisque'a bha*. They drank to each other, to their deliverance from starvation, to the arrival of Spring and to good fortune in the future.

But the words had been spoken, reminding them all of change to come. As the days grew longer and warmer Morag and Dougal worked with a will to do the work of the farm in repayment to their hostess for her hospitality. Morag tended the lazybeds, sowed the grain and saw to the beasts. Dougal cleared the byre, using the midden there to feed the land. Once again humans as well as beasts had the whole countryside to use for their toilet. He hunted for the pot and for meat Elspeth could smoke, hanging from the rafters, to see her bare larder replenished before they left her. Morag felt a restlessness she could not control and as the days lengthened Dougal's ill-humour returned. Again Morag found his eyes upon her and wondered if he regretted the invitation to his home. Elspeth Sutherland watched Dougal watching Morag and smiled.

Away from the house Morag and Dougal discussed their journey.

"I'm sure it's not so far from here that I'll find Mackays," said Dougal as they wandered along the river seeking trout in the shadows of the banks.

Sometimes they managed to get back to the happy comradeship they had enjoyed before the winter set in. Then they could laugh together and Morag teased Dougal as she was used to tease wee Rabbie back in the strath.

But Dougal was no wee boy and once took his revenge with a swiftness that caught her unawares. Firmly he gripped her arms and demanded she retract the latest insult. When she laughed up into his eyes he forgot their game and put up his hand to brush away a strand of her hair that had blown across his face. As he loosed it, the end curled around his finger. He was mesmerised as he wound it tighter and tugged it to him.

Morag laughed again. "Peace," she cried, "I surrender. I am your prisoner."

For a long moment he held her gaze. She was so bonnie, so trusting. With a final gentle tug he let go her hair. The moment passed.

Later, as he went about his share of the work the memory of that moment often came into his mind. The thought of Morag truly helpless brought thoughts to his mind he quickly pushed away. He gripped the wood axe in his hand with all his strength and vowed he would protect her to his last drop of blood.

The thought of their arrival at his father's house should have filled him with joy, had indeed pleased him – until now. But the reality would be Morag spending her days with the womenfolk. He would rarely see her and the idea of her marriage to one of his cousins was not to be borne. The axe came down with such force the log beneath flew apart with that one blow.

Dougal's thoughts troubled him through the following weeks. Like that wee curl around his finger, Morag had wound herself around his heart. But what could he do? She had no idea of him and he could never face showing his feelings to her for them to be rejected or, worse still, laughed at. He would keep his council and simply watch over her.

When Morag broached the subject of their leaving again, he forced himself to appear eager.

"We'll not leave the cailleach until she is sure of good crops and her beasts have regained their weight," Morag declared.

"Aye, indeed, for she's been good to us. But we must start to make plans."

"Is it missing your Mammy your are, wee man?" teased Morag.

Dougal grinned. "Take care, lassie, else I'll put you over my knee and skelp your arse for showing no respect."

"Respect!" Morag hooted with mirth. "And what respect would a feckless loon be wanting?" She took to her heels and ran as Dougal lunged at her to carry out his threat. He chased her round trees and bushes, not quite able to catch her, so fleet of foot she was. She glanced over her shoulder to mock him anew and tripped on a tree root.

"Ha!" he cried in triumph and bent to seize her.

She wriggled so fiercely he overbalanced and the two rolled together down a slight incline. They came to rest against the trunk of a small tree whose wind-pruned branches drooped to make a natural bower. Short-winded through laughter and exertion they lay in each others arms their breath intermingling as their heartbeats slowed. Morag smiled up into Dougal's eyes and watched his expression change as he looked down at her flushed face. Her eyes widened. Never had Dougal looked at her like this before. His was the face of a stranger, yet as kent to her as her own. Her lips parted in anticipation as he lowered his head and a fierce rush of gladness swept over her. Hidden under the leaves of the friendly sheltering tree, Morag found her true place in Dougal's strong arms. Gone was the ache of longing, gone the restless spirit that had plagued her through the dark days. In a passion of joy and certainty Morag gave herself to the man who would be her mate for life.

Of course they couldn't hide it. Elspeth Sutherland saw the bright eyes, the flush that rose so easily to Morag's cheek when, perhaps by chance, she touched Dougal's hand. Even the young man's voice had changed when he spoke to the lass he loved. It was deeper and warmer than before. Nowadays it seemed necessary for two to do the tasks it had only needed one before the winter came. Morag and Dougal spent long hours together away from the croft, always bringing home the beasts safely, or meat or fish for the pot. Morag usually had a bunch of herbs in her hands, but the flushed faces and conscious glances betrayed them. Elspeth hid a smile and kept her own council. She wondered how long it would be before they confessed the truth.

One evening Elspeth and Morag sat on stools at the door of the crofthouse. They were knitting with the last of the previous year's wool from Elspeth's sheep. It had been a fine hot day and the evening retained a pleasant warmth. Dougal lay on the ground at Morag's feet. He sucked at a grass stem between his teeth. His *sgean-dhu* lay beside him with the piece of wood he had been whittling. He laid a hand on Morag's ankle to attract her attention and jerked his head towards Elspeth. His eyebrows rose in silent interrogation.

Morag bit her lip. She valued Elspeth's good opinion and regretted the lies they had told, but they had to confess. She nodded.

"Elspeth, *mo gradh*," began Dougal. Morag smiled and Elspeth turned her wise old eyes on the handsome lad at her feet.

"Neither a lender nor a borrower be," quoted Elspeth. "If you think to cajole me with those soft words, laddie, think again. My pockets are to let and my barn is empty. But if you have need of the wisdom of my years, I'll give it you in plenty." She smiled.

Dougal laughed. "Aye, that you do have in plenty and grateful we are for it. But we have a confession to make."

Elspeth composed her face into a grave mien. "Alas, alas the day. What wickedness have you committed? Do I need to hide you from the sheriff? Or perhaps as a God-fearing, honest woman, should I give you up to him?"

Morag smiled, knowing full well the cailleach teased Dougal, but her heart was heavy at the deception they had played on their kind hostess. "I don't think we have committed any crime," she put in, "except perhaps against you?"

Elspeth showed astonishment, determined to wring the last drop of entertainment from the situation. They owed her that for their lies. "You too, lassie?" she cried. "Never did I think I had two desperate fugitives under my roof." She saw the colour drain from Morag's face and was instantly sorry. "There, there, lassie. I'm only jesting. I know fine neither of you would harm a hair of my head, nor break the law – without good intention," she added for in these troubled times, laws were passed and changed so quickly at the whim of the hated Earl, it was hard to keep up with what one could and could not do with impunity.

Tears stood in Morag's eyes. "We are fugitives," she said, "at least, I am, though not from the law."

Elspeth held her peace. Now the tale had begun she would wait until the end before she passed judgement.

Morag told with ease the story of how she and Dougal had met, their mad flight from the strath and onward north leaving the burning Dornoch behind them. She told of Dougal's wound and how it had become infected again, their meeting with the woman and child and her own fear of her father. She told of their meeting with Vhairi and then her voice faltered. She raised her eyes to Elspeth's face. "We lied," she said. "We're not brother and sister. We're not even kin. I am a Murray and Dougal really is a Mackay. But I was so afraid. Dougal lied for my sake," she assured Elspeth. "He said it to protect me. And I'm sorry, for you have been so good to us. I'm truly sorry to deceive you." She lowered her head and wept.

"Dry your tears, child," said Elspeth, "for I wasna' deceived, not for a moment." The two young people gaped at her. The tears dried on Morag's cheeks. Dougal's mouth was open in disbelief. "It would take more than two parents to produce so unalike bairns," Elspeth went on, "and the story of Mackay kin at Beauly? I think not. I lied too. My man came not from Forres but by Aultvaich. I know Beauly well and folks from miles around. Your story didn't ring quite true so I also trimmed my truth to suit the occasion. But it seemed you meant me no harm so I welcomed you to my home. You were keen to know the news of the battle at Dornoch when Hamish Mhor was here and that went with my belief you came on me from the East, from Dornoch direction, far though it is."

Morag nodded and smiled in relief. "I'm glad you didn't believe us," she said, "because there's something else that's happened now." She smiled down at Dougal, then laughed and shook her head. "This great loon here has stolen my heart. I don't know how it happened. I didn't see it coming, but the boy I tended in his pain became a man through the dark months and now we're handfast."

The old woman snorted. "Tell me something I don't know," she cackled. "Have I no eyes in my head? The pair of you nudging and winking and smiling and I'm supposed to be so foolish I can't read the signs. You young ones! You think you are the inventors of love, the only ones who know just how it is. I've been there, my dearie, and my memories are still green. I'm happy for you, child," she patted Morag's knee, "for both of you," she went on, "for he's not a bad loon. I'm sure you'll take him in hand," she grinned. "And now I suppose you'll leave me," she said to Dougal, "and take this lassie home to be your bride."

Dougal opened his mouth to agree, then stopped. His mother would welcome the girl who had saved her son's life, but would she welcome her as that son's bride? Without vanity he knew he was his mother's favourite. Surely he could talk her round? But he could hear the arguments now. A Murray! And penniless! No kin at her back, an outcast. It was not what his parents had intended for the son who had spent time at Court, been educated first at his mother's knee and then by the monks at Baile na Cille.

Morag watched the changing expressions flit across his face and read his thoughts as easily as if he had spoken them. Her heart sank. If Dougal abandoned her what could she do? Elspeth would take her in and be grateful for the help and company. But would she be safe here so near to Dornoch folk who might take news of her to her father in the strath?

Dougal sat up. "Marriage with Morag would not be what my folks would look for for me," he admitted.

"So we must not return to my home until a year has past. Then it is done and they must accept it. When the year is gone we shall be secure. No man can part us and any child we might have will have legal rights and status with my kin."

Morag's heart leapt, her eyes glowed. Dougal truly loved her.

Elspeth nodded. "Aye, that's the way it is. But where will you bide meantime? I get many visitors travelling between Laorig and beyond to Skelbo and Dornoch. There are ceilidhs for weddings and wakes for funerals when all the population gather. News is exchanged at the kirk and carried far and wide. It will not do to stay here, sad though I will be at your going."

"We'll go farther north and hide in the hills," cried Dougal.

"And next winter?" demanded Elspeth. "What then?"

Morag's hands twisted in her lap, the knitting fallen forgotten at her feet. "There must be somewhere we'd be safe," she cried.

Elspeth looked down the hillside towards the river and followed it in her mind's eye to the long strath leading north and beyond. She smiled. "Aye," she said, "I believe there is."

Mackay's Hotel 2010

At the breakfast table next morning Claire was quiet. Her companions realising the enormity of what she had discovered the previous evening left her to her thoughts and chatted about the weather, the fishing and Beanie's experience of British Rail.

For form's sake Claire nibbled a piece of toast, ate half a boiled egg and then excused herself from the table. She gave Angus a small smile as she left the dining room and went in search of Fiona. Having received permission to use the office telephone once again she made one call. Five minutes later she set off walking down the hotel drive to the main road. She was gone all morning.

'Angus, have you seen Claire?' queried Cynthia Butler as she made her way to the dining room for lunch.

'No, Mrs Butler. Not since breakfast,' he replied.

'I can't think where she can be. It's really very inconsiderate. I wanted to talk things over with her. She really needs some adult guidance at this time - a mature perspective of everything that's happened. She must be quite bewildered, poor child.' At this she realised she was almost confiding in someone who, although not quite a servant as such, was not the kind of person with whom one discussed private family business. She raised her chin and sailed into the dining room with Ernest following behind like a humble rowing boat towed by a stately galleon.

Angus controlled the twitching of his lips. He knew exactly Mrs Butler's dilemma. She would love to keep him at arm's length from her family but owing to the friendship between himself and Claire that was impossible. Add to that the fact he knew as much as she of the new turn of events, and the poor lady found herself in an intolerable position.

But where was Claire? He hoped she wasn't so upset about her new status that she was off somewhere licking her wounds. On that thought he hurried to the summerhouse, a place he had often used himself when sore at heart. It was empty. Angus frowned as he went back to the house. While he hesitated at the front door a car came up the drive. When it stopped Claire jumped out and thanked the driver who touched his forehead with one finger, turned the car in the gravel sweep and drove off.

'Where have you been?' demanded Angus. 'No. Don't answer. First I have no right to question your movements and second I know where you've been.'

Claire smiled. 'Yes. I suppose you recognise Lady Ross's car. She insisted on Tom driving me back.'

'How did you get there?'

'I walked.'

Angus's eyebrows rose. 'That's a good step, even for someone used to walking.'

Claire grinned. 'Yes, it is a bit of a long way, isn't it? But it gave me plenty of time to think what I was going to say when I arrived. I'd already phoned to let her know I was coming and I'd been thinking all night but the nearer it got the harder I found it.'

'I get what you mean. How did it go?'

Claire's face glowed. 'It was wonderful. You can have no idea. I never had a grandmother – well of course I didn't – but apart from Beanie there was never any other older woman in my life. Lady Ross - she says I should call her Aunt – she told me lots about my father, and she said Eilidh Morrison knew my mother well and will be able to tell me about her.' She gulped as her eyes filled with tears. 'She was a year younger than me when I was born. Poor Senga, my poor little mother. She must have felt so alone. I do wonder what happened to her. Do you think she was alright? Do you think she's still alive?'

Angus put his arm around her shoulders and gave her a comforting squeeze. 'I should think she is. Although she was young she was independent. And she was bright so I'm sure she would have got on alright once she'd been able to think about herself and not her lost baby. Lady Ross's detective traced her to a ship going to Canada. There was no mention of a child so no further enquiries were made. Now I imagine you should be able to find her if you really want to. There's the internet as well. I think there are all sorts of sites on it for getting in touch with people.'

Claire smiled. 'Yes, that's true. Angus, I don't know whether I'm coming or going. Everything's happening so fast. My life is all upside down and I have so much to sort out. I'm not really sure who I am.'

He turned her round to face him and with his hands on her shoulders he looked into her eyes. 'You are yourself, Claire. You are the sum of all your experiences, all your hopes, fears, and dreams. You are loved, respected and treasured for yourself, not for who your parents were or were not. Whatever you decide to do with your life do it for yourself, not to please others or because you feel some duty has been laid on you. You owe nothing to anyone. Be happy.' He pulled her gently into his arms and held her. He could smell the fresh scent of her hair. She felt so good close to him, so right. As they stood for a moment Angus realised, in spite of all his good intentions he had fallen in love with Claire Frobisher. He placed the lightest of kisses somewhere above her right ear and gently put her from him. 'You'd better go and face the music,' he smiled. 'Aunty Cyn was looking for you.'

Claire smiled at him. 'Thank you, Angus.' She raised her hand to his cheek and kissed him on the opposite one. 'Thank you for everything.'

Angus stepped back. 'Go on. Scoot,' he said, and watched as she ran laughing through the front door.

'You did what?' demanded Lady Ross. 'You just let her go?'

Angus shrugged. 'How could I stop her?'

Her arthritic hand gripped the knob of her cane with all her remaining strength. She filled her lungs. Angus looked her in the eye and braced himself for the tidal wave of her wrath to break over his head.

But Annabelle Ross saw the pain in his eyes and held her tongue. She wasn't the only person to regret the departure of the young woman who had come into their lives in such a dramatic fashion.

'When did she leave?'

'This morning. They packed up the car and drove down to Inverness to catch the London train this evening.' Angus looked at his watch. 'They'll take the sleeper and by this time tomorrow their time in the Highlands will seem like a dream or one of the romantic stories in magazines.'

Lady Ross's lips twitched. What did young Angus know of romantic magazines? 'Did she say when she was coming back?'

Angus's laugh was bitter. 'Do you really think she'll want to? Look what's happened to her here. She has been insulted by a crazy old woman; told she's not who she thinks she is; had her whole world turned upside down; and probably felt the earth move under her feet. She doesn't know who she is supposed to be anymore. No wonder she wants to run and lick her wounds, go back to her old familiar world and forget this ever happened.'

Lady Ross frowned at him. 'Do you really think that's what she is doing?'

'Best for her if she does,' muttered Angus in a voice so low he didn't intend it to be heard,

But the old lady's hearing could be sharp on occasion, usually when those around her wished it wasn't. 'And what is that supposed to mean?' she demanded. 'You wish to rob me of my niece, my only close kin?'

'No. Of course not. I didn't mean . . . I wasn't thinking of . . .' Angus strode over to the window and gazed out with eyes that looked back to the time he had first brought Claire here. She had stood just there on the gravel before the front door. She had laughed up at him with mischief in her eyes when she crowed over her new position as a distinguished guest, all the time averring she would be happy to enter by the kitchen as usual. He smiled at the happy memory, then sighed. That's all it was, all it could ever be. If Claire never returned to Mackay's and the Big House would it make life easier for him? It had to. She had taken his heart away with her and he must learn to live with that. But better leave him an empty shell for the rest of his days than have her come back and perhaps fall in love with him. He wasn't being vain when he thought there had been something developing between them. They had both felt it when saying goodbye. But he had to protect her from herself so he *would* wish her gone for good.

'Penny for them,' said Lady Ross.

Angus turned to her and tried to hide the misery in his eyes. 'I'm sorry. I wasn't looking at things from your point of view.'

'Whose then? Ah! Your own.' She smiled. 'Has my delightful niece made conquest of the inscrutable Angus? I wish it were so. I should be delighted to welcome you into the family on a legal footing as I always consider you a surrogate son anyway.'

Angus was touched and surprised. It was unusual for her ladyship to be so sentimental or openly affectionate. Was this Claire's doing? 'I thank you for that and I assure you your own kin could not have your welfare more at heart than I. But you mustn't make daydreams about Claire and me. If she does return then I shall leave Mackay's.'

'You can't Angus! Think of your mother.'

He bit his lip. 'Now you see what a fix I'm in. How could I possibly choose between the two women I love? Break Mother's heart – again – or put Claire in danger? Some choice!'

'But why?' She looked at Angus with growing compassion. 'It wasn't your fault, Angus. There was nothing you could do. You weren't even there.'

'Perhaps I should have been.'

'No. You had your duties. Ishbel knew that. She was always wilful.'

A spasm of pain crossed Angus's face. 'Aye. Wilful and daring - a true free spirit. It was a great part of her charm.' Lady Ross's expression was sardonic. 'If you say so. Perhaps to a besotted young man. But from the day she realised the difference between boys and girls I wanted to put her over my knee and spank her every time we met.'

A reluctant laugh escaped Angus's lips. 'Why?'

'She was selfish to the core, totally self-centred – which is something different – and manipulative. The day you announced your engagement my heart sank. I was so concerned for you. You deserved better, Angus. And it's about time someone told you so,' she added as she saw his jaw tighten and the storm signals in his eyes. 'I'm old enough to speak my mind. Perhaps I should have done it years ago and stopped you leaving, but your grief was too raw. I hope time has eased your pain, boyan, and your eyes can see clearly.'

Angus thought for a moment before replying. So much she said was true and time had healed so many hurts. Time and Luzia. If it had only been Ishbel then maybe . . . but then there was Luzia. They say things go in threes and he couldn't bear to put Claire in danger.

But Lady Ross didn't know the full story and he couldn't tell her now. 'She came to see you?' he said.

Annabelle Ross rightly understood they were once more talking about Claire. 'She did.'

'And did she say she would come back?'

'She didn't say she was going away. We talked of her father and mother, of her life in England and her home there. She seems to lead a very comfortable, if empty, existence.'

'Empty?'

'There's no purpose to her. Her mother - as she thought - intended her to marry well. That meant money. No harm in wanting your child to be comfortable. However if it was just to enable her to continue with the social round pursued by their set she did the child no favours. Her life is aimless. I think Claire has just realised that and it's largely down to Fiona.'

'Mother?'

'Yes. She admires your mother tremendously. Called her gracious, charming, warm-hearted and so clever.'

'Mum would be blushing.'

'It is no more than the truth. She is a gracious hostess and remarkable business-woman. In spite of losing both you and your father she kept your family home and business running and flourishing. And she did it in the midst of her grief and all alone.'

Angus winced. 'I came back as soon as I could after I heard about Dada.'

'I know and you were a great comfort to her. She has accepted the loss of your father but she still misses her son.'

Angus frowned. 'What do you mean? I'm here. I work with her. I do all I can to take the weight off her shoulders. I see her every day. We live under the same roof.'

'Your mother and I are good friends, Angus. I value her. A mother's heart takes a child's pain. Think about it. That is all I'm going to say. Now go about your business.'

When Angus had left the room she sat as the daylight faded, thinking over old times. What actions could she or should she take to shape the future as she wanted it to be? Was it so presumptuous to want the best for the people she loved?

Over the following weeks and months Angus watched his mother. He could see nothing wrong. Her health was good, her smile seemed ever present and she was quick to laugh when amused. The hotel bookings were steadily good and she had no financial worries. Surely Lady Ross must be mistaken?

There was no sign of Claire making a return to the Highlands. Fiona received a very warm letter of thanks for all her kindness. In it Claire asked to be remembered to Angus and the rest of the staff. He was hurt at her seeming lack of friendship but cursed himself for bringing that about. He had been her shoulder to cry on. Perhaps he had read too much in her reliance on him? He may have fallen in love but there was no reason Claire should reciprocate. He should wish she hadn't - be glad of it even. If love is great enough it should be unselfish. And he'd tried. God knew he'd tried not to fall for her. He must put her out of his mind and her silence should make it easier.

If only he hadn't given in to temptation. They say you never miss what you haven't had. They may be right but he had kissed her and the memory of what might have been would always be with him. What a fool he was. But how could he not have done it?

She had asked him to walk with her to the summerhouse after dinner and stood facing him.

'I want to say goodbye now, Angus, while we're on our own. Tomorrow there'll be Aunty Cyn and Uncle Ernest and your mother and everyone. It'll be different. It'll be hard.' In her flat-heeled sandals she had to tip her head to look up into his eyes. She had studied his face so long and so seriously he was sure she would never forget him.

Her face was already imprinted on his heart and mind; the one dimple that only showed when she smiled; the glints of auburn now in her natural brown hair; the way her delicate eyebrows winged up above those candid hazel eyes. He had felt the tug of attraction between them and done his best to hold back, to keep himself aloof from her warmth and charm. As well try to turn the tide. She took one step towards him and he was lost. Helplessly he had given in to the yearning of his heart. Gently he took her face between his hands and slowly bent his head to touch her lips. She had had plenty of time to pull back, to say no, but she did none of that. Her arms had slipped round his waist as she moved closer offering her lips to receive his kiss with a sweet gladness. That had driven the last sensible thought from his head. He had folded her in his arms and deepened the kiss tasting her as a thirsty man tastes sweet water. When the kiss ended he had held her with such tender love, her head resting on his shoulder where he could smell the scent of her hair. '*Mo gradh, mo gradh,*' he had murmured.

Cynthia Butler's voice had broken the spell that held them together. 'Claire! Claire! Where are you?' She had rounded the corner of the hotel and found Claire standing talking to Angus. 'There you are! I've been looking all over for you. Beanie wants to know which case you want your night things in. You'd better come and placate her. She's getting into a tizz with all this coming and going. Once we're home she can settle down again. Good evening Angus.'

'Good evening, Mrs Butler.' He had escorted them back to the hotel and that was the last time he had spoken to Claire. The following morning all had been hustle and bustle to make sure nothing was left behind. Angus had kept his face impassive as he wished them a safe journey.

'Do come again,' smiled Fiona Mackay. 'It has been such a pleasure to have your company.' She had winked at Claire as Cynthia Butler acknowledged the compliment with a gracious nod of her head.

Together mother and son had waved as the big saloon purred down the drive away from Mackay's hotel.

Fiona Mackay decided to keep the hotel open right through the winter. She knew there would be some quiet weeks but that was all to the good. She had work in plenty to keep her busy. There was the stock-taking to be done; next year's advertising to sort out; new menus to be planned with chef; as well as half the bedrooms to be re-decorated and brought up to her high standards. The other half had been done last year. Successive years had brought less and less snow to block roads for travellers to the North and bookings were well up for shooting and fishing parties. The hotel would be full for Christmas and the New Year. She was determined to keep her son so busy he wouldn't have time to miss Claire. Her plan was successful during the day.

Only Angus knew how many hours he spent staring from the window of his room or gazing sightlessly at the pages of a book through the long nights. He was surprised but not overly curious when Lady Ross declared she would be away for Christmas. 'She must at last be feeling her age,' he declared to his mother with a grin, 'says she's off south to warmer climes. Though I can't quite see her on a Pacific island complete with grass skirt.'

Fiona laughed. 'Wheesht! Angus. Behave yourself,' she said and kept her own counsel.

At the Hogmanay revels to welcome in the New Year Angus was the perfect host. The doors of Mackay's were opened wide as usual. At some time in the twenty-four hours everyone from miles around came to visit. Some stayed but half an hour to give greetings. Some joined the guests to dine and dance. Angus took every woman onto the floor. No-one watching him could doubt he was having a fine time of it - except Fiona. Her heart was heavy. Her son's ready smile never quite reached his eyes. When the last guest had departed or climbed the stair to bed it was almost dawn. Fiona had long since let her staff off duty to join the celebrations if they wished or go to *ceilidh* with their own folk. Together she and Angus cleared away the debris and laid up the tables to make all ready for the brunch that would be the first meal served on New Year's Day. When all was finished Angus kissed his mother and bade her sleep well. Fiona pretended not to notice him take a full bottle of whisky off the sideboard as he went past it on his way up to bed. She bit her lip and prayed the new year would bring peace to his heart.

But Angus couldn't rest. He took the bottle out into the garden, down to the wee summerhouse where he had sat with Claire while she confided in him. He gazed down at the loc, then up to the hills where the pre-dawn light began to creep over the landscape colouring everything in shades of grey. As the level in the bottle went down Angus at last relaxed. A soft peach blush tinged the sky and it seemed to him he was here and yet not here. Once again the houses round the loch had disappeared. He could smell the peat smoke from the long low stone house behind him. He could see the heather thatch kept down by weighted ropes and hear the voices of children and a woman calling. It was so familiar and so dear, he closed his eyes and slept. When he awoke stiff and cramped it was full daylight. He went up to his bed and slept again, not questioning what had happened to him.

The weeks passed. There was enough business in the hotel to keep Angus's life full. He heard nothing from Lady Ross but was not surprised. She knew he was capable of running the estate on a day to day basis without her input. As January passed into February Eilidh Morrison passed on Lady Ross's good wishes to her factor. 'She says she has perfect faith in you to be doing a good job, Angus, and will see you on her return.'

'Obviously,' grinned Angus as he reached for another piece of Eilidh's shortbread fresh from the oven. 'When were you talking to her?'

'She telephoned yesterday evening – just as I sat down to watch Coronation Street – and kept me blethering until it was half over. But it was good to hear from her and she sounded fine.'

'Where is she?'

'She didna' say and I didn't ask. It's no' my business to question milady's movements. But she did say her break was doing her heart good.'

Angus was alarmed. 'I didn't know there was anything the matter with her heart' he exclaimed anxiously. 'How long has this been going on, Eilidh? Why have you said nothing to me before?'

'Wheesht! Man. Don't be getting in such a lather. So far as I know there is nothing wrong with milady's heart – medically speaking. Sure it's just a figure of speech she was using.' Eilidh reached across the kitchen table and patted Angus's hand. 'It's gey fond you are of her ladyship, isn't it, Angus?'

'Aye. She's always been good to me, ever since I was a bairn. I suppose I almost look on her as kin. She's always been a fixture in my life. You know when away you think of home and see your granny's favourite chair and smell baking coming from the oven? That's the picture you carry with you. When I think of home she's there, somewhere in my picture'

Eilidh wiped her eyes on her apron and sniffed. 'Bye, that's a bonnie thing to say, Angus. Almost poetical,' she smiled. 'I didn't know you had it in you.'

'Away with your teasing, Eilidh,' Angus smiled and added with a shrug, 'I didn't know I had it in me either. I've never analysed my feelings about her ladyship before. I must be getting sentimental in my old age.'

'Old age. Ha!' scoffed Eilidh. 'Remember I knew you when you had no arse to your breeks from sliding down yon hill at the back. You used to creep in my kitchen looking for Minty to patch you up before you went home to your long-suffering mothers – you and Lachlan, as bad as each other. Have you heard from him lately?'

The talk turned to Lachlan Morrison's successful doctor's practice in Inverness, and no more was said of Lady Ross's holiday.

It was mid March before Eilidh gave Angus the news he had been waiting for. 'Her ladyship will be with us the morn's morn,' she said. 'And what she has taken into her head not to give me more notice, I don't know,' she grumbled.

'As if you didn't keep the house spotless and ready for her and any guests she might have to descend on you at no notice at all,' laughed Angus.

'Well, of course,' agreed Eilidh, pleased with the compliment. But her feathers were ruffled. She wriggled her shoulders as though settling them down and made Angus think of a comfortable pouter pigeon. 'She said nothing about it on Sunday evening when she phoned and now here we are on Tuesday and I'm needing more flour and butter if I'm to be baking for her arrival. You've eaten me out of house and home with your sweet tooth for the scones and shortbread.'

'I suppose that's a roundabout way of asking me to go down to the shop by the pier and get you some messages?' smiled Angus.

'Of course I wouldn't dream of putting you out so,' said Eilidh. Angus stared at her. 'It's just a wee bit flour and butter,' she went on. You can pick them up from Ernie's as you go home,' she continued, 'and while you're there perhaps I could do with some more lard and . . . '

'Make a list,' said Angus, 'and I'll get them from Ernie's – as you so graciously suggested, so as not to put me out,' he laughed. Lady Ross's imminent arrival had lifted his sombre mood. 'I'll see someone brings them by this afternoon if I can't make it myself.' He got up from the table and crossed the kitchen in the direction of the Estate Office.' Some of us have work to do and can't stay blethering all morning,' was his parting shot as he escaped from Eilidh's outraged reply.

He was still grinning as he entered Ernie's shop on his way home for lunch. As long as he could remember it had stood half way up the brae to Mackay's. It was a treasure-trove for any wide-eyed child. Tourists might not believe how long it could take to unearth exactly what was asked for. They didn't appreciate the extras you got from a visit to Ernie's. Time spent waiting for your order was never wasted and who was in such a rush they couldn't pass the time of day? Locals appreciated the amazing range of goods stuffed, squeezed and piled into the small space over which Ernie ruled with a monosyllabic geniality.

Angus handed over Eilidh's list and poked around while Ernie found the items on it. He gathered them on the foot-square space which was all that was left on the originally generous counter. It was no surprise when Ernie said, 'So her ladyship is back the morn's morn? 'Tis glad you'll be to see her.' For news travels fast in the North.

'Aye,' agreed Angus. 'I can't mind when she was last away so long.'

'When her man was in the politics and they had the big election,' supplied Ernie. 'That was the last time.' He continued calmly completing the list and didn't see Angus's appreciative smile. Trust Ernie to have such things at his fingertips. He was better than an almanac.

The following day Angus and Eilidh greeted Lady Ross's return to her home with equal pleasure.

She allowed Angus to help her out of the car while Tom held open the door. *'Ceud mile failte,'* said Angus. A hundred thousand welcomes, the traditional Gaelic greeting. He kissed her cheek.

'Tapadh leibh, Angus. Ciamar a tha sibh?' Thank you, Angus. How are you?

'Gle mhath,' Very well, he answered and laughed. This was the way Lady Ross had always greeted him on his return from school at Dornoch where he had boarded weekly and later when he came home from the

University. He believed it was her subtle way of reminding him who he was and where he belonged.

'Come away in your ladyship and don't be standing in this bitter wind,' scolded Eilidh by way of showing her employer that someone cared for her wellbeing.

'Thank you, Eilidh. Are you well?' said Lady Ross as she made her way across the gravel to the front door that stood open wide. 'Don't go, Angus. I want you to do something for me.'

'Will it not wait until you've had something to eat and a wee rest?' queried Eilidh.

'It won't take a moment and then I promise you, Eilidh, I'll do as you wish.' Annabelle Ross smiled up at Angus. 'How she bullies me. It's a wonder I came home.'

'You know fine she only does it out of concern for you. Now what is so important it can't wait?' he wondered as they crossed the hall to his office.

'I want you to organise a ball.'

Angus's eyebrows shot up in surprise.' A ball?' he echoed.

'Yes. I'm going to open up the house and do some entertaining. We'll start with the ball. Just before Easter I think.'

Angus looked across at the calendar on the office wall. 'That's not giving us much time. Easter Sunday's on 12th April. That's only three weeks away.'

'Are you saying it can't be done? Do you think no-one will come to my party because it's short notice?' she challenged.

'Of course not.' In these parts an invitation to the Big House was regarded as something between a Royal Command and a treasured treat. 'But if we leave it as long as possible you'll be in Easter Week. Not quite the time for festivities in some people's eyes perhaps? And there will be bound to be some folks off away on holiday.'

For a moment Lady Ross looked like a thwarted child. Then she pursed her lips and nodded. 'Alright then. The week after Easter but not a day longer. Make it the Saturday night. It will be the first Ghillies' Ball I've held here in ten years.'

'So it's to be a Ghillies' Ball?'

'That's what I said. Make sure all my people are invited as well as the usual list. Don't just stand there, boy. Get on with it.'

As he e:mailed the printers with details of the invitations for the ball Angus blessed modern technology. What bee Lady Ross had in her bonnet this time he had no idea but somehow he would manage all the details for her, as he always did. While he watched the screen of his computer tell him his message had been sent he ticked off details in his mind. Eilidh could safely be left with the catering arrangements. She only had to tell him what she wanted ordered. He had a handy list of extra local staff he could call on for the house-guests and he would hire waiters, waitresses and bar staff for the ball itself. When Lady Ross said to invite all her people she intended everyone who worked for her to enjoy themselves at her expense. They would bring their husbands, wives, and children too, who would sleep on piles of coats no doubt when at last they could keep their eyes open no longer.

Some of Lady Ross's personal friends would drive over for the dinner and dancing. Some would stay the night and some return home in the early hours – that group would include the minister and his family. It wouldn't do for him to miss morning service the next day.

What did she mean he wondered as he completed lists and made phone calls? She said she was opening up the house. He must pin her down if he was to know how many new permanent staff he should hire. The big house had been virtually closed up these past years. Dust covers shrouded furniture in rooms unused by her ladyship. The first people he must employ would be an army of cleaners to dust and polish. The ballroom floor - unused for so long - would have to be treated and the chandeliers lowered so the crystal lustres could be lovingly washed and dried. Once lit they would twinkle like a thousand stars and throw points of coloured light around the room. There would be no shortage of willing volunteers to get all ready. Beside the extra money coming in useful the *craic* would be good. To be able to carry news of the goings on at the Big House back to the rest of the community would give each speaker a special importance.

Fiona also was intrigued at the thought of the Big House being opened up. She made it her business to pay a call on Lady Ross and returned to Mackay's with a satisfied smile on her face.

As the weeks flew by all Angus's arrangements fell into place. The *ceilidh* band he hired would also oblige with some ballroom dances in between the reels and strathspeys so beloved of the more energetic guests. Lady Ross had invited ten coupes to stay the night and join her for a pre-dance dinner. Eilidh was in a flutter of satisfied excitement at such a challenge to her talents. She had five extra kitchen staff at her beck and call as well as the casual labour that would arrive on the morning of the festivities. They would be on hand to move tables and chairs, polish glasses and generally do her bidding.

    The local women swept, dusted and polished to good effect as the house emerged from its swathing covers and began to shine and hum as in the old days. There was constant coming and going with deliveries to be checked and signed for and questions to be answered.

Angus spent more time at the Big House than he did at the hotel but Fiona assured him they could manage without him.

Easter came and went following it usual pattern of Good Friday solemnity and Easter Sunday rejoicing. A squall of bad weather set in on Easter Monday as so often happens to ruin the Bank Holiday. On the following days many anxious looks were cast skywards and prayers uttered for better weather at the weekend. Lady Ross had ordained that Angus should organise a coach to fetch and return all her family of staff who lived at a distance. 'I'll have no-one driving home drunk from my parties,' she ordered. 'Nor will I have anyone not enjoying themselves so see to it, Angus.'

Angus hired a coach from Lairg, promising the driver plenty of alcohol-free refreshment, a good supper and a hefty bonus if he stayed on until all were ready to leave.

On Thursday Lady Ross summoned him to give account of the preparations so far. She was pleased with the result. 'You seem to have everything in hand,' she smiled. 'I don't want to see you tomorrow. No. Stop.' she cried as he would have interrupted her. 'Your poor mother has been coping without you I know. And I'm sure she has done excellently well but I want you to take a day off and run her into Inverness to buy a new dress and have her hair done. You are also to treat her to lunch at the Drumossie Hotel. I have already booked the table for one o'clock and the bill will be sent to me – so that you can pay it with the others at the month's end,' she grinned.

Angus and Eilidh had been a little worried when they realised the scale of the entertaining her ladyship was intending to do. They hoped it wouldn't tire her or cause her arthritic hips to give her more than usual pain.

But they had to agree she was thriving on the excitement.

Her eyes shone as she waved Angus away. 'Be off with you, boy, and see you make a good day of it tomorrow. I shall want all the details,' she added. 'Perhaps there's something on at Eden Court your mother would like to see? Why don't you phone them and find out? Now go. Go. Go.' She made shooing movements with her hands, laughing at him.

There was nothing Angus could do but shake his head and leave. Privately he thought her ladyship had overstepped the mark. His mother wouldn't take kindly to being ordered about in this way. But Fiona was delighted at the idea of spending a whole day with her beloved son. 'We'll play hookey,' she said, 'just the two of us. We'll run away and have a great time.' After wracking his brain to see if there was anything that could go drastically wrong in his absence Angus settled down to entertain Fiona and give her the spoiling that - in his opinion - she deserved and which was long overdue.

The morning of the ball dawned misty but bright with a hint of warmth to come once the sun was well up. Sighs of relief could be heard the length of the loch. Splashing through puddles to get into cars and coaches would not spoil festive raiment and no damp weather would cause carefully curled hair to droop or frizz.

When Angus arrived at the Big House Eilidh met him in the kitchen. 'Her ladyship says you're to concern yourself just with the ballroom and the catering staff. When all's ready you are to go home and have a bath or whatever you fine gentlemen do to array yourself for our pleasure,' she grinned. 'The fact is she doesn't want to see you today until dinner-time.'

Angus frowned. 'I knew she was overdoing it. I suppose you've been trying to get her to rest. I don't envy you. But is she having a lie-down, Eilidh? It's going to be a long night and you know what she's like. Any sensible woman her age would retire to bed and no-one would think any the worse for her. But not she. She is the hostess and won't budge until they've all gone home,' he fumed.

'Dinna fash yersel', Angus. She's in fine form the day and I promise you she will rest afore the night,' Eilidh assured with another huge grin. 'Away now and harass your hired-in minions. We'll be alright and I'd rather your room than your company in my kitchen this day.'

'Well at least you're cheerful enough,' conceded Angus. 'I know you love to have the house full. Quite like the old days now. But it'll be different when they've all gone and it's just her ladyship rattling round here all alone. I hope she doesn't come down from all this excitement with too much of a bump.'

'Aye, well, she'll just have to have more guests won't she? Don't look at me like that Angus Mackay. It's what her ladyship herself is saying. This ball is only the beginning.'

'What on earth's got into the woman?' muttered Angus as he made his way to the ballroom to see if all was as he had ordered.

For the rest of the day he was kept busy. Then at last when all was arranged to his satisfaction he went home to shave again, shower, change and escort Fiona back to dinner at the Big House. Happily the Easter guests had left the hotel and as soon as Fiona knew the date of the ball she'd taken no further bookings for that weekend.

Although Angus made sure he and Fiona arrived in good time for the pre-dinner drinks there were others already before them at the Big House. Some of Lady Annabelle's overnight guests had arrived in the late afternoon hoping for the opportunity of finding out what had induced their friend to open up her house after so many years. But when drinks were served in the Picture Gallery no-one was any the wiser. Lady Annabelle stationed herself at the end of the long room with Angus by her side. There was a spark of mischief in her eyes as she commanded Angus to call for silence. He clapped his hands and projected his voice down the gallery. 'Your attention, please, ladies and gentlemen.' The hum of conversation ceased and all heads turned towards Lady Annabelle. Two spots of bright colour stood out on her cheeks without help from make-up. Angus watched her closely - as Fiona told him later - like an anxious mother with an over-excited bairn.

'Dear friends and neighbours,' said Lady Ross, 'thank you for coming to help me celebrate this evening. I know the curiosity has been half-killing some of you,' she added with a sly grin at those who had been so un-subtly questioning her. 'So I will put you out of your misery. I have asked you here to introduce you to my special guest.' She turned her head towards the concealed door by which Minty MacPhee had left the gallery last year. It opened to allow Claire to step into the room. She hesitated a moment overcome by a sudden wave of shyness. Then she moved to where Lady Annabelle held out a welcoming hand. Her ladyship drew the young woman to her side. In doing so she positioned her beside the portrait of her father. For a moment there was a puzzled silence. Then among one or two of the older people present the penny dropped and a whisper ran through the company. Lady Annabelle smiled and nodded. 'I see some of you have realised the likeness,' she said with satisfaction. 'Indeed this is my beloved niece, Claire, my brother's only child and I hope you will all give her a truly Highland hospitable welcome. She has come to her rightful place in the home of her ancestors.' She pulled Claire towards her and kissed her cheek. Then said in a voice meant only for Claire and Angus's ears. 'There you are, my dear. The hard part is over and now you can go and enjoy yourself. Angus will look after you and introduce you around. I'm going to sit down and have a wee dram.'

Swiftly Angus pulled forward one of the chairs lining the gallery and made sure Lady Annabelle had a generous measure of whisky to sip. So this was the suppressed excitement that had kept his employer going for the last few days. He guessed she had been running on the adrenalin of it all and now fatigue had overtaken her. He glanced round the room and caught his mother's eye. He beckoned her over with a small jerk of the head.

Fiona pulled up another chair and sat beside her hostess. 'Run away you two and mingle until dinner so Lady Annabelle and I can gossip in peace.' She smiled at her son, appreciating his care for the older woman, then turned to her companion. 'Nice one,' she said dryly.

Lady Annabelle snorted a gust of laughter. 'Yes. I thought so. Do you think it will work?'

'Of course. Who would dare to snub her now? And you gave them the true information so no need to invent stories. Of course there'll be talk but nothing unkind I think. Are you happy now?'

Lady Annabelle watched Angus guiding Claire from one group to another and smiled. 'More than you'll ever know, my dear.' She turned to look Fiona directly in the eye. 'We've been friends for some years now, Fiona. You know more of my family than most and I've always appreciated your sense and discretion. Your Angus has been almost the son to me I never had. He is a great credit to you and his father. I know he looks after me – as much as I'll let him,' she added, 'and I always find his presence a comfort and a tonic. Thank you for lending him to me.'

Fiona smiled.

Lady Annabelle went on 'There is only one thing that would make me happier than I am at this moment.' She looked away to where Claire was holding on to Angus's arm as they chatted to the guests.

'Aye. If only,' agreed Fiona.

Claire nipped the inside of Angus's arm as they stood talking to the minister and his wife. She exerted a gentle yet persistent pressure until he took the hint and made their excuses to Rev and Mrs Macleod. She pulled him away from the gathering of guests who all knew each other and were quite happy catching up on the latest news – although none could have guessed just how exciting the very latest news would be. When they were isolated from the others and stood beside one of the windows, Claire at last had her chance. She grinned up into Angus's face. 'Surprise!' she said.

'God, you look like her,' he said.

Claire frowned. 'Who? My mother?'

'No. Your aunt. She's had just that same look of mischief in her eyes for the last few days. When did you arrive?'

Claire laughed. 'Two days ago and a hard job I've had keeping out of your way. Aunt Nell was determined to keep me secret and have her lovely moment this evening. She's great fun you know, when you get to know her – if you know what I mean?'

Angus smiled. 'How many drams have you had tonight already?'

'None. It's just excitement and just – everything.' For a moment she looked vulnerable and a small frown puckered her forehead. 'Sometimes I feel it's all a dream and I'm going to wake up back in Surrey,' she said quietly.

'And do you want to?'

She was shocked. 'No. Never. I'm never going back. Here I know who I am,' she cried passionately.

'Hey! No-one's arguing,' Angus assured her. He smiled. 'You've come home where you belong. You see I was right.'

'Right? How? What about?'

'Remember when you said you thought you'd found the right place and this was where you belonged? I said you must have some Scottish blood in you and you denied it?'

'Yes, of course. You were right but I didn't know then. How long ago that all seems.'

'Less than a year.'

'But so much has happened.'

'Aye,' said Angus. Far more than she would ever guess, he thought. He had never hoped or believed he could, or would, ever love again. But he had fallen deeply and irrevocably in love with Claire and he had to bear the pain of it in silence.

From the day of her homecoming Claire and Angus were rarely apart. In spite of his good resolutions not to spend his leisure time with her, Angus had little choice. Lady Ross had made her entertainment a 'ghillies' ball, although not at the traditional time of year. This ensured on that night all her people would know of Claire's existence and relationship to the Sutherlands. Next she commanded Angus to take Claire with him on his travels round the estate. He was to make sure she was introduced to everyone personally. There was to be no 'hole and corner' atmosphere to Claire's presence at The Big House. From the fish-filleters on the quayside to the ghillies on the river, Claire met them all. Her ready smile and open friendliness would have been her passport to general acceptance. But her intense interest in everything she saw added to her position in the community far more than she could ever have imagined. Soon 'the young mistress', as she came to be called, was a welcome sight anywhere on the estate and beyond.

Claire bloomed. She slept like a baby and ate like a young loon yet managed never to put on too much weight. Her eyes sparkled and her skin took on a golden tan as the year passed into summer. Her presence in The Big House gave Lady Annabelle a new lease of life. Invitations arrived with every post and Angus was roped in to escort Claire when her ladyship found so much junketing too exhausting. Lady Annabelle often blessed his existence as she found she could deny her niece nothing. Tennis parties or expeditions to climb Foinavon were impossible for her ladyship to join in. Tom, who drove her big Daimler, had better things to do with his time than ferry Claire around. Lady Ross intended to get Claire a wee car of her own but before then she wanted to be sure her niece knew her way about the county. So she made sure Angus was always available to run Claire here and there; make up a four for tennis; or give her a hand up the steeper braes on explorations of her extensive new home. She was constantly amused by Claire's prattle of her doings and astute observations on all the people Angus took her to see. Sometimes Annabelle Ross wondered how she had endured her solitary life before Claire's arrival on the scene.

For Angus this was a time of mixed pleasure and pain. He could not stop himself treasuring every moment spent with Claire. Yet sticking to his firm resolve not to betray his true feelings put him under a severe strain. To keep their relationship on a brother to sister footing was infinitely more difficult than he had ever envisaged. The main problem lay with Claire's affectionate nature. Surrounded now on every side with warmth and smiles, the diffidence that Angus had noticed on Claire's arrival at Mackay's with the Butlers was gone.

'It's so strange,' she said. 'Here I am with people I never knew a year ago and yet I feel happier in my own skin than ever before.' She took hold of Angus's arm and laid her head against his shoulder. They were standing on the lawn at Mackay's and looking up the loch towards The Big House. She gave a sigh of pure contentment. 'I am so lucky,' she said. 'Just think if I'd never come here?' She lifted her head and turned to face him. 'I wonder what would have happened to me?'

Angus shook his head. 'No idea. Probably you would have done the usual social round of your set and married some wealthy stockbroker or merchant banker,' he teased.

'Don't laugh. You don't know how close to the mark you are. Aunty Cyn would have touted me round the acceptable functions in search of a suitable husband.' Claire shivered, then frowned. 'But it wasn't meant to be like that. I'd almost forgotten why we came here. It was my dreams, wasn't it? Do you remember? I felt this urge to keep travelling northwards.' She smiled. 'Now I know why. I was meant to come home,' she pronounced triumphantly.

'Your Mum's been so good to me Angus. She and Kirstie between them have told me so much about my mother; and Aunt Nell is full of stories of my father. She loved him very much even though he was no angel. I feel I'm getting to know both of them. There's the portrait of Malcolm in the gallery but I wish I had a picture of my mother, Senga.'

Angus thought for a moment. 'Perhaps one of the staff has an old photograph? We could ask them.' But it seemed no-one had ever taken a photograph of Senga while she worked at Mackay's. So Claire tried to be satisfied with the face of her father and the kind memories others had of her mother.

Angus had not known at the time that Lady Ross had spent Christmas and New Year in Surrey with Claire and her aunt and uncle. She was introduced to Claire's friends and acquaintances and had spied out the lie of the land down there. Between them Claire, her aunt and the Butlers had decided nothing would be done in haste to change Claire's living arrangements. But after two months back in Scotland Claire came to a decision. She broached the subject one June evening after dinner. It was nearly the longest day and she and Lady Ross sat in the rose garden at The Big House sipping wine in the warmth of the evening.

'Aunt Nell, I think I'll sell the house in Surrey,' announced Claire.

Lady Ross's eyebrows rose and she quickly hid the smile of satisfaction Claire's words brought. 'Are you sure, my dear? Won't you miss your friends? And might it not be useful if you wished to visit London for shopping or going to the theatre? You could always keep it on, at least for a while longer. I'm sure your Beanie could be trusted to look after it for you.'

'Of course she could but that's not the point. First of all I don't ever want to live there again. I just don't feel 'myself' when I'm there. Which is ridiculous really, because I've spent far more of my life in that house than anywhere else. But that's the way it is. Second, if I want to visit London it would be much handier and cheaper to stay in an hotel in Town. Actually I can't see myself going down there that much when I have the Edinburgh and Glasgow shops nearer to hand and the theatre at Eden Court in Inverness. They have such a good diverse programme.

'And then there's Beanie. It's not fair to use her as a sort of watchdog cum house-sitter. Ever since Mother died Beanie's life has revolved around me. Which brings me to the next point,' here she looked anxiously at Lady Ross. 'I know it's a bit much to ask but could I please offer Beanie a home here, with us? She might not want to come, of course, but I really feel I can't abandon her. She's been good to me. She practically brought me up and I'm very fond of her.'

Lady Ross nodded approval. 'I am glad to see you concern yourself with the happiness and welfare of your people, Claire. Of course you must offer Miss Benton a home here with you. Heaven knows there's plenty of room. You can organise her a suite of her own. Perhaps she would like to occupy the old nursery wing. Nanny ruled supreme there in my childhood over the Day and Night Nurseries and the schoolroom. But she had her own sitting room and bedroom with, latterly, an ensuite bathroom.' She paused a moment deep in thought then nodded. 'You will have to give some thought to what your Beanie will do to occupy herself.

I know she is of retirement age and is very welcome here as your pensioner but you know the saying "the Devil finds work for idle hands". I do not wish my household to be disrupted by any unpleasantness in the form of jealousy or pride. Perhaps she might like to maid you? That shouldn't be too onerous but would let her feel she is still a large part of your life.'

Claire jumped up and bent over her aunt to hug her and kissed her cheek. 'Thank you so much, Aunt Nell.'

Lady Ross flushed with pleasure. She patted Claire on the shoulder then waved her away. 'Wheesht, child. This is your home. Where else would your Beanie go unless she has other plans?'

'I don't think she will have,' said Claire. 'I know she tried to warn me off coming to Scotland but it wasn't because she didn't like the place. She'd never been here. She was afraid if anything came out I should be hurt. She's always looked out for me,' she said simply. 'She could never have known how good, how right, everything would turn out. And I doubt very much if she has any life outside our family – that is Mother, Father and me. She was only a lass when she came to maid mother and she's been with my family ever since.'

Lady Ross's lips twitched at Claire's use of the Scottish word but she made no comment. The more her niece immersed herself in Scotland and its culture the better she would be pleased.

When Claire told Angus she was going back to Surrey she tried to read the expression on his face. She thought she saw alarm, regret, and acceptance show in his eyes in quick succession. What did that mean? Then there was just his usual friendly face. He was interested in all she had to tell him. Once the reason for her journey south was explained she was certain his smile was broader and more genuine. He seemed very pleased she was coming back. But it irked her to be unsure of his real feelings towards her.

She had met many men both young and not so young who would have been glad to marry her as the only Frobisher heir. None had appealed to her senses in any way. When she had first met Angus she had attributed the immediate attraction she felt for him to the romantic ideas the film Braveheart had put in her head. He wore his kilt with natural pride and his position of authority at the hotel gave him an air of easy assurance. She had put down to her love affair with all things Scottish that breathlessness she had felt on seeing him in the glory of his kilt and 'Prince Charlie' in the dining room of Mackay's. But during the holiday last year she had come to realise that Angus was absolutely necessary to her happiness and had made up her mind to marry him.

However, it was one thing to make up her own mind, quite another to discover if what she felt was reciprocated. Sometimes she thought he really cared for her then to her intense irritation he would become almost avuncular once more. She gritted her teeth and hoped the old adage of absence and increased affection would prove to come true.

It took Claire five weeks to settle her affairs in Surrey. She had to persuade Beanie she hadn't lost her mind and did really intend to spend her life in Scotland. She put the house on the market and packed up those of her possessions she wished to take up to Sutherland. Beanie decided to stay in Surrey until the house was sold. At that stage Claire would have to return to decide what to do with the rest of the furniture should the new owner not wish to purchase it with the house.

Claire returned to Bervie Lodge in the first week in August. Lady Ross was delighted and immediately made plans to host a shooting party for The Glorious Twelfth. Claire frowned and turned down her mouth when she realised what was involved. One day as they walked on the hill she confided in Angus.

'Don't knock it until you've tried it,' he advised.

'But I don't want to kill anything,' complained Claire. 'Why can't the grouse just be left alone on the hills?'

'If we did that the estate would soon run into trouble. The birds are bred for the shooting. That brings in revenue the first time as some people enjoy the sport of shooting. Then, apart from a few brace they take home as trophies or send off to friends, the rest belong to the estate and are sold, mainly to hotels, some as far away as London. That's the second revenue they bring.'

'But doesn't breeding them specially cost money?'

'Aye, of course it does.'

'So if we didn't breed them specially we wouldn't need all that revenue to pay for them, so we wouldn't have to shoot them.' Claire concluded triumphantly.

Angus shook his head. 'The people who do the necessary work to take care of the breeding don't only do that. There's other estate work and they have to be paid. There's the heather burning; the forestry; the lochs and the rivers to look after. There's the hill to keep and sheep to tend on the farms. The whole thing is interdependent and keeps many people in employment who, otherwise, would starve or leave the land which would become an empty wilderness. All very fine and beautiful perhaps for an artist or poet, but what a waste. All this,' Angus's arm swept wide to embrace the scenery as far as the eye could see, 'all this has to be husbanded, cared for to preserve it for future generations and for the enjoyment of folk today. Which brings us back to the Twelfth,' he teased.

'I still don't want to kill anything,' muttered Claire, sticking out her lower lip.

'Fine, don't,' said Angus. 'Nobody's forcing you. But next time you eat a delicious grouse or pheasant dinner, remember someone had to kill the bird for you to enjoy your meal. Then perhaps you won't be so judgmental.'

He strode off down the hill and Claire had to run to catch up with him. She smiled. This is what she relished. Angus never let her get off with anything. The other men she had met had agreed with everything she said – or pretended to. They didn't want to upset her or didn't care enough to have a proper discussion on any subject. Sometimes when she had been bored at a cocktail party or gallery opening she had invented an outrageous point of view simply to see if her latest escort would contradict her or take up an opposing stance. They never did.

Alright she would do what Angus suggested and see what happened. She caught him by the sleeve at the foot of the brae. 'Will you teach me to shoot?' she said and was rewarded by his shout of laughter and the bear-hug he gave her – but only in a friendly way. Claire sighed. What would it take to get him going?

On the anniversary of her first arrival at Mackay's, Claire plotted a day out with Angus. Fiona and Lady Ross colluded in her plans by arranging he should have no duties on that day. Eilidh Morrison packed a picnic fit for a king for Claire to bring from The Big House. With a shrug of resignation Angus agreed to humour her and the pair set off for the north coast not long after breakfast.

There was no hurry as the car climbed up to cross the high moor and descended the Gualin brae. Angus pointed out the water trough placed for the coach horses to drink after the steep pull up from the Durness side in the old days. Farther on he showed her the spot beside the road where he and Lachlan had brought their buckets to collect mussels when the tide was out. They drove through Durness to the Oasis cafe and stopped there for coffee, then on they went to Smoo Cave.

'I haven't been here since I was a loon,' said Angus as they scrambled across the wooden bridge that would take them inside where the waterfall fell into the pool lit only by sunlight slanting down from the hole high above in the roof of the cave. 'What made you think of it?'

'I asked Fiona. She said you hadn't been for ages so I didn't think it would bore you and I've never been so, here we are. It's great isn't it? Does it really make a noise?'

'Aye, indeed. When the tide is high and the wind in the right direction, the water surges into the cave and is pushed high into the funnel. It fills the space and displaces the air there. That has nowhere else to go so escapes through the small hole in the roof. I can tell you it sounds so weird. It's like a soul in torment if you are of a fantastical frame of mind and not prepared for it. On stormy days the spray itself comes whooshing out up high into the air. It's quite a sight.'

Claire shivered in delicious horror. 'Wow! I'd love to see and hear it.'

'Maybe some day, but not today. The tide is low and the day calm. Where do you want to have lunch?'

'I've got a picnic in the boot of the car. Where would you suggest?'

'We can go down on the beach at Balnakiel. It's such a warm day you should have brought your swimming costume, but at least you can paddle if you like.'

They enjoyed the goodies in the picnic basket on the long curve of silver sand that followed Balnakiel Bay right round to the rocks of Faraid Head. Afterwards they left the basket and Angus strolled along at the water's edge while Claire kicked off her sandals and paddled through the clear water.

'Do you want to go right along to the end?' queried Angus, but she shook her head. She shaded her eyes with her hand and looked across the bay.

'I want to go and walk along that cliff,' she said indicating the turf-topped jagged rocks that rose sheer out of the water on the far side.

'In that case we'd better turn back. We can dump the picnic basket in the car and park it in the Golf Club Car Park. That's the closest way to the footpath.'

In the Car Park Claire used Angus's handkerchief to dry her feet and brushed the sand from between her toes. She put her sandals back on and got out of the car. Behind and to the side of them the land rose in a rounded hump. Everywhere there was colour. She scrambled up the bank a short way and bent to examine the flowers at her feet. 'Come and look, Angus,' she cried. 'Have you ever seen anything so exquisitely beautiful?'

'No,' he said, but he wasn't looking at the flowers.

'What are they called?'

Angus focused his attention on the tiny flowers growing on the machair at his feet. 'I'm not sure of them all,' he said, 'but those are Scottish Primroses.

You're lucky to spot them. They're quite rare. And over there are harebells. The pink ones are Autumn Gentians and, of course, those are wild pansies.'

'They're perfect,' Claire cried. 'Just like the real ones but in miniature.'

Angus laughed. 'They are real ones. Somewhere along the way you might see a cream flower with orange stamens. I know that is called Mountain Avens and I could name Meadowsweet and either of the pink or purple orchids we might see but after that I'd be lost to put a name to anything.'

'I think that's pretty good,' Claire admired. 'I don't know any of them. I shall get a book and learn,' she decided. 'How do we get along the cliff?'

'Are you sure you want to go? The path can be a bit rough and the longer grasses could prickle your feet.'

'Don't be such a wuss,' she cried and Angus shouted with laughter.

'You are certainly widening your vocabulary,' he said, 'but I'm not sure your aunt would like to hear you using those words.'

'Why? Is it a swear?'

'Och, no, but perhaps not quite ladylike.'

'I doubt Aunt Nell would worry about that. I'm sure I've heard her use worse. You couldn't exactly call her mealy-mouthed,' retorted Claire.

Again Angus's hoot of laughter rang out. That was certainly not an adjective to apply to Lady Ross.

They crossed in front of the Clubhouse, skirted the eighteenth green of the Golf Course and came to the narrow footpath. They took care not to go too close to the edge of the cliff. After a while the path turned inland onto safer ground and they were able to walk side by side. They wandered along spying out the delicately coloured machair flowers. Soon the Clubhouse was out of sight and the path came to an end.

To their right and ahead of them beyond the long drop lay the sparkling waters of the bay stretching far out past the headland to the open sea. Claire walked a little faster and was soon a few yards in front of Angus. He saw her stop and take off her sandals. She carried them in her hands and walked on. He opened his mouth to shout a warning of prickles and rough ground but shut it again. Claire was no idiot and she had eyes in her head. She could look out for herself. He was simply enjoying a rare day of leisure when there were no phones to answer or guests to cater to. How long was it since he had had such a free, uncluttered, carefree day?

Ahead of him Claire stopped and looked out to sea. Graceful porpoises curved their lean bodies in and out of the water in playful mood. Angus reached Claire. She held wide her arms raised her face to the sky, eyes closed and breathed deeply. 'Och! Dougal is this not the bonniest place?' she cried, then turned and threw her arms around him.

Taken by surprise Angus couldn't build his defences quickly enough. Her body pressed firmly against his, fitting so well. It seemed right. His arms tightened round her and he drew her into him burying his face in her sweet-smelling hair which tumbled onto her shoulders. He was giddy with her nearness and warmth. Instinctively their heads turned, their lips met and Angus was lost. He could no more stop that kiss than take wing and fly back to the safety of Mackay's.

At length they both came up for air and Angus cursed himself for his loss of control. He would gloss over it, make some crack, a joke, apologise, anything to try and retrieve the situation. But Claire gently disengaged herself from his arms. 'We must get on,' she said and walked away.

Angus frowned. What on earth had just happened? That was only the second time he had kissed Claire and yet she had seemed so at home in his arms like a long-time lover returning to the place she belonged. He hurried after her. She had disappeared below the skyline.

When she came into view again surprise made him stop and stare. Below the knoll on which he stood and a sloping beach lay the ruins of houses, a line of them. Perhaps this had been some kind of croft or small settlement? He picked his way through the thick long grass to examine the stone structures. No roofs remained or any sign of tile or slate. This made him think they were quite old. The roofs had probably been made of turf or heather thatch. The whole seemed to be a row of small dwellings of no more than two tiny rooms each. The entrances all faced the sea and the remains of a circular wall enclosed a wide area of ground in front of them. What were they for and how had they got here? Angus had no idea. He had never heard of a croft or farm on this side of the peninsular. He looked about but could see no signs of land being tended and the beach seemed too shallow for fishing boats. He frowned. How odd. He crossed over to where Claire stood by the empty entrance to one of the small dwellings. Tears streamed down her face.

'Claire! What's wrong? Why are you crying?'

She turned to him. 'I don't know,' she wailed. 'I am so sad, Angus.' She reached out her hands to him in despair. He strode forward and cradled her in his arms. Shushing her like a bairn he rocked and comforted her.

'There now, there, there. I've got you. It's alright, my darling. I have you safe.'

Claire pulled back from his embrace and looked up into his face with anguished eyes. 'Something dreadful happened here,' she said.

Life at the solmar 1571

Morag was happy. She hummed a tune as she walked along the headland seeking the plants she used to make her cooking so special. Only last evening, Dougal had said even his mother could not set a better meal than Morag. She smiled. She must remember to go across to the woodland near Baile na Cille to gather some sorrel for Dougal's favourite soup. She would never forget the look on his face when she broke two fresh eggs into the cauldron and stirred them quickly round in the hot broth so they cooked in strips of white and yellow. But he had appreciated the resultant meal.

Morag stopped and looked about her then dropped onto the short turf and breathed in her joy. Out to sea the sun shone on the wavelets making pinpoints of light to rival the stars in the heavens. Below where she sat the cliffs dropped sheer to the water. No matter how calm the day, at this spot there was always sound and movement as the surging waves rose up the rock-face then sucked back into the waiting sea. Far over on her right the beach was washed clean and white by yesterday's storm. It reached out to the distant headland which gave some protection to the whole bay from the anger of the weather. Later she would go down to the jetty in the cove below the houses and gather any branches or jetsam that had been washed up. She loved the colours and pictures in the flames of a driftwood fire. She could gaze for hours letting her imagination run free.

How lucky we are, she thought. And how strange is life? If Elspeth's father had not rebelled against his own father's rule and come here to try his hand at the fishing with his uncle, she and Dougal would never have known this place existed.

"Follow the water," Elspeth had told them. "The other side of Laorig begins a long loch. Keep to the north bank always. Follow it for several days until it ends. There you will find a stream that joins it with a shorter loch. At its northern end climb the saddle you will find in front of you on the skyline, and you will come to yet another loch. Keep going always with the water. It dwindles to a stream and then opens to the last of the loch chain. This one runs between two big hills. Follow it to its end and then the river down to the sea. You will have reached Laxford.

"Then you must strike right, up steep braes, picking your way between the rock outcrops until you reach the summit. Go north by east then, sticking to the high ground as far as possible for there are bogs and lochans all around. One day you will see the sea ahead of you. Aim for that and you will arrive at Baille na Cille. Keep this smoke on your right hand and follow the cliff until you reach the solmar. Give my greetings to my kinsmen there and they will give you shelter." She smiled at Dougal. "You can learn a new trade, laddie."

"What's a solmar?" asked Morag.

"What new trade?" said Dougal.

Elspeth smiled. "A solmar is where salt is made and fish are salted," she said. "My kin serve the monks at Baille na Cille. When the herring, or the salmon or even the mackerel are running they go out fishing and then salt the fish in the barrels provided by the monks. These are taken by sea around the coast for the monastery use. Do you fancy such work, Dougal?"

He shrugged. "If it's honest and will keep me and my woman safe, I'll do it," he said.

And so they had followed the *cailleach's* directions. It had been hard saying goodbye, for who knew if they would ever meet again. If Elspeth had had her way they would not have been able to leave for the weight of gifts she pressed on them. But they could take only what they could carry, which wasn't much more than they had had on arriving. One thing Morag did insist upon was to keep the spinning wheel Elspeth offered her. The *cailleach* had two more, so Morag felt able to accept this gift. And she dearly longed for it. Even Dougal with his clever whittling couldn't make her such a wondrous thing. Now it rested in their room at the solmar.

They had been happy days making their way along the path the water lead them. The weather was kind and food plentiful in loch, burn and plant. Rabbits abounded and they were never hungry. They were young, healthy, free and in love. Answering to no man, they felt invincible.

Their arrival at the solmar wasn't quite what they had expected. Elspeth had described a row of stone-built houses occupied by her kinsmen with their women and children. But it seemed the hard life of the solmar had reduced the number of Elspeth's kin left there to just one old man. Two younger had been drowned and a third together with his wife and children and the widows left behind, had moved away to easier living the other side of Durness. Of the five houses only one was occupied.

But Old Willie Sutherland had been overjoyed to learn they wished to stay with him – although no-one would ever have known this by his behaviour, for he was a solitary and dour man. Until Morag learned better, he reminded her of her father. But it wasn't long before Old Willie was doing small tasks to help her and bringing home a pretty pebble he thought she might like or a glossy bird's feather he had found on the hill. Morag became very fond of the old man and made sure she always cooked enough food in their own house to leave some for her to take along for the *bodach*.

Dougal bit down on his temper many times as Old Willie laughed at the younger man's attempts to fish, steer the boat, carry the slippery harvest, skim the salt from the pans or build the right type of fire beneath them in time of need to hasten the evaporation of the salt water within. At first it seemed everything Dougal did was wrong or ill-timed, but at last he got the hang of it and felt no greater pride than on the day Willie clapped him on the back and declared he would make a fisher of him yet.

When the wildness of the winter storms kept them close indoors, the old man's company was very welcome. They told him of Elspeth and he told them tales of his childhood. They didn't feel the hunger of last year's winter, for there was always salt fish to augment the hares that seemed to abound on the headland. When the new year came around the three celebrated it together and Morag looked to the future with more joy and confidence than for many a long day.

She enjoyed making a comfortable home for Dougal and through the spring and summer months her sweet voice singing as she worked brought a smile to Old Willie's face.

"Good day to you, child."

At the sound of a voice, Morag whirled around. She had been so absorbed in her thoughts she hadn't been aware of anyone approaching. Her heart beat fast in alarm for no-one came this way. There was no reason. Beyond the solmar there were no smokes on the rest of the headland. They were surrounded on three sides by the sea and inland there was no-one for more than a day's travel. Willie had told them so.

Morag's heart rate slowed as she realised the speaker was a woman, and alone. "Good day to you, mistress," she replied. "Have you lost your way?"

The woman smiled, softening the features of a face worn by time and weather. "No, lassie. I wager I know this land better than you do. Where do you bide?"

Morag bit her lip. The habit of fear and concealment was still with her despite the months they had spent here with Willie. But the woman was alone and quite old. What harm could she do them? But still. "Not far from here," she answered cautiously.

The woman smiled again. Her eyes lit up with amusement. "Don't tell me you are staying with Young Willie Sutherland? You must be, for his is the only smoke in this area."

In her surprise Morag nodded. How did this stranger know Willie? And why did she call him young?

"I am on my way home from the kirk," said the woman, "but I will turn my steps from the path and *ceilidh* awhile with Young Willie. I have not seen him these many weeks. Come, child." She held out her hand and helped Morag to her feet. It was the stranger who led the way, which eased Morag's worries. It seemed the woman knew Old Willie and where he stayed, so perhaps it didn't matter if she knew Morag and Dougal were also there? But as they walked along Morag was puzzling where her companion had come from and was going to? From the kirk, she had said. Of course, today must be the Sabbath, but where was her home?

"Greetings, Young Willie, may the Lord be with you," were the visitor's first words as Willie waved to the two women. He was carrying driftwood up from the small beach beside the jetty. "And why do you work on the

Lord's day?" she went on. "Has He not given you time enough to do your tasks?"

"Is it yourself, come to chastise me, Peggy Campbell?" smiled Willie. "You're a sight for my old eyes. Come away in and take a bite with us. Don't be afraid to eat the food. It's not my making," he snorted with laughter, no doubt remembering some past occasion. "My wee lassie, Morag, can draw wondrous flavours from God's bounty."

So now Morag had the visitor's name at least, but it was not until they had eaten she learned more of the stranger. Willie was as anxious for news of the outside world as a bairn for courageous tales of his ancestors. But the news was grave. Unrest still stalked the land as the great lords wrestled for supremacy. Morag heard the names of Caithness, Sutherland, Duffus, and Gordon, but they meant little to her. It wasn't until Peggy Campbell spoke of the Murrays who had fled Dornoch to join Huntly, ready to serve Earl Alexander on his majority, that Morag pricked up her ears. Did this mean father and the boys were gone from the strath? Or had her cunning father returned to his farm and kept his head down through the past two years? Would she ever know the truth?

The talk turned to Peggy's visit to the kirk. She told them of the grand sermon she had heard that day and how she had enjoyed it. The priest had taken the opportunity to speak to his congregation who came from far and near on this holy day. He knew many had walked for miles to hear his words and be blessed. He hoped they would take his message back to those too old or too young, perhaps infirm, who could not be there in person. Then, to Morag's amazement, Peggy had repeated the priest's words, interpreting them for her listeners. For a good hour she spoke and then prayed with them for another hour.

Morag's heart was full. Peggy could not forgive her sins, but she told Morag to be constant in prayer and the Lord would be gracious unto her. When Peggy Campbell finally went on her way, she left a changed young woman behind her. Morag resolved to embrace her new life with no regrets for the past. She would put herself in the Lord's hands and follow the path down which He led her. She would not fear for the future but look ahead with confidence. And she would take the goodwife's words to heart and try to make up for the many weeks she had ignored her prayers.

When their visitor had departed Dougal turned to Old Willie. "Who in the name of goodness was that? I've heard of wandering priests, but never a woman who quotes the Bible"

Willie smiled. "Aye, she's unique right enough. She stays way over in the West by Sheigra. On a Sabbath she walks from there to Baille na Cille for the service and then home again."

Dougal frowned. "But how far are you talking about? She said she crossed the water in a coracle. Is it on Eilan Dubh she stays?" he asked for the name Sheigra meant nothing to him. He looked across the narrow strip of water that separated them from the 'black isle'.

Willie smiled. "No, laddie. It's the Kyle she speaks of. She'll be crossing below Beinn an Amair and then walk across to the sea. Her home lies near Sheigra which is on the West Coast where the great ocean lies. She will follow the water round the hills, the Movallys, Meall na Mone and Meall Dearg until she reaches the shores of Loch More a Chraisg and so home. She is known far and wide for her virtue and godliness. Many a lost soul has she brought back into the bosom of the church – or so they tell me."

"I didn't know you were a religious man, Willie?" said Dougal.

Willie shook his head. "Aye, you've a deal to learn yet, laddie. When the storm rises and the boat is swamped then every sailor is a religious man. Keep to the fishing and you will learn to pray."

"I learned it at my mother's knee," retorted Dougal, "but you're right, it is a habit I've fallen out of."

"Me too," admitted Morag, "but not one I'll forget again in a hurry."

She was true to her word as the happy weeks and months passed. Peggy Campbell became a frequent visitor and, although Morag was too nervous to accompany her to the kirk, Peggy shared the services with the trio at the solmar. Morag loved her visits, not only for the comfort of a church service she could not attend, but to be able to talk with another woman. She hadn't realised how much she had missed the company of Elspeth, and also her female friends back in the strath. Joyfully she confided in Peggy that come the next Spring there would be a new inhabitant of the houses at the solmar. Peggy promised to come and bide with her when she judged Morag's time was near. Childbirth was a frightening experience for a young woman, especially the first time around when everything was strange and unknown. Although from her work with the animals Morag was knowledgeable enough to cope, without the comfort of her mother helping her, she would have felt apprehensive indeed. Once reassured of Peggy's help and expertise, Morag could enjoy her pregnancy with confidence. Dougal was beside himself with pride and joy. And Willie was determined to be the best grandsire any child could have.

One day in October the sun shone hot on the heather. Morag wandered up the slope behind the row of wee houses. Dougal had already mended the damage the wind had done to the roofs of the other three since their occupants left. Now the whole row of five stood weatherproof and useful for storage. In the coming winter they would not want for supplies. Willie and Dougal had stocked up on salt fish. One of the houses would be used as a chicken coup to stop their precious five hens from being blown into the sea, or eaten by foxes or wolves, and the berries she was seeking today would be dried to join the others already sealed away from hungry mice.

Morag's hair flew free in the gentle breeze. She had grown tired of pulling fish scales out of it with the comb Dougal had whittled for her. Today might be one of the last hot days when she could be sure of drying her long thick hair quickly, so she had washed it in the running burn just beyond Willie's house on the end of the row.

She had already filled one of the birch-bark containers she carried with berries, and the second was nearly half full when she heard an unusual noise. Someone was whistling. Old Willie rarely ventured far from the solmar these days and not in this direction. Dougal was out in the boat, so who was this? Morag crouched down as much as she could for her waist was thickening and her belly growing. She waited. The whistling got fainter and fainter. Whoever it was they were going away. She sighed in relief. Dougal had made several trips with Willie in the boat to the monastery to help him deliver the filled barrels and bring back empty ones. While there they had gone on to Durness and made the few purchases they needed, drunk some ale and listened to the latest rumours and counter-rumours as to what was happening in the outside world. But folk had accepted Dougal as one of Willie's kin and no questions were asked. From the day of their arrival, Morag had never left the vicinity of the solmar and she was happy to stay there. If no-one knew of her existence she couldn't bring trouble to her loved ones. She waited a few moments longer then heaved herself to her feet and continued to pick her berries. She had found a good patch of blueberries and was determined to fill her poke.

She picked with a will moving slowly up the slope. She hadn't realised she had reached the summit until she nearly fell forward, but she regained her balance and stood on the skyline looking all around. From here she could see the way the land rolled away from her. Between two summits to her right there gleamed the water of a small loch. She must suggest Dougal tries his fishing there. Perhaps there might be trout for a change? As she turned towards the direction of Baille na Cille she saw a movement, and studied the place more carefully. As she looked over rock and heather and down the brae, so a man stood looking up at her. He was too far distant for her to make out his features, but it was clear he had spotted her for he raised his hand to his eyes. With her red hair blowing free, back-lit by the bright sun and making Morag appear a dark silhouette on the sky-line, who knows what he thought he saw? She dropped to the ground and crawled swiftly below the summit. Her heart thundered against her ribs and she had no care for scratched hands or spilled berries. Why had she been so foolish? Why had she wandered so far from the solmar? Why had she ignored the warning of the whistling?

As she made her way back to the houses Morag furiously berated herself for her carelessness. But when she related the incident to Dougal he soothed her fears. "No doubt he thought you an apparition. If he has a guilty conscience he could have taken you as a dreadful warning of retribution. If he is a good man then he might think a saint has promised him good fortune." He wound his fingers through her silky hair and pulled her gently into his arms. "If he knew the truth he would congratulate me on loving the most beautiful and bounteous angel dropped from the Heavens."

Morag's laugh was shaky, but she let herself be comforted. Indeed there were always tales of sightings in lonely places. Boggarts and will 'o the wisps abounded here, especially when men walked on unfamiliar ground. That night she prayed she might have been taken for just such a one.

The day of Morag's fright had been the last gasp of summer. It seemed autumn was short-lived and then winter was upon them. Often Dougal and Morag spoke of the winter they had spent with Elspeth. Old Willie was always happy to hear any stories of his kinswoman. "Aye," he said, "I mind fine when she and her father came to stay here. He was a sad man. His woman had died and left him with the bairn. I think he was seeking a new life away from his memories, but the fishing wasn't for him. He married with my cousin Sheena and took her away back to Laorig with him. Glad she was to go, for this is a hard life for a woman."

"How long did they stay here?" asked Morag. Elspeth had said nothing of her mother's death or her father's remarriage.

"The lassie would have been about five or six years old when they came. Her father took them back to Laorig in the summer of her ninth year. I was a strapping loon then but I mind I always had a fondness for the wee lassie. She had a quaint look on her. Ye couldna' tell her a lie," he cackled.

"You still can't," said Dougal and exchanged a rueful smile with Morag.

They celebrated Christmas with a good meal and some prayers around the fire in Willie's house, but for

Hogmanay Willie took himself off to Durness where he still had kin. Dougal and Morag cuddled close as the weather grew stormy. Morag gazed into driftwood fires and dreamed the sweet dreams of any expectant mother. She and Dougal argued about naming the child. He wanted a son to be named for himself or his father, with perhaps Morag's father's name included. She would have none of it. "A new life, we're making, Dougal and we should give our bairn a new name too. Perhaps Willie for the bodach? He would be gey happy at that."

"Aye, so he would. But we should take the best of the old life into the new. And if we have a lassie I would like fine to call her for my mother – or yours," he said.

They still hadn't made up their minds when Willie returned from Durness. He brought them New Year gifts. A fine knife for Dougal and an ivory comb for Morag.

"How beautiful, Willie," she cried. "Wherever did you get it?"

"There was a seafaring mannie staying with my cousin, Robert. I think he has an eye to Robert's daughter. He told us wonderful tales of his travels, no doubt trying to impress her. He said these were made from the bones of a sea monster bigger than their boat. It blew water from its back in a spout and they chased it with metal poles called harpoons until they could spear and kill it." He laughed. "That'd be right. The weaver of tales had two of these and gave one to Vhairi, Robert's daughter. Robert frowned on that so to make less of the gift he offered me the other one. 'For my sweetheart' he said and the company laughed. 'Aye, that'll be right', I said and little did they know I meant it. So here you are sweetheart girl of mine."

Morag's eyes shone at the story and at the gift. "Thank you, Willie," she cried. "I will treasure it always."

"And of course, being a faery woman you must keep your word," said Willie.

"What's this?" cried Dougal.

"I met with the one who saw you on the hill," said Willie. Morag's eyes grew huge. She held her breath. "Seems he told the tale to everyone he met. How he had seen the red-haired woman appear, as if by magic right before his eyes, where no-one had been before. She stood there above him and there were flames in her hair and then she disappeared. He had crossed himself and said a rosary in case it was an ill-omen, but seemingly all has gone well in his life since that day and he is mightily pleased with himself. Some say he was drunk, but others half believe him. One or two have gone to that spot hoping for a sighting, but with no luck." The old man chuckled. "Be calm in your heart, lassie. No-one knows you are here."

With that Morag had to be content. She put it out of her mind and made ready for the birth of her child. As the months went by, Peggy Campbell made it her business to visit regularly in spite of the hard weather. Usually she would not have ventured to the kirk in mid-winter for there wasn't enough daylight to make the journey from home and back in one day. But when she was offered shelter overnight at the solmar, she made the trip on a regular basis and her presence was both a joy and a comfort to Morag as her time drew near. Dougal had Willie for company and blether, such as men do, and now Morag had Peggy. All was well.

With love and pride Dougal looked across at his wife. For wife she was to him now. They had been handfast for a year according to custom and now she carried his child. The union was binding, recognised by all, including his kinfolk – should he ever meet with them again. She looked up from the stool where she sat sewing. By its size her work must be something for the coming child for she used the finest of the bone needles he had made her and the stuff between her hands would certainly not fit Dougal, not even as a new bonnet. He smiled at the thought and she returned his smile then lowered her head again to see her stitches in the light of the driftwood fire. His heart swelled with pride in this girl-wife. Despite all her worries and the alarms which kept them constantly alert, she was so brave. And who can measure courage without it is accompanied by fear?

He remembered with awe their first coming together. He had had many lasses before her, young as he was. For he knew he was comely. As a child it had been his bane. 'Mam's wee lassie' his brothers had called him, jeering at his prettiness. And it was true their mother had longed for a girl child all the time she carried him.

He hated his fine features and Catriona Mackay had barely stayed her son's hand when he snatched up his brother's dirk and tried to duplicate the fearsome scar Andra carried as memento of a skirmish some years past.

"Have patience, laddie," she cautioned. "You'll not always feel the same about your bonnie face."

And of course she had been right. Once he was of an age when lassies were interesting he had only to give them a glinting look from his laughing eyes and they were only too willing to roll with him in the hay at the shieling, during harvest, or creep into a corner of the byre in winter. But he was careful never to break a heart or give a promise.

He had never been any lassie's first man until Morag. At the memory his heart swelled, even his breathing deepened. It had been so unexpected. She was more than willing, but untutored, following only the natural desire of her urgent young body. But he had never felt so powerful, so strong and yet so gentle towards her. The carefree couplings of his earlier days were like a puppy playing heedlessly in the sunlight. This union with Morag was so much more. From that moment they were bound together, until only death could separate them.

He watched the firelight outline the swell of her expanding belly. There under her heart she cherished his child. Son or daughter it made no matter. This child created out of this almost holy love her felt for Morag would be the greatest blessing God could bestow on them. And one day they would find a priest to bless their union and baptise the child.

Dougal had never thought to become a fisherman and salter, but now he knew what to do he was prepared to make a good life for them all. The houses here were a bonus they hadn't looked for when they left Elspeth. There was room and to spare for a growing family and perhaps this year he could buy Morag a few of the pretty sheep she prized so much. She had her spinning wheel but nothing with which to use it. Dougal smiled as he gazed into the fire and saw how it would be here in the future as their family and livestock grew.

Mackay's Hotel 2011

Claire knew there could be no turning back after the events at Balnakiel. She was absolutely convinced that Angus loved her, deeply and passionately. Her heart raced when he held her and the blood grew hot and heavy in her veins. This was for her. Of that she had no doubt. The kiss shared on the headland of the Golf Course; the comfort of his strong body as he soothed her distress; all this she wanted for the rest of her life. And everything else that would come when he confessed he loved her too.

But since their return on that day Angus had treated her if possible even more like a young niece to be indulged and he the kind uncle. Claire ground her teeth in frustration. What could she do?

Her first ploy was to get Fiona on side. Claire knew Angus's mother was always to be found in the hotel office after the breakfasts were finished. One morning Claire timed her arrival at the hotel to catch her there. But when she questioned Fiona about Angus's reticence his mother shook her head. 'No, Claire, I'm sorry I can't help you. This is something you and Angus have to work out together.'

'But I love him, Fiona,' Claire paced the length of the office then swung round to plead with Angus's mother again. 'You must help me. I know he loves me too, but he just won't say it, or show it. Why?'

'I love him too,' said Fiona. 'But he's a grown man and cannot be forced into anything he believes is wrong.'

'Wrong? How can loving someone be wrong? Am I so bad?'

'Of course not. I'm sorry to be so clumsy.' Fiona was distressed at having upset Claire. 'You see. I knew I shouldn't have said anything at all. And now I've made it worse.' She took the younger woman by the hand. 'Speak to him, Claire. I can't help him in the dark place he has put himself. Perhaps you are the only person on earth who can. Help my boy, my dear, and I shall be eternally grateful.' She squeezed Claire's hand then wiped away a tear she couldn't prevent and hurried from the room.

Claire went out into the hotel garden and made her way to the sheltered summerhouse where she had sat with Angus. It seemed so long ago. She nibbled on her thumb nail as she pondered her present situation. Obviously there was something about Angus she didn't know. Something in his past? Fiona knew but wouldn't talk about it. Was that because she was ashamed? No! Fiona had never shown any signs of being ashamed of anything Angus had said or done, now or in his past. So what? She said he was in a dark place - but he had put himself there. Why would anyone do that? Shame? No! She would rule that out. Guilt? But why? Claire gazed up the loch seeking inspiration from the still water. On the far side below the banks that rose steeply the water was dark and took on a menacing appearance. Who knew what lay beneath the placid surface? A bit like Angus really. And that brought her back to the beginning.

She looked down at her ruined nail. She had gnawed off all the clear polish she habitually wore these day. She shook her head and got to her feet. A line of Gilbert and Sullivan sang through her mind 'none but the brave deserve the fair'. Well she had to be brave and hope Angus would be fair to her, even if that wasn't exactly what the song had meant.

'Angus, will you please take me to Oldshoremore?' she asked in her sweetest tone.

Angus frowned. He didn't mind taking her anywhere she wanted to go, but he remembered their last visit when she had behaved so strangely. 'Are you sure you want to go back?' he said

'Yes. It was so beautiful and I do want to go again.'

'Very well. We can go this afternoon if you like.' After all that last visit was months ago when she hadn't know of her parentage. Perhaps she had sensed something strange and not known how to deal with it?

'May I drive?' Claire smiled and held out her hand as she asked. Lately she had often driven the Mondeo. Soon she would have her own car and be independent. Angus had mixed feelings about that day.

'Why not?' he said and handed over the keys.

Once the car was parked they made their way up beside the graveyard wall onto the dunes and down the wooden steps to the beach. Claire kicked off her sandals and ran ahead. She would find the perfect spot. Angus followed more slowly and watched her with an aching heart. Once she no longer needed him to chauffeur her around there would be little need for them to spend time together. He could tend to his duties at The Big House and make sure he didn't run into Claire too often. He had to . . . for his own sake. Being with her and not touching her was a torture he could barely endure. He constantly schooled his expression and guarded his tongue. Since he had held her at Balnakiel she had said nothing more to him on the subject. But sometimes he saw a look of hurt in her eyes and the guilt he felt attacked him again. He felt torn between his need and the determination to keep her safe.

Claire had chosen an indent into the dunes at the top of the beach. The tide was on the turn and small ripples ran across the hard flat surface. Each one reached just a fraction higher up the beach than the last. They spread like a frill of lace upon the sand. It was a process she could watch for hours, but not today. She sat with her back to the dune sheltered from the wandering breeze that usually blew here. She patted the sand at her side. 'Come and sit, Angus. Isn't this view glorious?'

'Aye, it's bonnie enough. But you know you can see better and farther from higher up.'

'I think we're in just the right place,' she said and pushed the car keys deep into her pocket. She was determined they would not leave this spot until she had the answers to her questions. 'Now turn round and face me. Can you sit cross-legged?'

He laughed 'Yes. I don't think I am so stiff and ancient yet that I can't manage that. Like this do you mean?'

'Exactly.' Claire sat herself facing Angus. Short of staring over each other's shoulders there was no escaping looking into each other's eyes, or at each other's faces at least. No hiding of expressions now. 'Angus.' She waited until she was sure of his attention then, 'I love you,' she said. 'Do you love me?'

The statement was unexpected and the question even more so. Without volition Angus told the truth. 'Yes. That is . . . I mean . . . I don't . . .'

Claire held up her hand. 'Stop right there. I asked. You answered. So why are you now trying to wriggle out of it?'

'I'm not. That is . . . oh, hell, Claire, what have you done?'

'Got the answer I wanted and needed,' she said triumphantly. 'We love each other so nothing else matters. Now we know where we stand.'

'No, we don't,' Angus said savagely. 'You don't know what you've done. I can't love you.'

Claire frowned. 'Why not? You say you can't love me but you do. It doesn't make sense.'

'Not to you perhaps but you just have to trust me on this. I can't love you.'

'That's silly,' she burst out. The hurt he had inflicted made her eyes sting but she was determined not to lose her argument with tears. 'You can't *not* love me, can you? I know you can't because I couldn't stop myself loving you if I tried till Doomsday, and I think it's the same with you.'

Angus groaned and hung his head. She was right. How could he get her to understand it was for her sake he was denying himself, denying both of them. 'It's a long story,' he said.

'Fine,' her tone was short, her lips tightened as she made a performance of sitting back against the sand. 'I've got plenty of time and you're going nowhere until we've sorted this out.'

Claire's heart raced. She clenched her hands into fists to stop them shaking. Whatever the next few minutes would bring could change her life completely. Her whole happiness, and Angus's, rested in what he said and how she accepted or refuted it. She must persuade him that loving her was the only option. He had to love her. He just had to. Anything else was unacceptable, unthinkable. 'Go on then,' she swallowed on a suddenly dry mouth. 'What's so dreadful about loving me?'

Angus sighed raised his eyes and looked at Claire. He shook his head. His heart was heavy. The last thing he would ever want to do was hurt her. In spite of the belligerent tone of voice and the aggressive angle of her small upturned head, he was not deceived. She had pushed her fists into her pockets but there was tension in every line of her body. He saw the faint quiver of her chin and his heart broke. She was on the verge of losing control but her courage wouldn't let her give in. He sighed again. 'Very well, here goes. The story of my life.' His lips quirked in a grimace of self-mockery.

'I was a very lucky youth. I had a good home, friends and parents. God had given me enough brains to do well in my studies and my folks made sure I towed the line and applied myself. Everything in the garden was rosy. I even had the girl of my dreams. Ishbel.' He paused remembering Ishbel. 'She was a wilful, wild child and grew into a headstrong young woman. But no-one could deny Ishbel. Everyone loved her and fell under her spell. She could have had any of the fellows around, but chose me. Her hair was as fiery as her temper. We argued and quarrelled and kissed and made up more times than I can count. But we always knew it was meant that we should be together. We got engaged and everyone was happy for us. It was no more than they expected.'

If Angus's tale was unwelcome news to Claire she gave no sign but concentrated on his face watching every expression of regret and affection.

'One day she told me we were going to a dance up at Durness. I told her I couldn't go. The hotel was busy and I had to work. That was alright, she said, we'd go after I was free.' Angus shook his head. 'I don't know what got into me. We'd done that before. I'd finish at the hotel and then we'd go up to the dance but that day I was particularly tired. The hotel was full and we were all working flat out and long hours. She just rubbed me the wrong way. It was like she was ordering me about. There was no question of would I like to do this. She said we would go and that was that. I said no, again. I was too tired. We'd been busy. It was all very well for her, she didn't have to work like I did. And so on, and so on, until we were having a right royal row. She flounced off and I went to work.' Angus paused, closed his eyes and gathered himself for what came next. 'It wasn't the first row we'd had. We always used to make it up. But that was the last time I saw her . . . alive.'

Claire's gasp of dismay broke the silence that followed his words. She reached for his hand in quick sympathy. 'What happened?' she breathed.

'She went to the dance with one of the tourists she'd met at the Seamen's Mission where she occasionally helped out. He had a motor bike. I suppose they had a good time but he had drink with his. It probably gave him a feeling of invincibility. Perhaps he was showing off? Who knows? On the way back, not knowing the roads, he went too fast round a bend and skidded. He escaped with a broken leg but Ishbel was thrown off the bike and killed instantly, they said, as her head hit a rock beside the road.' He raised pain-filled eyes to Claire. 'If only I'd agreed to go to the dance she wouldn't have died. I took such care of her.' His voice broke.

Claire's eyes were full of sympathetic tears. She squeezed his hand. 'But it wasn't your fault. It was her choice to go and her escort chose to drink. None of that is to be laid at your door, Angus.'

'I know that now.' He paused as he remembered just how long it had taken for him to acknowledge the truth of it. 'It took some time but at last I forgave myself. After Ishbel died I couldn't bear to stay here. She's buried up there,' he jerked his head towards the churchyard they had passed on their way from the car park. 'The day we wandered around I visited her grave. It was the first time since I came back home. I felt at peace with her then but at first I saw her everywhere. She was so much a part of me and of everything here. There was nowhere we hadn't been together, no corner that didn't hold memories of her. So I had to get away,' he shrugged. 'I wasn't bothered where so Dada arranged for me to go and work in Switzerland at the hotel of one of his friends. It had always been on the cards that I would travel o other countries, work in other hotels and gain experience before I came home to take over here. After that I did a stint in France and then moved on to Mexico. Finally I ended up in Brazil – where I met Luzia.'

Claire's eyebrows rose in surprise. What did a Brazilian girl have to do with anything?

Angus smiled. 'She couldn't have been more different from Ishbel. Where Ishbel was quicksilver - flashing here and there, never still or settled, always on the go, impatient and wanting something new - Luzia was like melting chocolate, smooth and warm. Her lazy smile could dissolve an iceberg and her indolence was as soothing as the murmur of a burn. It was impossible to worry in her company. Everything would work out right, don't worry so. That was her motto.'

Gently he released his hand from Claire's grip. 'By the time I reached Brazil, I had come to terms with the loss of Ishbel. I never thought I could love again - until I met Luzia. She healed me and taught me how to appreciate life once more instead of just going through the motions. I loved her deeply.'

Claire frowned. A weight settled on her chest. 'Loved?' she whispered.

Angus bit his lip squared his shoulders and went on with his tale. 'All went well. I was accepted by her family as a possible son-in-law and arrangements were made for my parents to come out for a visit so that formalities could be completed for our betrothal – all very much more formal than back home,' he smiled briefly, remembering. 'There was also the question of Luzia being chaperoned in public – for form's sake at least – but we got around that. Then one day she had a headache. She'd been suffering from a cold but it was better. The headache persisted. It got worse by the hour. She was in such pain I couldn't bear it. I was helpless. I could do nothing for her. Twenty four hours later she was dead.' Angus's face was stony. He could still remember his incredulous disbelief when he heard those words. The world had gone mad. How could such a beautiful warm, healthy young woman be dead, and so quickly?

Claire was stunned. Whatever she had expected to hear from Angus on this beach it had not been a tale of such tragedy – double tragedy. 'How can that be?' she asked.

'It was meningitis. It all happened so quickly there was barely time for a diagnosis when the doctor arrived. She died in the ambulance on the way to the hospital.'

Claire shook her head. 'Poor Angus.'

'Aye, that's what I felt too, once I had taken in what had happened. I would have left Brazil after the funeral, but Luzia's family seemed to feel I was a contact with her. I couldn't leave them so we grieved together for a year. Then my father died and I came back to Scotland, to my mother and Mackay's'

'My poor love,' cried Claire and knelt up to take him in her arms. She wanted to comfort him but he held her off.

'Now do you see why I can't love you?'

She was puzzled, confused. 'No. What do you mean? Don't I measure up to them? Aren't I good enough?'

Then he did take hold of her to shake her, 'Don't be a fool. Of course you're good enough, no-one could be better. But I can't risk your life. I can't put you in such danger.'

For a moment she stared at him then started to laugh. Her laughter verged on hysteria but she managed to control it, pulled away from him and sat back on her heels. 'Angus Mackay! Are you telling me you're superstitious?'

He shook his head slowly. 'No. Not superstitious as you mean it, but you can't deny I bring ill-fortune to those I love.'

For a moment Claire was silent. How could she get through to him? 'And what does Fiona say to all this?'

He frowned. 'Mother? What does she have to do with it?'

'A great deal I should say. You love her and yet I think she would say you bring her great happiness – except, of course, when she's worrying about you.'

'That's different.'

'Of course it is. But you said anyone you loved. A pretty sweeping statement don't you think?' She saw his jaw set. He was going to be stubborn about this she could tell. He had nursed this sense of doom for so long. How could she persuade him to let it go? She sat quietly while her thoughts skittered around her head like frightened mice. She must conjure up all her arts of logic and reason. She bit her lip. This meant everything to her. At last she felt calm enough to speak. 'Angus, I am so sorry for your loss. I can see how you must have felt tragedy followed you around. First, Ishbel, then, Luzia, so far away, then your father. But none of those deaths are connected.'

'Except by me.'

'And your mother who loves you and grieves for you. She has a part in this story. But think. If you had been away from home Ishbel would still have gone to the dance with the guy on the motorbike. If you had never set foot in Brazil Luzia would still have died from meningitis. You didn't infect her, just as you didn't tell Ishbel to go to the dance without you. That was her wilful nature talking. You didn't cause your father's death either or are you claiming to have godly powers and can bring about these things from afar?'

He was shocked. 'Of course not.'

'Well, it seems very arrogant to me that you have claimed responsibility for two out of the three deaths that have occurred. That is hubris indeed if you didn't actually kill them.'

Angus looked thoughtful. A frown puckered his forehead. 'Do you know I never thought of it that way before?' In his heart hope stirred. 'Can I let myself really love you?' He looked with agonised eyes at the girl beside him. 'But if it happened again I should die too. I couldn't live if I brought harm to you. I love you so much.'

That was just what Claire wanted to hear but she couldn't let herself rejoice yet. 'Let's think of the worst scenario. We love each other and something happens. Perhaps I get run over.' She shushed him as he would speak. 'Or maybe something happens to you? That's how life is sometimes. Your father died far too young and your mother has been left alone. But do you think if she had known at the beginning how it would end she would have done anything differently? Their love gave her you and years of happiness together. No-one can take that away from her. Are you more of a coward than your mother, Angus? Are you going to let your fear deprive you - deprive me - of the happiness we can know? Please, Angus,' she begged, then waited. She had done all she could. She watched the expressions flit across his face as he went over all she had said. When he smiled at her she went weak with relief. She held out her arms and he drew her to him.

'Claire Frobisher,' he said, 'you don't know what you've got yourself into. You're stuck with me now, my love, for ever.'

Neither Claire nor Angus could hide their shining joy when they returned to Mackay's. They met Kirstie crossing the hall. 'Your mother's seeking you, Angus Mohr,' she said. Her eyes narrowed a she saw the smiling pair. Her head cocked to one side. 'Hmm. And what have you two been up to?' she queried. 'You'd best come clean. You know you can never keep a secret from your Mam.'

Angus laughed. 'Aye. I'll take your advice Kirstie. Where is Mam?'

'I last saw her in the office.'

'Okay. Thank you. Come on, Claire.' He grabbed Claire's hand and the two ran off giggling like a couple of bairns. Kirstie shook her head and smiled indulgently. It was good to see the boy she had known all his life was happy again. Long may it last. She looked over her shoulder and round the empty hall then made the sign of the horns to ward off evil spirits.

Fiona looked up from her computer as Angus and Claire erupted into her office. It took only one look for her to realise what had happened and her heart rejoiced. She sent up a silent prayer of thanks for the look on her son's face when his eyes met Claire's. And the flush on the young woman's cheeks told its own tale of happiness. Fiona stood up, came round the desk, hugged Claire and turned to Angus. Her throat closed with tears she was determined not to shed. She couldn't speak but reached her hand up to pull his head down to her and held him close, cheek to cheek. Angus's arms went round his mother and held her tight. He knew something of the anguish she had felt for his sufferings and now was grateful he could ease that burden off her heart. Gently he put her from him. 'Wise old owl, Mam?' he smiled.

Fiona's laugh was shaky. 'I'd need to be blind and stupid not to read the signs,' she said. 'What now? Are you going to . . .?' She paused and changed what she had been about to ask. '. . . go and tell Lady Ross your news?' Let the young people enjoy their love with no talk of engagements or future plans. For now, it was enough they had found each other.

And so it seemed. The good news flashed from one end of the loch to the other in the way news has of travelling in small communities. Angus stayed at Mackay's helping Fiona. Claire slept at the Big House delighting her aunt with her company. But it seemed if Angus was working at the House there was a message she must deliver to the Estate Office. Or she needed to call him in for a cup of coffee; or tell him her aunt wished to see him. He didn't complain and spent as many hours with her as he could.

The house in England sold quickly. Angus took a few days off and went with Claire to sort out what she wished to keep that must be sent up to her new home. Beanie travelled back with them in the comfort of the Mondeo and settled into the Big House with surprisingly little bother. On the face of it everything in the garden was rosy.

Why then did Fiona notice dark circles under Claire's eyes? For a day or two she said nothing but worry creased her forehead again. One morning she came on Claire huddled in front of the fire in the drawing room at the hotel. Angus had left early for Inverness to meet a visitor off the night train from London. Claire gazed into the flames with such a sad look on her face. Fiona was concerned.

'Claire?' she said gently. There was no response. 'Claire,' she said more loudly and touched the young woman's shoulder. There was no startled jump or exclamation. Claire just turned her head gradually and it seemed to Fiona her blank eyes focussed so slowly it was as though she was returning from far away. 'Are you alright, my dear?'

Claire didn't reply at once but nodded and reached to hold Fiona's hand as it rested on her shoulder. 'I'll be alright. I just need Angus. Where is Angus?' Fiona reminded her where he had gone. 'Of course. He did tell me. I wish he'd come back soon. I must talk to him. I must tell him. I'm sorry.' She gave Fiona a weak smile then stood up and drifted out of the room.

Fiona stood looking after her. What did it mean? Why did Claire seem so sad and why had she said sorry? What was she going to say to Angus on his return? Fiona's hand went to her mouth in distress. Not more heartache for her boy? No, please, not that.

'I'm sorry, Angus.' Claire's eyes were strained as she looked up into his face. They were sitting in the summerhouse looking up the loch. She had lain in wait for his arrival back from Inverness and waylaid him as soon as he had passed the new guest into Fiona's capable hands. 'I don't want to keep you from your work but if I don't tell you soon, I think my head will burst.' Her lip trembled.

Angus took her in his arms. 'What is it, darling? Don't look so sad.' He sat back in alarm as a thought struck him. 'It's not Lady Ross, is it? Is she unwell? Tell me quickly.'

'No. No. Aunt Nell is fine.' She watched him relax in relief. 'It's me.' Angus frowned. 'They've come back, Angus, and I don't understand it.'

'Who's come back?'

'Not who, what. The dreams are back and they're even more vivid than before. I'm remembering and . . . you're there. You're in my dreams, Angus.'

'I should hope so. If you're going to start dreaming about any other man I can tell you, love, I shall take a very dim view of it.' He smiled.

She beat his chest with her fists. 'Don't laugh. Don't joke about it. It's serious.'

'Sorry! What do you mean, you're remembering? Didn't you remember your dreams before?'

Claire shook her head in frustration. 'I don't mean that. I don't know what I mean. I think I'm going crazy.'

'Hey!' Angus took her by the shoulders and shook her gently. 'Come on now. Stop talking like that. Just calm down and try and tell me what it's all about. I'm sure we can sort it out between us.'

Claire took a deep breath. 'You remember I used to have dreams?' He nodded. 'They told me to come north, always north, and they brought me here. Once we knew about Aunt Nell and my mother I thought that was why I was brought here, or guided here - that I was meant to find out who I was. And the dreams stopped.'

'So you were right?'

'I thought so but they've started again - although now they're different.'

'How?'

'It's as though I'm living another life. And you're there too.'

'Well, I am here. But how do you mean another life? A dream is living another life, I suppose. The life of the subconscious.'

'No.' cried Claire. 'It's another life, but here, long ago. The scenery is the same but there are no houses and our clothes are wrong and . . . I don't understand. I am seeing things so clearly that I never knew about.'

'What things?'

'The clothes we wear and our house. It's made of stone with a turf and heather thatch roof. I helped you build it. Don't look at me like that. It's not a joke. I could tell you how to do it. How to lay every stone - to place the house on a slope so the muck from the byre at the end would drain away but the heat from the beasts rise in the winter to keep us snug and warm. Now where did that come from?' she demanded.

Angus shrugged. 'I don't know. But you did read a lot of books about Scotland when you first came here. You read about the cathedral in Dornoch being burnt.'

She shivered. 'I remember that.'

For a moment Angus wondered whether he should share with Claire the times he had seen the well-loved view without its roads and houses; about the time he too had seen the stone house with the heather thatch roof. But of what use would it be to her? She seemed so agitated by what she had experienced whereas he had always been soothed by his 'vision'. So he tried to comfort her. 'So you probably picked up this knowledge from those or from seeing Braveheart,' he suggested.

Claire sighed and shook her head. 'You don't understand,' she said. 'You don't believe me . . . and I don't blame you.'

Angus wrapped her in his arms. 'I think,' he said, kissing her forehead, 'you've been running on adrenalin for too long and now you're having a reaction. We've had such lovely excitement and then there were two long car journeys and sorting out the house in between. You're exhausted, darling. A couple of good nights' sleep is what you need and perhaps some fresh air first to help you get off. I'm going to take the rest of the day and we'll go for a good walk up Foinavon. The weather is fine and though we won't get to the top because the days are too short now we'll have some good exercise and lovely views. And tonight you'll sleep like a baby,' he promised her.

Claire put her arm around his waist as they walked back to the house. She wished he could be right but knew it wasn't as simple as fresh air and exercise. If only she knew why she was dreaming again? But there seemed no answer. She was so happy with her aunt, in love with a wonderful man, accepted into her new life. What was the dream trying to tell her this time?

Over the next few weeks Angus thought he had soothed his love's alarms. They were always happy to be together and she joined in preparations for Christmas and New Year with enthusiasm. But Fiona and Lady Ross noticed that when Angus wasn't around the worried look of strain returned to Claire's face and her shoulders slumped. As soon as he appeared she straightened up and smiled a loving welcome but the two women knew she was hiding something from him.

'Do you think she needs a tonic?' Lady Ross asked Fiona one day as the two sat in the Blue Drawing Room at the Big House. A roaring fire supplemented the central heating because, her ladyship said, 'it was so comforting'. 'I know she's not sleeping well. I even had Beanie in here demanding some action.' She looked across at Fiona with a meaning smile.

'At least she knows who's boss round here,' commented Fiona with a grin. 'How is it all working out with Miss Benton?'

'For Heaven's sake, Fiona, call her Beanie. Even I do that now. It has worked out surprisingly well. I feared there might be some friction but apparently Eilidh, who is very fond of Claire, has taken a liking to Beanie who tells her all about Claire's childhood. You know Eilidh. She has to know everything there is to know about The Family. But even Beanie doesn't have the answer to what ails our Claire now.'

'Angus thought she had filled her head with tales of long ago and they surfaced in her dreams. He seems quite happy to believe it will pass.'

'Of course he does,' snorted Lady Ross, 'because she never lets him see her anything but smiling and ready to join in all his ploys for the holidays. Perhaps she should go and see Lachlan. He's a good lad and getting a fine reputation.'

Fiona smiled. She knew why Annabelle Ross wanted her niece to visit Angus's friend rather than call in the local GP. 'That's quite a good idea. He could give her a general going over. Dr Henderson would probably give her a bottle or a pill and assure her she must be pregnant as in his opinion all pregnant women have strange fancies.'

The two were laughing at the elderly doctor's well-known pronouncements when Claire walked in. She smiled at them. 'Hello, Fiona. You sound happy which is more than can be said of your other visitor, Aunt Nell.'

'What visitor, my dear?'

'The baby. I don't know why its mother doesn't do something about it. I've been hearing it crying for the last half hour. As it's not in here, is it a friend of Eilidh's? Perhaps I should go to the kitchen and see what's wrong. I'll see you later, Fiona. I'm coming to pick Angus up in my new car,' she smiled proudly, 'Aunt Nell gave it to me and I love it. I want to show it off to him. Bye.' She went out of the room and left two puzzled women behind her.

'I didn't hear a baby,' said Fiona.

'Nor I,' said Lady Ross, 'and it would be very unusual if Eilidh was having visitors without telling me of it. It must be someone arrived on the spur of the moment. I wonder who? Who has a young child now?'

They searched their memories but neither could come up with the identity of a local woman with a young babe.

In Eilidh's kitchen Claire had no better luck. 'But you must have heard it, Eilidh,' cried Claire. 'The poor wee thing's been crying piteously for the past half hour. If it's not here perhaps one of the maids has got a visitor?' But the maids' whereabouts and companions were all accounted for. Claire began to get annoyed. 'This is ridiculous,' she said. 'I didn't imagine it so where is the wretched child? Gone presumably as I can't hear it any more but to pretend there never was one is just stupid.' She flounced out of the kitchen and the house and got into her beloved new car. Perhaps a drive along the coast would put her in a better temper.

She drove down the lochside up the brae past the hotel and down through Kinlochbervie where she took the fork to Oldshoremore. Since her first visit with Angus she had loved this spot. They had returned many times since he had admitted he loved her. Soon she was walking along the beach breathing in the bracing air. She felt her taut muscles relax and decided to go right to the end, scramble over the rocks and climb to the highest point of the islet. From its summit she could look all around.

Starting from the machair above the beach behind her she turned her head to take in the views of the road and the scattered houses, then the coast and out to sea. She scanned the horizon until her eyes reached the rocky coastline on her right. She smiled. This place was the best medicine anyone could need. She sat down and hugged her knees. Her thoughts wandered over the past happy weeks with Angus and their preparations for Christmas. What would the new year bring? Where would they live when they got married – for married they would be. Neither of them had said the word but they both knew it would happen when they were ready. She had just wondered if Aunty Cyn and Uncle Ernest would come up for the ceremony when she heard the baby cry.

She looked round for the family or mother and child. It was unusual for anyone to be on this beach so late in the year. In fact now she felt quite chilled. She shivered and stood up still seeking the child who had cried but there was no-one in sight. Claire shrugged. They must be up on the machair in a dip in the ground and the breeze had blown the sound to her ears. She strolled back along the beach at the edge of the water where foam tipped each ripple with froth as it crept across the sand.

When she reached the entrance to the hotel Claire turned the car up the brae. She would phone Aunt Nell to tell her she was going to have her dinner here with Fiona and Angus. Then later she would go back and have a game of canasta with the older woman who had become so dear to her.

She met Fiona in the hall and invited herself for the evening meal sure of her welcome.

'Of course. That would be lovely, Claire. I think you'll find Angus through in the kitchen checking things with chef.'

Claire smiled. 'Poor chef. I'll go and drag Angus away.' She stopped with a half-smile on her face. 'What's with the babies today, Fiona? They're everywhere I go. Has this one just arrived? Perhaps if they all cry as much as the ones I've heard today you may never get a grandchild,' she teased and disappeared in the direction of the hotel kitchen.

Fiona stood in the hall listening. She could hear no baby crying. Which wasn't surprising as there was no-one with a baby checked into the hotel. She frowned as she remembered Claire vowing she had heard a child crying at the Big House. But no-one else had heard it. What did this mean? A guest approached with a question and Fiona put the matter out of her head.

But it was a question Claire began to ask herself. Everywhere she went it seemed a baby cried. By the third day this happened she was beside herself. She vowed to tear the Big House apart if the child was not produced for her to see. Like a thing possessed she raged through the house opening all doors. Now and then she stopped to listen and then ran on. At last she finished by Lady Ross's chair. 'You can't hear it, Aunt Nell, can you?' she cried. She grabbed two fistfuls of her hair and dragged her head from side to side. 'Am I going mad? What's happening to me?'

Lady Ross put out a hand to restrain her. 'Stop it, Claire. Control yourself.' Her stern voice had good effect for Claire's hands dropped to her lap and she burst into tears. Lady Ross patted her shoulder and drew the sobbing girl towards her until Claire could rest her weary head on her aunt's knee. 'Don't fret, my dear. We'll get to the bottom of this - together. You're not alone. Have you told Angus what you hear?'

Claire shook her head. 'He already thinks I've lost the plot with my dreams,' she said. 'I don't want to worry him any more.'

'I think you should tell him. Don't shut him out. I also think he should take you to Inverness to see his friend Lachlan who will give you a thorough physical.'

Claire took her aunt's advice. Angus was shocked and a little angry she had suffered in silence and let him think she was alright. 'I feel a right eejit,' he said, 'bobbing merrily along in a Fool's Paradise. Promise me, darling, you'll not keep secrets from me again, 'specially if they are worrying you.'

'I promise and I'm glad to. I hated trying to hide my troubles from you. But I know you don't believe me and I don't blame you.'

He took her by the shoulders and looked into her eyes. 'I believe that you believe and that's good enough for me. We'll get Lachy to give you the once over and if there's nothing medically wrong we'll have to think again.'

'Strong as a horse and fit as a flea,' was Dr Lachlan's verdict once he had given Claire a battery of tests urged on by Angus. 'Of course I can't say as much for your brain,' he joked, then stopped and looked closely at his patient as distress showed on her face. 'What is it, Claire? Do you think you might have something wrong with your brain? Have you any symptoms?'

She shook her head. 'Not my brain as such, Lachlan. It's my mind that's playing tricks on me.' And she told him from the very beginning of the strange dreams, imaginings and visions she had had ever since coming to Scotland.

'And you came north to Mackay's on the strength of those dreams?'

'Yes.'

'Well that turned out alright, didn't it?'

'Yes,' she said and reached for Angus's hand. 'It made me the happiest person in the world.'

'So if that has been achieved and now the dreams are back, what do they want you to do this time?'

Claire's face shone as she beamed at Lachlan. 'You believe me, don't you?' she said.

'Obviously. You aren't in the habit of telling lies, are you?'

She laughed. 'No. Of course not. But I don't know what I'm supposed to do this time. The dreams seem to be of Mackay's, or at least that spot. I am content but with a small weight on my heart. Angus is with me and life is good. I don't feel any urge to move on.'

'What else is happening now, then?'

'There is the crying baby.'

'When do you hear it . . . during the dream?'

'No. Never. It's in the daytime – everywhere. But I can never find it and no-one else can hear it.'

'So the baby would seem not to be associated with Mackay's even if you've heard it there. I think that is your answer.'

'What?'

'Find the baby.'

'But I've looked. It's never there. I'm sure now it's not a real baby, not of this world.'

Lachlan shook his head. 'That is your answer, though. Find the baby. Listen to your heart, think of your dreams, but do it gently. Let the knowledge come to you and I'm sure it will. I do believe there is a reason for what is happening to you, though I can't explain it and most of my colleagues would think I'd flipped.'

Claire took Lachlan's hand. 'Thank you, thank you, Lachlan. You've made me feel so much better. I'm going to do just what you said. I'll relax and let it happen. Perhaps when I hear the baby cry next time I should ask it to show me the way,' she laughed.

'Do that,' said Lachlan.

On their way home, a more contented Claire quizzed Angus. 'Did you think Lachlan would believe me? Is that why you agreed with Aunt Nell?'

Angus smiled. 'I wasn't sure what he would say or do but I knew if there was nothing physically wrong with you he would keep an open mind.'

'How?'

'Lachie's grandmother had 'the sight'.'

'You mean second sight?'

'Aye. And apparently a very uncomfortable gift it can be too. But it means his mind accepts things that happen which other folk might dismiss as nonsense.'

'I am glad you took me to see him, darling. I feel so much calmer now.'

'Good. Always happy to be of service, ma'am,' he grinned.

'Eejit!'

The solmar 1572

'There are strangers at Baille na Cille.'

Peggy Campbell's words filled Morag's heart with fear and dread. 'Who are they? What do they want? Where have they come from?' she demanded.

'I ken not the answers to your questions, child. I but heard of them as I left the kirk and didn't want to appear too interested. Folk know my mind is usually upon my prayers at that time,' she smiled. 'I didn't want to rouse too much comment, but I think maybe Young Willie should go into Durness and listen to the *craic* there.'

'Are you recommending me to take drink, woman?' Willie cackled. 'For you ken fine the alehouse is where I'll be hearing all the details of any strangers.'

Peggy wagged a finger at him. 'Aye, that'll be right, Willie Sutherland,' she said. 'Just this once I must bless your visit and pray you will have good news for our girl on your return. These folk are probably some kind of pilgrim, come to visit the monks for a blessing. I did hear Dornoch mentioned, but that's nothing to get worried about,' she added quickly as Morag's face paled. 'You ken fine that Baille na Cille collects tithes from the rich farm land around here to support the Cathedral. After all it is the Bishop's summer residence. I'm told the tithes from the monks at Baille na Cille pay for all the candles used in the cathedral in Dornoch. Of course the money has to get there somehow and perhaps this party is here to fetch it. Is your father a religious man, my dear?' Peggy knew the whole of Morag and

Dougal's story. They had no secrets from this 'woman of great faith'.

In spite of her anxiety Morag's lips twitched with amusement at the thought of her father doing any errand for the priesthood he castigated as a band of thieves and robbers taking poor folk's money for their own aggrandisement. She shook her head. 'No. My father would not be about the cathedral's business. And is it so quickly restored then? We knew of the burning only – what is it now – two y ears ago?'

'Aye, you're right. But perhaps they are seeking funds for the rebuilding? It's no use wondering. Willie must go right away and find out more. I'll bide with you this night and wait on his arrival back before I set off home.'

Morag was grateful as always for Peggy's presence. The year had turned and soon her child would be born. The goodwife's presence always helped to calm Morag's fears, but this time she had stirred them up.

'Watch and pray, child, as the Good Book says,' counselled Peggy. 'Bring your fears before the Lord and He will provide.'

It was an anxious wait they had for Willie's return. When he arrived his face was grave. 'I know not for certain if they are your kinsmen, Morag. I found them reticent in their answers to any questions. Not put by me,' he hastened to add, 'but there is always a general interest in travellers. They said they came from Laorig which is on the borders of Mackay country,' he went on, looking across at Dougal. 'But they are no kin to any folk I ever heard of when I was back there. My belief is they do come from Dornoch way and don't want to tell the fact for fear of the Mackays.'

'Why are they here?' said Peggy.

'Business with the monks is what they said. You may be right,' he nodded to her. 'Funds for the rebuilding. But there are two groups together. The men I saw in the alehouse were the type who would bear arms for their lord, but I'm told there were three who might be scribes or townsmen. They bided with the monks and didn't come into the township. I believe the three I saw were guards or protectors for the others' journey.'

'What were they like?' demanded Morag.

'All fairly young,' said Willie.

Morag relaxed with a smile. No-one could call her father young.

'But they were gey interested in the woman with the red hair,' went on Willie and Morag sat forward in alarm.

'Who told them of me?'

'You know what it's like lassie – or no, perhaps you don't. When men get together and drink is taken they start to blether.'

'Tell lies to each other, more like,' said Peggy severely.

'Wheesht! woman. I'm trying to explain to the lassie. They'll tell visitors, travellers and the like, of anything that makes their town or smoke better than another. And that's how they came to speak of you. They were boasting no doubt that their visitors didn't have such a vision in their part of the country.'

Morag wrung her hands. 'How I wish I had never been so foolish.'

'Be calm, child,' said Peggy. ''Tis just man's talk over the alepots.'

'Not so, mistress,' said Willie. 'These strangers questioned closely on the subject of the red-haired woman and determined to see her for themselves. They intend to get up an expedition. They were laughing when they said it, but there was a strength of purpose in their eyes. I believe they will not rest until they find us here,' finished Willie soberly.

Morag wrung her hands. 'What can we do?' she cried. 'If, as I fear, they are my brothers then they will kill you, Dougal. Aye, and me too no doubt - even Willie for helping us.' She cradled the bulk of her belly in her arms. 'My child!' she cried. 'I must save my child. We must hide. But where?' She looked around wildly as if the answer would come to her seeking eyes.

Up to this point Dougal had been quiet, listening to the talk. Now he leaned forward. 'I have had enough,' he said. The other three looked at him in surprise. 'We have run ever since I was wounded and I will run no more. My child shall live in one place and my woman will not fear her own shadow.'

'Fine words, boyan,' said Willie. 'But what do you intend to do about it? Kill the lot of them? I think there would be others coming after if you did that.'

Dougal smiled. 'I'll not kill them,' he said. 'I will kill us.'

'What?'

'You're mad, I'll not let you hurt the lassie!'

Willie and Peggy spoke as one, but Dougal turned to Morag. 'Well, *mo grabh?'*

For a moment she looked puzzled, then smiled. 'How?' she said.

'When these men arrive here, as they will, for the place is known, they will find Willie. Folks have seen me with Willie and taken me for his kin. He need neither confirm nor deny it, for they'll not ask him. They must find everything in place just as though we had stepped out for a breath of air, and an anxious, even grieving Willie. He saw us go out into the bay in the boat, saw you, Morag, fall over the side and as I reached to haul you back in the boat turned over and we were both lost.'

'But surely they'll search the beach for our bodies?' said Morag.

'Nay, lassie,' interrupted Willie, quite taken up with the story. 'The tide was on the ebb at the time and all folks hereabout know how swift the current makes around the headland. Your corpses might appear months hence along the coast or never. It's a good tale, laddie and I believe it will do fine,' he went on. 'And when they're gone you can come back.'

Dougal shook his head. 'No, old friend. We can never come back. This must be the final end of our wanderings. There must be no doubt we have perished or we will never know a moment's peace for the rest of our days.'

'I thought you could hide over yonder towards the kyle. Peggy Campbell could show you the path to the water's edge. They'd not go that far seeking you if they thought you dead.'

'But if I then turned up with you in Durness, it would be all over the country in the wink of an eye. You know how stories travel, and I have no mind to spend the rest of my life in hiding.'

'I'll miss you sorely and never see your child,' said the old man sadly. 'But you are right. Where will you go?'

'I don't know. I thought perhaps, with your permission Mistress Campbell, we might accompany you across to the ocean. Now I have learned to fish I can keep my family from starving if I am near the sea.'

'Come with me and welcome,' said Peggy, 'but you should not bide long. News travels as fast along the West as the North coast and there are several smokes in the area I live.'

'If you will take us with you, we'll not make any trouble for you, but journey on once we're across the water.'

'Aye, laddie. You say so. But your wife is heavy with child and cannot move far or fast. How much time have we got?' she asked Willie.

'They will not move this night for they had much drink taken and no-one would guide them for fear of boggarts or the red-haired woman herself. The morn's morn they are bidden to the kirk for some heavy work, for I heard them grumble they were not garrons,' Willie grinned. 'I believe the earliest they might come would be the day following for they are to return back to Laorig by the Sabbath.'

'Then we must leave tomorrow,' cried Dougal. 'We will set everything up to look normal, leave the fire heaped up with peats against our return. There must be food in the pot and porridge too. Our winter stores must be left behind, except for those we can take without it showing.'

'I'll not leave my spinning wheel,' cried Morag. 'Dougal, please don't make me. Elspeth gave it to me and no-one knows I have it.' She looked beseechingly at her husband.

He smiled at her. 'I'll not ask you to make that sacrifice as there will be so many more. Your best clothes must stay and cooking pots, the bowls and platters I have made you. They must believe we intended to return.' He looked at Willie. 'What about the boat?'

'Dinna fret,' grinned Willie. 'Lang syne I let it be known we have two fine boats now, since you came to work with me.' He had the grace to look sheepish. 'Perhaps I wanted to boast a bittie. I made no mention of Morag, but they believe you brought your own boat with you. When the locals see only one pulled up at the beach it will add to our story.'

Peggy shook her head. 'The Lord is merciful to you Willie Sutherland for your lies have wrought a good thing. So be it. Now pack up the things you wish to take with you, and Dougal shall carry them to the kyle with me. Thank the good Lord there is a fine moon this night. I will take them across and those I cannot carry farther I shall hide until we come again. The morn's morn, Dougal, bring the rest of the things you are taking to the crossing place and hide them close by. When I return we shall both be able to help Morag to walk to the boat. Once I have taken her to the other side there will be little need for haste. She may rest as often as necessary until we get to my home.'

'But where will we go after that?' queried Morag. 'You say we may not stay near you, so where shall it be?'

For a moment Peggy Campbell didn't answer. She closed her eyes and they saw her lips moving, then for a long time she stayed quiet. At last she smiled and opened her eyes. 'The good Lord has shown me a place that will be perfect for you. He minded me of a place my late husband knew of. South of where I stay a two-pronged sea loch goes far inland, pointing to the eternal hills. There is a shelf high above the water, a piece of flat land Nature cut out of the hill. And at the far end a cave. That will be your home. You can clear the slopes to grow the seed I shall give you, and rear hens and sheep. The waters teem with fish and the rocks with shellfish. The Lord will provide for you and your descendants.'

'Do you have the sight?' said Morag fearfully.

Peggy shook her head. 'I prefer to say that the Lord shows me what He will. You must track south until you find the loch. There you will find your home. Come now, Dougal,' she went on, 'hurry and choose what you will take and what leave for the day is far advanced and night will soon fall.'

When their bundles were ready, she kissed Morag and blessed her. 'I will return by noon the morn's morn and take you to safety before anyone can arrive. Have faith, my dear and be of good cheer'.

Mackay's Hotel 2011

Once she had told Angus what had been troubling her Claire calmed down. She no longer felt her nerves stretched to breaking point. She had put everything into words and that had seemed to make sense – somehow. At night she slept without dreaming and during the day she no longer strained her ears for the cry of a baby.

Angus said nothing about her 'fancies' but daily watched to see if she was agitated. As she showed no signs of being upset he almost managed to forget she'd told him how he was involved in her dreams. If he had wondered about it he would probably have dismissed it all as part of the excitement of finding her true parentage. Since moving into Bervie Lodge everything had been strange and new. She had adapted marvellously, but had it taken its toll?

One morning Claire came to Mackay's and told Angus she had heard the baby cry again. His heart sank

'Darling, I thought you'd got over all that,' he said, pulling her into his arms and holding her tight.

Claire moulded herself to him for a pleasurable moment then gently released his hold on her. 'Dear Angus, you've tried so hard to bear with me over this. I do appreciate it because I know you don't believe a word of it. But please humour me. I could do it on my own but you asked me not to shut you out and I really would prefer you to come with me.'

'Where?'

'Back to the solmar.'

'But Claire, why do you want to go back there? It made you sad last time. You said something bad happened there.'

'I know I did and I don't know what it was that happened. But when the baby cried yesterday I tried to do what Lachlan said.'

Silently Angus cursed his old friend. 'And what was that?'

'To be still and sort of ask the baby what was the matter.'

'And you got an answer?' Angus tried not to sound incredulous.

'Not really. Not then, but this morning when it cried again I just concentrated and I felt the need to go to the solmar. Will you come with me, Angus darling? Please.'

'Of course I'll come. I'd go anywhere you wanted me to.' And take care of her if she should have another strange 'attack' he promised himself When they got back he would phone Lachlan and ask his advice about getting hold of a good psychiatrist. Perhaps someone Lachlan knew in Edinburgh would be able to help dispel these troubling dreams?

'Are you feeling alright?' Angus asked Claire as they left the Golf Club Car Park and headed for the solmar. 'Can you hear the baby? Does this seem the right thing to do?' For himself he felt like an idiot chasing after a mythical baby across the cliffs of Sutherland. But Claire needed him to be with her, so here he was.

She smiled at him and held out her hand. 'Poor Angus. The things you do for love.' She linked her fingers with his and hand in hand they crossed the machair. 'I must confess I don't have any wonderful feeling of being on the right track. No-one is calling out that I'm getting warmer. If nothing happens I'll just have to wait until I feel something else.'

'What do you expect to happen?' he asked.

She shook her head. 'I have no idea.'

Enlightenment had still not arrived when they stood above the line of ruined cottages. Claire let go Angus's hand and descended the slope. She tried to listen with her heart; tried to tune into whatever feelings lingered here - but there was nothing. She looked out to sea where the weak winter sunshine glinted on the tops of the waves. In spite of her conviction something sad had happened here she loved this place. What must it be like to live so close to the water; to have the sound of the surf on the rocks constantly in her ears and smell the salt and sea wrack on the inshore breeze? She turned back inland in time to see Angus striding down the slope towards her .

He had walked this path before, thought Angus. To his left the wee cottages stood whole and strong, their roofs of heather thatch secured against the storms by ropes weighted down with stones. And over to his right was the narrow beach between wicked rocks where he had pulled up the boat to high water mark safe from the cruel sea. He knew this place. As he strode onwards he caught his foot on a buried stone and pitched headlong into the long grass not far from the end cottage wall.

'You should look where you're going,' Claire called remembering how often he had warned her to mind her step. But when he lay still she hurried to his side and fell to her knees. 'Angus! Angus! Are you hurt?' He didn't move. Claire's heart leapt to her throat. Swiftly she ran her hands over his body. Nothing seemed to be broken, but she wasn't a doctor. If only Lachlan was here. Angus lay almost on his back. His head was turned to one side. Had he broken his neck? With trembling fingers she felt for a pulse on his wrist and then below his jaw. Thank God! His heart beat quite strongly. She brushed the hair from his forehead and realised his head lay hard against a rock. Carefully she moved it away and found her fingers covered with blood from an oozing wound at the side of his skull.

Frantically she looked around. There was no help in sight. They had never seen anyone else on this side of the headland. She patted her pocket and remembered she had left her mobile in the car in case she dropped it on their walk here.

Angus's face was pale although his breathing seemed to be regular. Claire bit her lip. What should she do? There was no way she could get him back to the car like this. She didn't dare shake him awake. She might do worse damage. Water. That was the answer. She fished in Angus's pockets until she found the large clean handkerchief she knew he tucked away there each day. Then she got to her feet and ran, with care, down to the sea. In her cupped hands she carried the soaking fabric back to where Angus lay and trickled the cold water over his brow. She made a pad of the handkerchief and cleansed the wound with gentle hands. Again she wet the cloth and returned to repeat the process. Angus showed no sign of regaining consciousness. Claire held the wet pad to this forehead which was rapidly swelling into an impressive 'egg'. There was nothing more she could do. She settled herself beside him and prayed for a miracle.

Once again Dougal went out of the house and looked along the path where he could expect to see Peggy Campbell. But there was no sign of her and the wind was rising. Behind him he heard Morag cry out and winced at the sound. Her pains were on her and he could do nothing to help her. It shouldn't have been this way.

When they had risen betimes this morning he had agreed with Morag they wouldn't wait for Peggy but set out to meet her. Morag had slept little the night before. Her fears would not let her rest. They had packed up the few remaining belongings they were taking with them and said a tearful goodbye to Willie. In spite of Dougal's reassurance they had plenty of time Morag pressed on as fast as she was able. Dougal helped her up the first steep slope on the kyle side of the solmar. At the top they rested and Morag took one final look back at the place that had given them shelter and been a happy home for over a twelvemonth. They would never see it again. She turned her face towards the west and pushed on.

It was hard for Dougal to be of much help to her for the ground was rough. Tough grass and heather roots caught at their feet and it was easier to walk in single file than side by side. The first time Morag fell forward onto her knees Dougal was swiftly at her side to help her rise. 'Why don't we wait for Peggy here?' he cried. 'She will surely know the easiest way for you to take. I think I have wandered away from the path she took yesterday. It was little more than a rabbit track but easier than this.'

'No. No. We'll go on. I am fine,' cried Morag. She eased her aching back and gripped his arm as she waded through the knee-high heather. Do what he might Dougal could not make it easier for her.

When she stumbled forward a second time Dougal called a halt. 'Enough. Enough. We shall wait for Peggy here. I'm sure we're not so far off the track that I won't see her. Sit you down now and rest, *mo grabh*. What is it?' he called out in alarm as Morag doubled over and gasped with pain.

'The child. The child is coming,'

'No. It can't be. It's far too soon. You said yourself there was plenty of time to get to our new home. And Peggy said so too. Are you sure?'

Morag laughed through the receding pain. 'I know I've never had a bairn before but believe me Dougal this is not in my imaginings.'

'Of course not. But a touch of sickness, perhaps? Surely it can't be the child?' He was practically wringing his hand with worry. 'What must we do?'

Morag doubled over again her face contorted with pain. 'Peggy says children are born every day. Nature will take its course. We just have to wait.'

'Wait? Are you mad? My child will not be born in the heather. We must go back.'

Morag shook her head. 'No. We cannot. I will not give birth to a child to have it slaughtered by my brothers.'

'If we stay here it will die without any help from your kin,' said Dougal as a soft rain began to fall.

At last he had persuaded her. He shuddered now as he remembered that tortuous journey back to the solmar. When he thought them close enough Dougal had run ahead to fetch Willie. Together they had almost carried Morag back to the cottage.

While they had struggled along the rain fell more heavily, the wind rose and when they were finally inside the house the weather broke with a crash of thunder. The storm snarled like a hungry beast and buffets of wind threw lumps of rain against the house. Dougal thanked God for the sturdy roof he had been at pains to secure against winter gales. He built up the fire and tried to make Morag as comfortable as possible.

'Peggy!' she cried. 'Where is Peggy? Why doesn't she come?' She gripped Dougal's arm with a strength that made him clench his teeth against his own pain as her nails dug into his flesh. When the worst had passed and she collapsed once more back onto the bed he freed himself and built the fire up with fresh peats. As the flames flared he could see how Morag's skin gleamed white. Drops of sweat stood on her brow and her eyes were full of fear.

'Do not be afraid, Morag. This storm is our friend. No-one in their right minds would venture out looking for spirits or strange red-haired women.' He tried to smile and instil some confidence into her. He bit his lip. She was so tired. How much longer could this go on?

The hours passed. Dougal bathed Morag's face with cool water. He heated some broth and encouraged her to drink to give her strength. If only he knew what to do? But it had always been Morag who tended to the beasts when they gave birth. She had assured him it wasn't a cross-birth but that was of little consolation. If only Peggy would come. But the storm that kept them safe from strangers also kept Peggy away. She couldn't cross the kyle in this tempest.

At last when it seemed Morag could stand no more she gripped his hands and forced her body forward and with one drawn-out agonised cry she expelled the child from her body and fell back, exhausted. 'See to it,' she whispered.

In the long hours she had told him what to expect and what to do. He loosed her hands and knelt between her knees as the afterbirth appeared. He tied the cord and cut it then lifted the tiny limp body in his hand. That something so small could cause so much pain.

Dougal moved nearer the fire and tried to bring life to the child. Gently he rubbed the chest as he had seen Morag do with lambs. Carefully he held the wee one closer to the warmth, brought the little body up to his cheek, willed the blush of life onto the waxen skin. His heart cracking with grief he looked across at Morag, but she had dropped into the sleep of total exhaustion. He tried all he could think of but it was no use.

Like an old man Dougal stood up. With one glance back at Morag he moved to the doorway. The storm had eased. The gentle rain washed away the tears that streamed down Dougal's face as he carried the body of his son out of the house.

Angus's eyes fluttered then opened fully. Claire helped him to sit up. 'Are you alright, Angus? You gave me such a fright.'

He looked at her and frowned then turned to look all around him. 'I don't understand,' he said and shook his head then winced as pain lanced through his skull.

'You fell. You must have tripped. You hit your head on a stone and I didn't know what to do. We left the mobile in the car. I bathed your face with sea water.' The explanations rushed out of her.

Angus smiled. 'So that's why my hair is soaking.' He looked round again at the ruined houses, the overgrown grass and the small beach to his right, then back to Claire. 'You are, Claire, aren't you?' he queried.

Her mouth dropped open in shock. 'Of course! Who else would I be?'

'Morag?'

This time surprise rendered her dumb. She gaped at him. Then finally, 'I was never Morag. At least, I don't think so. I just knew what was happening to her.' Finally the truth of what he asked sank in. 'You believe. Angus! You really believe. You don't think I've lost my marbles?'

'No. Or if you have then I'm in the same boat. Do you remember Morag's son?'

'Iain? Yes.'

'No. Iain was her second child.'

'How do you know? That day at Oldshoremore I remembered the time they came to the beach and Dougal made a sand ship for Iain to play in. There was no other child then.'

'The baby died,' said Angus. 'He was born right here. Over there in our house.' He pointed to the third of the ruined cottages.

Claire looked at him. 'Our house? Where did that come from?'

'I was there.' Angus said quietly. 'It seems such a short time ago I can still hear her cries, feel the pain. The child came too soon. A wee boy. He couldn't survive.' Angus lowered his head as the grief of that small death tore him apart again. Claire put her arm around his shoulders and laid her head gently against his.

'Did he cry?' she said.

Angus shook his head. 'No. There was never a breath in him. He was so small. He fitted into my two cupped hands.' He held them in front of him, seeing, remembering, the feel of his – Dougal's – son.

'Then I don't understand. If he never cried who was it who did cry? Who did I hear? What child was it that drew us to this place?'

Angus sat still wondering the same thing. Gradually he pieced together his thoughts. 'You have been seeing, in dreams and memories, the lives of those two you told me of. When we found the solmar that day you were distressed. You said something bad happened here. It did. The baby died and Dougal and Morag had to flee her kin – possibly her kin – no-one really ever knew if it was them. But they had to go where they would feel safe. They made their new life and had their family far from here but they had to leave their first-born behind.' He turned to Claire. 'Why do you think you are the one to have these – visions –or whatever they are?'

'I have no idea. I thought it was to bring me here to find out who I really am and to find you,' she smiled.

'Perhaps that's a part of it. Now you are in your right place. Do you think it possible you are being used to right a wrong? To put someone else in their right place?'

'Who? How? From scepticism you've certainly taken a great leap to true belief.'

'I have reason,' he said and told her what he had experienced while his body lay unconscious under her hand. 'So I do believe in everything you told me from the first.'

Claire smiled. 'That day when we arrived at Mackay's I couldn't understand how there were so many houses below us. When I walked to the edge of the lawn I expected to see nothing but scenery and water.'

Angus smiled. 'Yes that must be here they went - where they made their home. I've seen it as it used to be. And the cave and everything. It all fits. That's where we used to play - I'll show you. Of course! Dougal was a Mackay. He must be my ancestor.' Angus's eyes were shining. 'Wait 'til I tell, Mam.'

'And what about me? Where do I fit in? I'm not a Mackay too, am I?'

'No. But then neither was Morag. She was a Murray. Perhaps we'll never know why you were chosen but I'm so glad you were.'

'That's all very well but what about the crying baby?'

Angus's smile faded and he became serious. 'Perhaps I can answer that. Give me a hand to stand up. I'm still a bit dizzy.'

Claire helped him to his feet and he leaned on her shoulder. At the end of the row of cottages Angus stopped and looked about him. 'I'm trying to remember it as it was,' he said. 'Round the back, I think'. Once they had arrived at the rear of the row where the walls still stood shoulder high he took his arm from Claire and used the stone-work for support. He made his way along, eyes searching the ground as he went. At the back of the third cottage he stopped and went down on his knee. He pulled up clumps of long grass and moved stray stones until he had uncovered a patch of earth about eighteen inches square. 'I think it's here,' he said. Claire moved closer and watched over his shoulder as he scooped the earth away with his bare hands. Pulling up the grass roots had loosened it but still it was hard going. Angus fished in his pocket and brought out his knife. With that as a tool he worked faster. Unconsciously Claire held her breath.

'Here.' cried Angus as his knife hit stone. He worked on until he had uncovered the surface of a piece of stone about a foot wide. With his knife he scraped around the edges until he could get a purchase at the sides and underneath. Once his fingers had hold he pulled until the stone moved, then slid his hand beneath it and lifted it clear of the surrounding earth.

Claire gasped on an indrawn breath at what lay beneath. In a shallow hole lined with stones rested a small skeleton.

Angus laid aside the stone. 'I wrapped him in the finest wool woven by his mother's hand from her own sheep in the strath,' he said, 'but that's long since rotted away. What can we carry him in?'

'I have it,' cried Claire and lifted her skirt to pull off the silk waist slip she wore beneath her dress. 'Here,' she offered it to Angus. 'Be careful with him.'

Gently, almost reverently, Angus lifted out each of the minute bones that lay at his feet. Last of all he picked up the tiny skull and cradled it for a moment before placing it with the other remains on the silk Claire had laid out on the ground. Carefully he wrapped up the bones and he and Claire made their way back to the car.

'Who can we tell?' she asked.

'I think Reverend Macleod would give us a sympathetic ear,' said Angus. 'This wee fellow must be buried with his kin. The Mackays lie in the graveyard at Oldshoremore and there he must sleep also.'

'Will you tell him the whole story?'

'Aye. He can make of it what he wills but he is from the Islands and I am sure he has heard things equally fantastic in his day. I think he is the man for us. But first we must tell Mam and your Aunt Nell.'

'Give him to me while you drive,' said Claire once she had settled herself in the front seat of the Mondeo. 'Once he is at rest I don't think I'll be bothered by any crying again.' She smiled as she cradled her precious bundle all the way home.

A week later the remains of the wee boy Claire had named Malcolm for her father were laid to rest with God's blessing in the foot of Angus's father's grave. No-one asked Reverend Macleod how he had got permission for this to happen but each heart was grateful to the minister. Only Claire, Angus, Fiona and Lady Ross attended the minister at the graveside. Before the burial Angus had dug the pitifully small hole needed for the wee white coffin he had made. Then followed a short service of blessing inside the church.

At the end it was a thoughtful group who watched Angus smooth the replaced earth and cover it again with quartz gravel.

Claire turned to Lady Ross. 'I think I shall rest as quietly as that wee boy now, Aunt Nell. He is where he should be, and so am I.'

Christmas and Hogmanay were celebrated with renewed joy amid plans for a wedding just before Easter. The business of the hotel had still to carry on but Fiona closed for a week around the wedding date to accommodate the overflow of guests who could not be fitted into The Big House. Obviously the Butlers would stay with Lady Ross. Angus's lips twitched as he imagined Cynthia's conversation leading up to the celebrations. She would revel in the fact she was staying with Lady Ross in the largest house in the area. Och, well. Let her enjoy. It did no harm.

With two loving families to help her arrange 'the happiest day of her life', everything should have been perfect for Claire. And it nearly was.

'What is it, my dear?' asked Fiona, seeing Claire lost in thought.

'I'm just being silly. I am so lucky. I have Angus and you and Aunt Nell. I have found out who my father really is – was – and that should be enough for anyone.'

'But . . .?'

Claire smiled. 'I keep thinking of my little mother.'

'We can try and trace her if you would like that. There are all sorts of avenues to explore.'

'Yes. I think that's what I'll do, but carefully in case she has a new life. Perhaps she has family who know nothing of what happened before. It's just that I'd like to be able to think of her - how she looks - imagine her really, being there on my wedding day. I said it was silly,' she finished with a shrug.

'Not silly, quite reasonable I would have thought. I'm only sorry I can't wave a magic wand and make it happen,' said Fiona.

The weeks leading up to the wedding were stormy. March roared in like the proverbial lion. Anxious frowns appeared on foreheads and local forecasters were questioned constantly. Would there be time for the weather to improve before Easter?

With a week to go to the wedding Fiona walked into her office where Claire was sitting on the corner of the desk talking to Angus. She held a letter in her hand. 'I'm so glad you're both here,' she said. 'You will never believe what I've just received. Do you remember the American couple who were here for the Twelfth last year, Angus?'

Angus frowned and thought a moment. 'Do you mean the Mackenzies? He was trying to trace his ancestors in between shooting the birds.'

'That's right.'

'Is that letter from them? Are they coming back?'

'No . . . I don't know . . . maybe. Apparently they went to a Thanksgiving dinner last year where they met the Coopers.' Angus and Claire looked blank. 'You wouldn't remember them, Angus,' went on Fiona. 'When they came regularly you were only a child. Later they came when you were at University. But when the Mackenzies spoke of Mackay's and their holiday here, they and Mr and Mrs Cooper got to exchanging memories. The Coopers didn't know your father had died.' Fiona fished a handkerchief from her pocket and blew her nose. 'Some people are so kind. This letter is from Mr Cooper.' She riffled through the sheets of thin blue airmail paper. 'He says . . . our condolences . . . no that's not the bit . . . here it is . . . remembered you were always the one to take photographs for us so thought you might like to have this one as it shows you together.' She handed the photograph to Angus.

'May I see?' said Claire.

'Is anyone doing any work this day at all?' came a voice from the doorway as Kirstie stood with her hands on her hips. 'There's the Sheridans standing in the hall waiting on that lazy Fergus Beag to carry their bags down. But not hair nor hide of him's to be seen.'

'I'll go,' said Angus and passed the photograph to Claire. 'I can see this later. Nice of them to do that, Mam.'

'Yes, it was,' agreed Fiona. 'I thought you would be particularly happy to see it, Claire.'

'I've seen a picture of Angus's father before,' Claire reminded Fiona as she looked at the photograph in her hand. 'But it is nice to see you together. When was this taken?'

'A while ago now. It must be at least twenty-two years. See there's Kirstie standing with Minty. I remember it was just before the Coopers left us and he gathered together as many of the staff as were around at the time. Do you see who is on the other side of Minty?'

Claire looked at the young woman with red hair and a sweet expression. 'I don't know her do I? Is she still here? Of course she'd be older now. Who is it?'

'That's Senga, my dear, your mother. She must have been visiting Minty. They were always close.'

Claire caught her bottom lip between her teeth and gazed at the face before her. 'She's younger than I am now,' she marvelled. 'I wonder what has happened to her.' She raised shining eyes to Fiona. 'Thank you so much. This is the best wedding present I could possibly have.'

'I thought you'd be pleased,' said Fiona.

Claire traced her mother's face with one finger. 'Brave little Senga,' she said. 'Senga Morrison, my mother.'

'Oh, no.' said Fiona. 'Senga wasn't a Morrison. When her father was widowered she kept house for him. She came with him when he moved here for his work in the forest. She was a Murray – from Dornoch.'

So the wheel of time turns . . .

ACKNOWLEDGEMENTS

I owe thanks to Graham Bruce, the former Headmaster of Durness School, for advice on the crops in the 16th Century; to Alick Mackay for being the first to tell me about the burning of Dornoch Cathedral; to Euan Currie of Burghfield, Dornoch for sharing his vast knowledge of the history of the area and Scottish history in general; to Wilma Ross for telling me the story of 'the woman of great faith'. I hope I can be forgiven for borrowing it and putting that story into the 16th Century; to Peter Wild of the Historylinks Museum in Dornoch for answering my historical questions. And to the late Bill Macdonald of Dornoch for taking me on my first journey from Lairg to Laxford along the 'chain of lochs' and showing me the wild beauty of the Sutherland countryside. To Peggy Savage for, as always, being my helpful proof reader and critic, and to Alick Mackay who supports me in all I do.

For more information go to

www.lulu.com/spotlight/4booklovers

Printed in Great Britain
by Amazon